Talk
of the Town

by Tonya Ridley

A Life Changing Book in conjunction with Power Play Media
Published by Life Changing Books
P.O. Box 423 Brandywine, MD 20613

Library of Congress Cataloging-in-Publication Data;

www.lifechangingbooks.net

ISBN - (10) 1-934230-92-8 (13) 978-1-934230-92-3
Copyright ® 2007

Talk
of the Town

By Tonya Ridley

*D*edication

I would like to dedicate this novel to my grandma Ruth Watkins---R.I.P. Momma you wouldn't believe how many times I still dial your number. Some days I'm too weak to come out the house, but I'm a big girl now, so I keep pushing on. You have no idea the impact that you've made on your family. Chanel and Elijah are doing great. You would be so proud of them. It's not a day that goes by that I don't stop and look at our picture. I LOVE YOU MOMMA.

To Grand-Da Frank Ridley, Grandma and Grand-Da Vandergriff, Roberta Young, Grandma Ruth, Grand-Da Floyd Robertson, Derrick, Devon, Soul, Big Shawn, Pokey, you all are truly missed.

acknowledgements

I thank God for giving me another year to say thank you once again. I want to thank my Mom and Dad for being so strong for me this year. This year has been hard, with me losing my Grandma and my father hospitalized. Da, I know you're trying to be strong for me, Josh and Meme, but please all we want for X-MAS is you. Thanks to my Grandma Mary Ridley and step-Grandma Ethel Ridley. I also want to thank all of my closest friends from NC, SC, DC, GA, NY, W.VA, FL, Philly, Cali, Bahamas and Jamaica. Thanks for being who you are. To my Aunt Joyce, you are so fun and crazy. I'm glad you're a part of this.

To my God children, Shemar, Poobie 32, and Sherrill, Aunt Tonya loves you all and I'm so proud to be apart of your lives. Also to my new God child coming in July, push Johnelle. PETEY-PABLO, you are the best brotha, so keep your ass off that You Tube video so you won't give V a heart attack out there in Cali. To my TALK OF THE TOWN HAIR SALON family, Nicky, Bell, Brandi, Kim thanks for holding the shop down while I'm gone. I really appreciate it. To CAROL GIST aka MONEYBAG, I can't believe you're gone, but I know heaven is busy now for sure. People say you can't meet good friends and love them in six months, but now I know that's not true. We sit around the shop and laugh at you all the time, and yes E-man and Josh act just like you now. We miss you, Moneybag.

To my LCB family, it's a joy and privilege to work with all of you. Danette Majette (I Shoulda Seen It Comin' and Deep), Tiphani (The Millionaire Mistress), J. Tremble (Secrets of a Housewife and More Secrets More Lies), Tyrone Wallace (Double Life and Nothin' Personal), Mike G (Young Assassin), Ericka Williams (All That Glitters) and Mike Warren (A Private Affair) we've had a good year so far…let's keep it that way. You know I'm security!!! Also to all of those who made this book and my first book "The Take Over" possible, I thank you from the bottom of my heart. To my BOSS LADY, AZAREL, what can I say…you're the shit! Leslie Allen, thank you so much for helping me with this book. What would I have done without you??? You always make it happen, fa'real. To Davida Baldwin, thanks for the bomb cover. Keep'em comin'! My publicist, Nakea Murray thanks for all your hard work. CORNBREAD!!!!! A special thanks goes to my cover model, I. Marie.

A special shout out goes to my fellow authors, Hickson, Erick Gray, Treasure, Danielle Santiago and K. Elliott.

To all my people on lock down, Cuz Harvey, Beefy, Trick, Red, E-man, Rhamel, Kiko, Salaam, Troy, Butta, Ski, T-bone, Scooter, Mookie, Lil Chris, Black, Ty, Country, Debo, Block, Paul Streeter, Scarface, Hardy, Money, June and Quanita Winston, the sun will shine again. Please write to: Tonya Ridley 4501 New Bern Ave, Suite 130 #315, Raleigh, NC 27610-1550.

Tonya Ridley

Chapter 1

Diamond

Mya and I pulled up to the exclusive Swiss Hotel in downtown Atlanta around midnight. I had instructed her to park in the back of the hotel so I could get myself together. My stomach seemed to be doing flips, and my hands wouldn't stop shaking. Even though this was my third score, I was still a nervous wreck. Mya must've sensed that I was uncomfortable by the way I kept shifting in the passenger seat, and decided to give me a pep talk.

"I'm not gonna ask if you're ready because I can tell you're nervous," she said.

"I don't know how you do this shit, Mya," I replied. "I keep thinking something is gonna go wrong."

"Ain't nothin' gonna go wrong if you keep doin' everything I taught you. I've already done my homework on this niggah and trust me, he's harmless. He's just a fake ass thug with some money to burn, that's all."

I guess she thought that was supposed to make me feel better, but it didn't. I still hadn't gotten use to robbing dudes yet, and hadn't planned on it. I couldn't wait until I had enough money, so I could get out of this crazy game.

"It's time to get up there, Diamond," Mya said, looking at her expensive Cartier watch. "Do whatever you gotta do to get hype because it's almost show time."

I took a deep breath and closed my eyes for a second before hopping out the burgundy Ford Expedition we rented just for this occasion, and stared at my reflection in the passenger window. I looked like a true Diva, in my tight fitting Seven jeans, and black low cut shirt that exposed my perfect 36C breasts. Luckily for me my mother had passed down her shapely figure.

As Mya and I walked toward the front of the hotel, I concealed the .380 automatic in my brand new Chanel bag, compliments of our last score. The one good thing about my new lifestyle was the frequent trips to Lennox Square Mall. I watched as Mya walked confidently in the tight mini-dress she wore that looked like it was painted on. You would've thought she was headed to a business meeting with a Fortune 500 company the way she strutted in her four inch stilettos. Mya loved attention, and she always expressed that through her skimpy outfits.

When we entered the plush Art Deco lobby it was nice and desolate just how we liked it. The last thing we needed were a bunch of witnesses who could point us out in a lineup. Even the two hotel clerks behind the front desk were so busy talking, they didn't notice us as we walked by. I wanted to go to the bar to get a drink so I could calm my nerves, but I knew that was out of the question. Mya was a drill sergeant when it came to being on time. Her philosophy was in and out, so distractions were never apart of the equation.

Mya stopped right before we reached the elevators and put her hand on my shoulder. "I hope you're ready now because there's no turning back."

I sighed and nodded my head, "Yeah, I'm ready. Just make sure you keep looking at the time."

"Don't worry I got you. Now go up there and do your thing. Make momma proud," Mya responded with a smile that made her eyes squint.

I made my way to the elevator, stepped inside and pressed the number five on the panel. Before the doors closed, I glanced at my best friend, who looked like a proud parent sending her child to their first day of kindergarten.

When the elevator stopped on the fifth floor, I stepped out and slowly walked toward room 507. I was still nervous, but I knew we needed to get this money. Besides, I had my eye on a heart shape pendant that was iced out in princess cut diamonds. However, I needed to get it with the target's money, not mine.

On the way to the hotel, Mya had schooled me about our next victim. His name was Sky and he was from Philly. Apparently, he loved Atlanta and its women with a passion. Mya had met him at a club the week before, and sized him up the same night. She said he was a loud mouth who constantly flashed his money, which was a complete mistake on his part because he had caught the attention from the wrong person. Mya lied and told him that she was a Madam, who would be happy to send him a girl to his hotel, and officially welcome him to ATL, but little did he know he was about to be welcomed the hood way.

I reached his room and knocked softly, so the other guests wouldn't hear anything. As I waited for him to answer, I stood in a sexy posture, and tossed my long sandy colored hair over my shoulder.

Suddenly, the door opened, and my eyes widened. Sky stood in front of me looking sexy as hell with his beautiful smile and a body that was cut to perfection. *Damn, Mya didn't tell me he was fine*, I thought as I admired his muscles in the tight wife beater he wore. Even all the tattoos that covered every inch of his skin was a turn on. I had to keep reminding myself that I was here to do a job.

"Damn girl. You look good enough to eat!" he shouted. "Precious didn't tell me you were gonna be this bad!"

I laughed to myself at the thought of Mya telling him her name was Precious. She was far from that. "Ssshh, be quiet baby, are you trying to wake up the whole floor," I said, gently pressing my finger against his lips.

He followed my order and moved aside so I could enter. I felt him staring at my ass as I walked into his suite. As soon as I heard the door shut behind me, Sky didn't waste any time putting his hands all over my body. He instantly pulled me into his arms and started fondling my breasts and ass.

"Damn, Precious hooked me up. I've been thinking about this pussy all week. I can't wait to fuck the shit outta you," he said, licking his lips. "You feel my dick growing?"

He was pressed against me so tight; I could definitely feel his hard bulge against my ass.

"Are we alone, baby?" I asked seductively.

"Yeah, we alone," he replied. He put his lips against my neck and started sucking on my neck like a fuckin' vampire.

"Ouch, that hurt. Did you just bite me?" I barked, pulling away from him.

"Yeah, I like it rough and want my woman to be the same way," he stated.

"Your woman? You're moving a little too fast aren't you? Besides, I don't want any fuckin' marks on me... I don't play that shit," I said sternly.

He looked at me and flashed his sexy smile. "C'mon, baby, how much is it gonna cost to get it on like Ike and Tina Turner up in this mutha-fucka?" he asked.

"Niggah, I just told you I don't play that," I said with an attitude.

My reply must've pissed him off because he looked at me and frowned. "Well, I do," he returned.

Is this niggah crazy? "Listen, I came here to have a good time with you, not to be a fuckin' punching bag for your enjoyment."

"Look bitch, tonight, you up in my suite and I call the fuckin' shots. If you expect to get paid, then you're gonna have to obey me. You ain't leaving here till I fuckin' say so," he scolded.

His whole demeanor had done a three sixty on me. Obviously, Mya had underestimated this fool. *So much for being harmless*, I thought. My plan was to be in and out, but I guess Sky had other plans. He walked up to me and pulled me toward him, snatching my purse out of my hand and tossing it across the room.

Instantly, I knew I had fucked up. I had let him get too close which was my first mistake. Now I couldn't even get to my gun.

"We gonna play my games tonight, you dirty whore," he said, slapping the shit out of me.

My face felt like I had just gotten stung by a bee. "Niggah are you crazy!" I asked holding my face.

"Bitch, shut the fuck up!" he shouted, and then slapped me again.

I instantly punched Sky on his chin with a hard right, but it didn't faze him much.

"Oh, shit, that's what I'm talking about. You a feisty bitch, but I like that," he said, smiling at me wickedly. He punched me back, causing me to stumble and fall against the wall. "Yeah, bitch, let's do this," he snapped.

Shocked, I looked up at him like he was the devil himself. I quickly jumped up and tried to throw a few more punches to his face, but he grabbed my arms.

"I told you, bitch…we're playing my games tonight," he responded, tossing me onto the sofa. "Yeah, you got me horny now, you whore. I'm gonna put my big long dick up that tight little ass of yours," he said, walking toward me.

I couldn't believe what was happening. Even though I was scared to death, I had to get myself together. In my mind, I could hear Mya telling me to stay calm and think of a plan. I needed to get to my purse, but it was on the other side of the room. He grabbed me by my legs and began pulling me off the sofa. I could feel the hot friction on my back as he dragged me across the carpet.

"Please, stop…let's just do it right," I begged, trying to distract him from doing any further damage. I needed time to get my gun.

"What did you say, whore? You came up here to fuck, right? C'mon, you know you love it. You should love a niggah from up north to work that ass out because all y'all country bitches are some freaks." He picked me up and tossed me onto the bed.

"Yeah, baby, I'm gonna definitely fuck you up tonight," he said, standing over me.

I knew I had put myself in a bad predicament. I needed my gat badly. As Sky reached down to grab me, there was a knock at the door.

He paused for a moment, looking at the door, then back at me. "You came alone right?" he asked.

"No, I invited my girlfriend too," I informed him.

"Oh word, does that bitch look as good as you do?"

I gave a slight smile. "Yeah, she loves to fuck. I knew you probably needed to handle two girls like me, so I told her to meet me up here just for you, baby. I didn't want to handle that dick alone," I replied, stroking his ego.

Niggahs think with their dicks, especially when you bring up a threesome with two beautiful women, so I knew he would fall for it. Men were stupid like that.

I knew it was Mya at the door. We had a system, if I didn't come back within twenty minutes, then she would come looking for me. And when Mya came looking with the 9mm she carried, trouble would soon follow. Mya didn't give a fuck, so she didn't have any problems with killing someone. She was always known around the hood as a pitbull in a skirt.

The knocks at the door continued. At first, Sky looked reluctant, but then I'm sure he thought about the threesome, and decided to change his mind.

"Don't move," he ordered.

"I promise, I'll be right here," I replied, trying to look helpless.

His dick seemed extra hard as he turned around and headed toward the door. As I watched him walk away, I slowly maneuvered myself toward my purse.

"Yo, who is it?" he shouted.

"I came with my home girl," I heard Mya shout from the hallway. "Are you gonna let me in?"

"Oh word, well we were just getting things started up in here.

You're definitely welcome to join in," Sky said, as he opened the door.

I felt an instant relief when I saw Mya standing in the door-way looking flawless as ever. Mya was a beautiful girl, who always reminded me of Alicia Keys with her fair complexion, slanted eyes and long jet black hair. Even her voice was a little husky like Ms. Keys herself.

"Damn, Precious. I didn't know you were the girl she was talking about," Sky uttered, stepping back and gazing at her per-fect figure.

"You like what you see?" Mya asked, doing a little twirl for him. I could tell Sky was about to lose his mind.

"Hell yeah. I wanted your ass at the club last week," he responded, "come on up in here and join our party."

As Mya walked in she winked at me. I knew that meant her nine was ready. I'd already pulled out my .380 and cocked it, so it was about to be on. I was more than ready to fuck up Sky's world. I was pissed at him for hitting me in the face. As Sky shut the door and turned around he was more than surprised to see two beautiful women armed and ready to fuck his shit up.

"Yo, what's good, is it like that?" he asked. I'm sure he was shocked by how things had suddenly turned on him.

"Yeah, niggah, it's like that!" Mya barked. "What you doin' to my girl?"

With his arms stretched out like eagle wings, he looked at us wide-eyed. "Yo, we were just having some fun, right baby?"

I was furious. I couldn't believe he had the nerve to say that shit. I walked up to him, and bashed the gun across his nose. I could hear a bone crack when I hit him.

"Aaahhh," he screamed out, clutching his nose. "You fuckin' bitch!"

"You wanna play Ike and Tina, remember!" I shouted. I hit him several more times until his face was completely bloody.

"Niggah, strip," Mya ordered.

"What?" Sky asked with a confused look.

"I said, strip," she repeated.

He looked at her and laughed. "Bitch you must be crazy."

"Oh, you think I'm playin'," Mya said. She walked up to him and pressed the gun against his dick. "Do you think it's funny now?"

"Yo, hold up! Don't do anything stupid," he said, taking off his jeans. Both Mya and I stood in shock as he pulled his boxers down exposing his huge dick.

"Damn niggah, why you have to be an asshole and beat up my girl like that. I would've definitely given you some ass wit' that big dick. What a shame," Mya said.

He gave her a slight grin. We made Sky lock his fingers behind his head and walk backwards butt-naked out onto the balcony.

"Yo, y'all bitches are definitely gonna see me again, this shit ain't over," he threatened.

Before we closed the terrace doors, I glared at him one last time. I was still pissed that his punk ass had hit me. A part of me wanted Mya to shoot him, but I knew the gunshots would've definitely gotten us unwanted attention.

"Niggah, get on your fuckin' knees," I demanded.

As he followed my orders, I kicked him between his legs. When he fell over in pain, I dug the tip of my heel down into his balls. He cried out and balled up into a fetal position holding onto his nuts for dear life. I closed the glass doors and locked him outside to drown out the sounds.

We took everything he had, from money, jewelry and drugs. We even walked out of his suite with all his clothes, which left Sky with nothing but the skin he came to town with.

Fuck him, I thought as I wheeled his luggage down the hall.

Shortly after, we were back in the truck and drove off with another successful score under our belt. As we drove down 85 South, I looked at my face in the small mirror in the sun visor. "That mutha-fucka!" I muttered, staring at my black eye.

"See, that's why I told you to never let those niggah's get too close, Diamond," Mya replied. "Don't you remember anything I taught you?"

"Yeah I know I fucked up. I think when his fine ass opened the door, it threw me off my game."

Mya shook her head. "I don't care how good the marks look. You're there to do a job, so you have to stay focused at all times."

"I shoulda shot him," I replied.

"You're not at that point yet," she responded. "I think you fucked him up pretty good though. He'll probably never forget your ass, especially when he goes to pee and his balls ache."

"I shoulda shot him," I repeated, staring at my eye.

Mya laughed. "You can't get caught up like that anymore."

"Oh trust me, it won't happen again. You can be sure about that shit," I guaranteed.

Mya laughed again and then pressed down on the accelerator. She was soon doing over ninety miles on the expressway. The girl was always a speed demon behind the wheel.

Twenty minutes later, Mya pulled up at my crib. I stayed in the hood, Bank Head Projects to be exact. It was a very rough neighborhood, but I was comfortable. I'd been living there for three years, and everyone knew me. Bank Head wasn't much of a step up from me and Mya's old neighborhood Kimberly Court, but it was where I called home for now.

"I got you home in one piece," Mya said, nodding to a Jay-Z song.

Thank goodness. I don't know who gave your ass a fuckin' license," I said laughing. "So, what's going on for tomorrow?"

"You know me, I gotta check out this niggah," she said.

"Business or pleasure?" I asked, knowing her M.O.

"He's cute, and got a big dick, so mostly pleasure. Shit, I need some right now, but I can hold off 'till tomorrow."

I let out a small laugh. Mya loved dick just as much as she loved the thrill of the game and the money we made. "You want me to keep the goods, or are you gonna stash everything at your place?" I asked.

"Nah, you take that shit because you know me. I might get into somethin' tonight and if I do, I don't want nobody all in my fuckin' business, so it's better at your spot."

"Cool, come by tomorrow afternoon so we can split every-thing."

"Ayyite bet. You go and take care of that eye; before you start lookin' like Tyson hit you. You need a patch over that shit?" she joked.

"You're a real comedian," I replied smiling.

I got out of the truck and pulled out the black suitcase from the back seat. We'd taken two suitcases from Sky, but the sec-ond one was only filled with his clothes, so we quickly tossed that shit out the window on the way to my house.

As I walked toward my building, Mya made a quick u-turn, and honked the horn, speeding off like a mad woman. All I could do was shake my head. *She's gonna kill somebody one day.*

Once I was inside my apartment, I placed the luggage in the coat closet and walked in my bedroom with anticipation. I could-n't wait to take a nice hot bath and relax. It had been a rough night for me. I hated my place, and was glad that I would have to move soon. In my new line of work, it wasn't good to stay in the same place for too long. I was told by Mya that I couldn't stay in one spot longer than two months, so no one would know where I lived. In order to be successful at this game I had to follow her rules, so how I'd just fucked up with Sky was unacceptable.

I didn't want to come home one night and find a crew of nig-gahs sitting up in my living room, so I was saving enough money to get me a place somewhere in Buckhead or Midtown. I had plans for the future, because I knew robbing and hustling niggahs wasn't gonna last forever. I loved doing hair, and wanted to open my own salon one day, and even a small part of me thought about having a family. But that was one dream I kept to myself.

In my bedroom, I took off my clothes and put on my sexy pink Victoria's Secret robe. I loved the way the fabric felt against my nude skin. As I prepared my bath, I turned on the stereo and placed an old school R. Kelly CD in the drive. I pressed the button to play one of my favorite tracks. I loved the way R. Kelly's sexy and masculine voice serenaded me when I was alone. When my bath was ready and the bubbles were almost overflowing, I dropped my robe to the tiled floor and slowly got in. Lying gently in the tub, I turned to my left and stared at my reflection in the mirror that was parallel to the tub.

Looking at my black eye made me furious again. I could've murdered Sky for what he'd done to me. I closed my eyes, and let Mr. Kelly's smooth voice take over for the night. I loved R. Kelly to death because he looked just like my first boyfriend. He was a hustler, and the twenty five year old man who took my virginity at the age of sixteen. His dick game was serious, and when he fucked me, he would play his R. Kelly tape throughout the night. He was a beast when it came to fuckin'. He knew my spots and always put me in a zone when we fucked. He always penetrated my pussy deep and made my walls swell with each thrust. I loved the way he did things; he was smooth and rough at the same time.

Hearing R. Kelly sing *'It Seems Like You're Ready'* was making me horny. Masturbating always seemed to calm me down, and after tonight pleasing myself was definitely needed. I started playing with my kitty in the tub and twenty minutes later, I let out a serious orgasm.

Chapter 2

Diamond

I woke up the next morning to a loud knock at my front door. It had been weeks since I'd gotten a good eight hours of sleep, and now someone was depriving me of that again once again.

"What the fuck!" I said, opening my eyes. I turned over and stared at the clock on my dresser. It was only eight fifteen.

As the knocking continued, it became even louder, which immediately made me nervous. I sat up in the bed and looked around my room before tossing my duvet comforter aside. *I know it's not Mya because her ass doesn't even get up before noon*, I thought. *Damn, what if it's Sky? Maybe he found out where I live.* I opened my dresser near the bed and retrieved my .380. I wasn't taking any chances. I quickly put on my pink robe and slowly made my way toward the door with my gun in hand.

"Diamond, I know you're in there…c'mon, you told me to come through around eight," I heard a woman shout from outside. "Diamond, I need my hair done before noon," she continued.

Oh shit. It was Alaina. I'd completely forgotten about doing her hair. So much had been going on over the past few weeks, I was losing track of all my hair appointments.

I stashed the gun inside one of my dying plants and quickly opened the door. I apologized to Alaina as she came rushing into my place with a red scarf tied around her head.

"Damn Diamond, don't be doin' that shit to me. You got me all nervous thinkin' your ass wasn't home. Shoot, you know I gotta be at work by one."

"I'm sorry, I overslept. I forgot all about your appointment," I replied.

"That's cool; you still got me though, right?" Alaina asked, looking at me with a nervous expression.

"Yeah, I got you. Just let me get set up in the kitchen and throw on some clothes."

"You an angel, Diamond," Alaina said, following me.

"Shit, I'm sorry about the mess," I said, removing all the hair magazines that were lying on the kitchen table. "I shoulda cleaned up last night, but, I had a late night."

Alaina laughed. "Girl, I don't care about that. Shit, I might be havin' one of those tonight."

"What you got planned?" I was curious because Alaina was known for her crazy rendezvous.

"After work, I'm going to the Bank Roll concert, and see my boo Lil' Moe perform." She did a little dance with her shoulders.

"Alaina, why do you like that scrawny, lookin' mutha-fucka?" I asked.

"Please, Lil' Moe is sexy as hell. He's a thug the way I like them, and got it goin' on. You know I met him at Club 112 last month and fucked him in the V.I.P. Girl, he could work some pussy," she informed with a huge smile across her face.

I looked at her in shock. I'd heard rumors about Alaina being a hard core groupie, but I didn't think she would go that hard. "Me personally, I like 'em hefty. I need something to grab onto when he's putting it down in the bedroom."

She laughed as she untied the scarf from around her head. "Shit all that money that niggah's makin', he's finer than a mutha-fucka right about now."

I had to laugh. Alaina was crazy. I pulled my hair in my face to make sure it was covering my black eye, so she wouldn't start asking me a thousand questions about what happened. But she was so concerned about getting her hair done and talking about Lil' Moe, that she probably wouldn't have noticed my eye anyway.

"Let me get this kitchen cleaned up so I can get started," I replied, cutting the conversation short. Once Alaina started running her mouth there was no way to stop her.

I washed the dishes, and put a few plates away, before I was ready to have Alaina looking like a million bucks. I did hair in my kitchen while I was still attending Arnold Patrick's beauty school. I had over two dozen clients that came to me for everything from weaves, to perms and braids. I had hoped to be out of school within the next three months, so I could get a game plan together and finally pursue the profession that I really loved.

"Diamond when is your last month at school, cause I heard you're takin' all the clients from the salon up the street," Alaina asked.

"Why? What do I have to do with the clients up the street?"

"Because everybody around the way is sayin' you're gettin' a salon soon, that's why. Girl, you know you're like the best in Atlanta. And you know, Tonia is pissed, because you're takin' all the clientele out of her shop."

"Fuck that bitch! If she brings me any problems, I gonna definitely fuck her up. She acts likes she's the only fuckin' person in Atlanta that can do hair." Tonia had always been my competition, and since she was probably talking shit about me, now I was really gonna make it a point to take all of her clients. "It won't be long before I can leave this damn kitchen and get my shop, but I gotta save some money so I can have the best salon Buckhead has ever seen."

"Well, when you do that, let a sistah in, so I can quit my bullshit job and get down wit' you. Cuz I know you're about to blow up doin' hair, girl," she responded.

"Thanks, you know I got you," I replied with a smile. "Now what style are you getting today?"

"I need a perm around these edges and some spirals so my hair will have time to fall before I go to the concert," she said, looking at herself in the mirror.

"No problem." I sat Alaina in the kitchen chair and began messing around with her hair.

"Damn, Alaina, I gotta get outta this little ass place before I lose my mind. I'm so tired of all these fuckin' roaches that are coming in from next door," I said, applying the chemical to her hair. "Plus these grimy, broke ass niggahs that are always outside my building trying to holla at me every night is really getting on my nerves."

"I hear you girl, shit where I'm at ain't any better. My fuckin' neighbor's dog be barkin' all damn night. Then tell me why my landlord tried to push up on me the other day, wit' his bald fat ass. That niggah only got about four teeth in his mouth," she said, pointing to her own teeth. "That's why you need to hurry up and open up this shop and put me down."

"Don't worry, Alaina, I'm on my grind. Give me a few months and I'll be good. I'm getting the fuck outta here." I looked around at my apartment that could use a lot of attention. The only thing that I enjoyed looking at was the nice Italian leather sofa and dinning room set that I'd just purchased from the Z Gallerie furniture store.

"Diamond, I think you have a nice place. Shit, I wish I could have somethin' like this. I'm tryin' to move me and my kids from Garden Walk Blvd. It's changed since the Freaknik days."

"Yeah that's why I'm trying to take my ass to Buckhead," I replied, focusing on Alaina's hair a bit more. "Let me wash out this perm before we talk too much and all your shit falls out."

"Please don't do that. I'm already two strands away from being bald-headed," she joked.

"After I put you under the dryer, I'm gonna jump in the shower. If it cuts off turn it back on for twenty more minutes."

After putting Alaina under the dryer, I raced back to my small cramped bedroom where I had no business having a king size bed. I could barely move around, but I had to stay fly. I jumped in the shower, and gave myself what my Aunt Faye called a hoe bath, which meant to hit all the right places quick and fast. I let out a huge sigh as I began to think about my family, who I missed being around especially my brother. I'd always looked up and cherished my older brother growing up since I never had anyone else to call father. Becoming a hustler at the age of sixteen, my brother spoiled me with all the finer things in life and treated me like a princess. He always said his plans were to get me and our mother out the hood, but those plans were cut short when he got caught selling drugs and received a fifteen year sentence. After my brother went to prison, my mother and I began to struggle and our relationship became extremely distant.

However, after receiving the news that another inmate had killed my brother during a fight in the yard our world turned upside down. My mother turned into a cold heartless person, who didn't seem to care about life anymore. Instead of the tragedy bringing us together it drove us further apart. After his death, she had to take on two jobs to make ends meet, so things really took a turn for the worst. We argued everyday about the smallest things, and I would definitely get upset when she wouldn't spoil me like my brother used to do. This situation continued until I was eighteen and began sneaking out the house at night to work at Body Tap, a well known strip club.

In my eye, I wasn't doing anything wrong. I just needed money to keep up with Mya, who always rocked the latest gear and even had her own apartment. I managed to keep up my routine for about a month before my mother found out, and kicked me out the house. I ended up having to move in with Mya, and since that day, my mother has never asked me to come back home and has refused to talk to me, which hurts like hell. I made plenty of money dancing nude and enticing the endless ballers that populated the club, but soon I grew tired of dancing and having men ogle over me. After striping for almost a year, I managed to save enough money to quit and move into my own spot. Now three years and several bullshit jobs later, I'm still on the grind and trying my best to finally be able to make my mother proud.

A tear rushed down my cheek as I thought about my mother and how I had disappointed her. I was starting to get depressed and wanted to crawl back in bed, but I thought about Alaina, so I quickly got myself together and jumped out the shower. Several moments later, I returned to the kitchen wearing my favorite white terrycloth Juicy sweat suit. I had to be comfortable while I worked my magic.

"Damn, I thought you weren't comin' back!" Alaina yelled from under the dryer.

"Shut up, before I send your ass to Tonia's shop," I said jokingly.

I finished Alaina's hair by twelve. I took my time and made sure she was looking like a diva when she stepped out my door. She gave me my fee, plus a five dollar tip and thanked me for hooking her up. I admired my work by taking pictures from my digital camera for my portfolio. I had to make sure none of my master pieces went unnoticed.

When Alaina left, I opened my closet and pulled out the suitcase Mya and I had stolen from Sky and rolled it to my room. I sat on the edge of the bed, dumped all the contents out and looked at the items from our recent score. It had cost me a black eye, but now it seemed to be well worth it.

Staring at the jewelry, drugs and the large bundle of cash rolled tightly in a rubber band, I imitated the same dance that I had seen Alaina do earlier. Between all the items, it had to total over fifty grand. "Sky, you definitely got taste," I said, picking up the diamond encrusted bracelet. If Mya and I kept racking in this amount of money, I'd have more than enough to open up a salon. I could finally live like a diva and get out of this hell hole I was in. As I inspected the package filled with white powder, I realized that it was at least half of a kilo. We had definitely hit the jackpot because that amount of cocaine was big chips for sure.

Suddenly, I heard a knock at my door. "Shit, who is it now. I don't have another appointment," I said, throwing the contents back into the suitcase and quickly placing it in my bedroom closet.

The knocking continued and the person at my door seemed relentless. "Diamond, open the door. Why you got me out here waitin' in the damn sun?" I heard Mya shout.

I looked at the clock on my dresser and smiled. "Damn, it's only twelve-thirty. I can't believe her ass is up already," I said to myself. When I finally opened the door Mya walked in like she owned the place.

"Why you got me waitin' outside so fuckin' long? You know I hate to sweat, now my hair is all fucked up," she said, lightly punching me on the arm. "I know your ass wasn't still sleep. You know I think you need some dick to wake you up every morning, fuck an alarm clock."

I laughed and placed my hands of my hips. "For your ghetto ass information, I've been up doing hair since eight o'clock."

"Oh, yeah well maybe you can do something to this frizzy ass shit," Mya replied, rubbing her hands over her hair.

I ignored her request, because for some reason I wasn't in the mood to fight with Mya's uncontrollable hair at the moment. Mya had what most people called, *good hair*, but it was always frizzy. "So, how did it go last night?"

"It was great. I did my thing as usual, but I'm gettin' tired of that niggah, because he always wants to be all over me after we fuck. You know how I need my space," she stated, being loud and ghetto. "That niggah acts like I'm his fuckin' wife wit' that cuddling shit."

"Mya, you're so crazy," I replied.

"I swear Diamond, niggahs around your way be actin' like they've never seen pussy before. As I was gettin' out my truck niggahs were lookin' at me like Jesus was walkin' through the projects or something. I mean damn, they were makin' me nervous. I'm gonna end up shooting a couple of those fools if they come at me wrong," she stated with authority.

Looking at the tight booty shorts she wore, and the snug red t-shirt that accentuated her breasts, I could understand why the guys outside were probably undressing her with their eyes.

"Calm down, Mya. What do you expect if you come out here looking like you about to start swinging around a pole? And stop acting like you don't like it, because your ass craves for the attention, that's why you dress the way you do."

Mya smiled. "So true…so true."

"Well stop complaining all the damn time, hoe," I said jokingly.

"Yeah I may be a hoe, but at least I'm a paid hoe," she responded. "Anyway, where you stash that niggah's shit?"

"In my bedroom closet, I was just about to call you."

"Well, I'm here, so let's do this so I can go shoppin'. I need to get my party on tonight."

We went to my room and I pulled the suitcase out my closet and dumped the contents on my bed for the second time.

"Oh my goodness, my pussy just got wet staring at all this," Mya said. "Damn, that niggah had taste. They doin' it big up in Philly, huh?"

I nodded my head. "I guess so. I was just saying the same thing."

"Yeah, he woulda definitely got some of this pussy if he wasn't such an asshole. What a waste of dick."

First, we divided up about thirty thousand dollars worth of jewelry, then split the cash. I agreed to let Mya have the coke, because she had people who could move it. Ever since my brother got locked up, I was never interested in the drug game, and besides I wasn't greedy. In the end, I had about twenty five thousand from the hit, so I was satisfied. That was more than enough to pay off some bills, go shopping, and more importantly invest in my salon.

"Diamond, what you doin' tonight?" Mya asked, putting the new items inside her denim Louis Vuitton bag.

"Why?"

"I got us another score," she replied.

I'm never gonna get any rest. "So soon?" I asked.

"Of course, you know I stay on this money!" she responded with a smile. "Did you think we were on vacation or some shit?"

"No, I just didn't think we would do a job back to back, that's all. So who's the victim this time?" I asked.

"This white boy from Buckhead, who's so fuckin' paid. He owns a few restaurants downtown, and a club down in Miami. He's into other things too, but I don't have the rundown yet. He's a baller, Diamond. I know we can get this dude for an easy hundred thousand a piece. But I need for you to be the front girl."

"Again, why me? I thought we were supposed to take turns."

"Well normally we would, but I heard this dude is into Puerto Rican type chicks, and since you could pass for one, I know he's gonna love you."

I looked at her with a frown. "What about you? You're damn near white yourself."

"Honey, I'm far from a Spanish chick. You're the one with the beautiful complexion."

I hesitated for a moment before I continued. After the Sky incident the night before, I kinda wanted a break before being the front girl again. I wanted to wait at least a week. "What's his name?" I asked in a low tone.

"They call him Scottie, but I don't know if it's his real name. He's cute for a white boy. I know for sure that he's gonna be at Visions tonight doin' his thing."

"But look at my eye, Mya. I can't be seen like this!"

"Girl, just throw on some sunglasses, and you'll be good. A niggah ain't gonna give a fuck about your eye when he's starin' at that ass, and thinkin' about pussy," she stated with a bold tone.

I looked hesitant, thinking that it was still too soon, but Mya was straight hood, and didn't give a fuck about risk or chances. All she saw was paper and opportunity.

"C'mon, this is major mutha-fuckin' paper we talkin' about.

You can open up two fuckin' salons after we hit this dude," she continued, trying her best to encourage me.

"Okay, I'm in. But after this, we need to chill for a minute. I don't wanna make it too hot for myself. We live in this town too, Mya," I replied. "I keep telling your ass we shouldn't shit where we eat."

"I know, but do you think I actually give a fuck about these niggahs out here? We need to ride this shit until we fall back."

I knew once Mya had her mind set there was nothing I could do or say to convince her otherwise. Even if I would've told her no, she probably would've found someone else to take my place. Mya and I went over a few more details before she headed out the door. When she left, I looked outside my window thinking to myself. This game was cool for now, but I had dreams that I wanted to see happen.

Several minutes after going over my future plans in my head, my phone rang interrupting my thoughts. After answering it, I realized that I had another hair appointment at three. Even though I was tired, doing hair wasn't a problem for me. It kept me busy and most of all, focused. I even enjoyed hearing all the gossip that was told to me by every woman who sat in my kitchen chair. They talked about everything, from their cheating boyfriends, their kids, to who was fuckin' who around the way, and the craziest topic, who was gay. I probably knew every man on the down low in Atlanta. People could waste their money on magazines or newspapers, but the best resources in the world, were gossiping women.

Chapter 3

Diamond

At eleven p.m., I was in my white convertible Toyota Solara cruising down 85 South, on the way to Visions nightclub. I loved convertible cars and couldn't wait until I stacked enough money to buy the new 650i BMW. Every so often I would go to the dealership and drool over the stunning vehicle.

When I arrived, the place was packed with people waiting to get inside. I guess some people got tired of waiting and decided to move the party outside because I could barely drive through the large crowd. I parked my car, and stepped out in my sexy cream Nicole Miller halter dress that hugged my body in all the right places. If I wanted to make an impression on this Scottie guy, I had to start with a gorgeous appearance. I had decided not to take Mya's suggestion about the sunglasses in order to cover my eye, but had applied tons of makeup. I didn't want Scottie to think that I was being abused.

As I walked toward the club, the line seemed even longer to get in and stretched down the street like a damn slinky. I knew I wasn't about to play myself and stand in the back, so I strutted my way up to the front entrance to see if any of the bouncers I knew were at the door. When I passed by all the losers standing in line, I could hear several men trying their best lines on me. I had to laugh when I heard one of them say "Damn, I'm glad I'm not blind because you're fine as hell." I'd never heard that one before. I didn't even entertain the comment and continued toward the club.

When one of the bouncers saw me coming, he smiled. "Diamond, I had a feeling that you were gonna show up tonight. It's too much money inside for you to stay home, right?" Brian joked.

"Why did you say that?" I responded, trying to act offended. "I'm just here to get my party on." I lied.

"Yeah right," he responded.

I turned back around and looked at the crowd. "It's packed out here tonight. What's going on?"

"This is the after party for the Bank Roll concert. Petey Pablo is hosting it."

Even more ballers to choose from. "Oh, so that's why these money hungry tramps are out here." I stood in front of Brain, who looked at me like I had some nerve by saying that. Brain was a handsome six-four, muscular brotha that had a thing for me since we both worked at Body Tap. I was close to him, but it was strictly platonic. Brian and I always had an arrangement. At Body Tap he would put me on to all the dudes with paper before any of the other girls could get to them, and in return I would introduce him to some of my freaky girlfriends like Alaina and Mya.

I stood behind the red velvet rope and barked, "So what's up, Brian, you gonna have me standing out here all night, or do I gotta get Mya on your ass."

"Shit, is she comin' up here?" he asked with a frown.

"Maybe, why, do you miss her?" I joked.

"Man, hell no. You better keep that crazy bitch away from me. The last time I got wit' that, she damn near snapped my dick off. You would've thought she was tryin' to win a race. That girl needs help, she's too damn freaky. I ain't into that S&M shit."

The other bouncers laughed including me. Shit, if Mya was too much for Brian, then she had some serious issues, because I heard Brain liked it rough.

"Get your ass inside, Diamond and behave yourself," he said, removing the rope.

"I always do," I returned, and strutted passed the bouncers like the diva I was.

Once inside, I noticed that it was even more crowded, than I thought. The place was so packed you could barely move. I watched as the crowd went wild, when the popular DJ Smooth played '*Get Low*' by Lil' Jon. After shaking my bare ass in front of hundreds of men as a stripper, dancing was the last thing I wanted to do when I went out, so I made my way to the bar. I seemed to catch every man's attention as I navigated my way through the thick crowd. I wasn't as nervous from the score the night before, but I wanted to get a drink so I could blend in with the crowd, just in case the white boy saw me first.

I was at the bar for less than a minute, when a guy came up to me and offered to buy me a drink. Reluctantly I accepted, and decided to hold a conversation with him. As I sat there and listened to him go on forever about his job as a record producer, I realized he was very attractive and well dressed, but I had to remain focused because he wasn't my target.

I decided to scan the room for the white boy that resembled the description Mya had given me. Luckily for me, there weren't too many white boys in the club, especially cute and rich, so it was easy to weed out the crowd.

I cut my conversation with Mr. Unknown short when I noticed a small entourage of men making their way over to the V.I.P section. As I continued to look, I quickly noticed a white guy in an expensive looking suit walking with the same group of men. *That has to be him*, I thought. He was tall, about five-eleven, and sported a short spiky hair cut. He looked like money and I admired his style.

"Thanks for the drink, but I have to run," I said to Mr. Record Producer.

"Wow, so soon. Well, can I at least get your number?" he asked.

I looked back and noticed the entourage of men were almost to the V.I.P. door, and I hadn't made my move yet. "Umm, sure but let me run to the ladies room first," I replied. I didn't even wait for his response before I turned around and walked away.

I quickly made my way toward the group of men, with my Apple Martini clutched in my hand. I had to quickly think of a scheme to get the white guy's attention. I didn't want to come off desperate for his attention and look like a fuckin' groupie. That was the last thing I needed him to think. I needed to do this without playing myself somehow.

Luckily when I got closer, Scottie still hadn't reached the V.I.P from all the people who were stopping him, so I still had time to go in for the kill. It was now or never. As Scottie turned around I pushed myself forward, tripping over him and spilling my drink. He quickly caught me in his arms and I acted as if I was so embarrassed.

"Oh my goodness, I'm so sorry," I apologized. "Some asshole just pushed me. Damn, I spilled my drink all over you."

"It's okay," he responded with a smile. "It happens."

"I'm so clumsy. Let me get you a napkin."

"No, I'm good. I have three more of these at home," he stated.

"Well, send me the cleaning bill, it's the least I can do."

"Nah, don't worry it's an old suit anyway. Like I said, accidents happen. I'll give it to charity tomorrow."

Damn, give it to charity. That suit looks like Armani. After apologizing a few more times, Scottie stared at me for several seconds without saying a word. It was if he was looking at me for the very first time.

"Are you okay?" I asked.

"Yeah, I'm fine," he responded, never taking his eyes off me.

Indeed you are, I thought gazing into his beautiful green eyes. "Well, thanks for not blowing up about this. You're a true gentleman."

When I attempted to leave, I felt him grab my arm gently.

"Um, you're not in a rush, are you?"

"Why did you change your mind about me cleaning the suit?"

"No, not that. I just want to know if I can have the pleasure of knowing your name?" he asked with such charm.

In my mind I could hear Mya telling me the rules of the game, so I had to come up with something. "Dee and yours?"

"Scottie."

"Nice to meet you, Scottie."

"Listen, I was just on my way to the V.I.P, would you like to join me?" he asked so smoothly.

I hesitated for a moment. I already knew my answer, but I didn't want him to think I was too anxious. "Hey, I owe it to you for ruining your suit, so sure I would love to join you."

He smiled and extended his hand as a sign that he wanted me to walk first. As I took my place in front of him, I thought his gesture could mean one or two things. That he was a true gentlemen or that he was trying to look at my ass from behind. Either way, I liked it. Phase one was already in action.

Once inside, Scottie introduced me to his crew, and everybody looked like they had money. *Mya would be on cloud nine if her ass was here right now.* When he finished introducing me to his friends, we found a private section of the room and sat down on a comfortable red chaise. I made sure I sat with class.

"So, I assume you came alone tonight, Dee?" he asked, pouring me a glass of Veuve Clicquot.

"Yeah, my girlfriend was supposed to meet me tonight, but as you can see…"

"Hey, everything happens for a reason," he said.

"So Scottie, if you don't mind me asking, what is it that you do for a living?" *Fuck all the small talk, I came here for business.*

"No, I don't mind at all. I own a few restaurants here in Atlanta, and also own a few clubs in South Beach. Have you ever been to Miami?"

"Actually no, I haven't," I said embarrassed. It was crazy how

Mya and I had never even thought about traveling or getting out of the hood before.

"Well I would love for you to come down sometimes, as my guest, and even bring a friend if you'd like. I know you would have a wonderful time," he replied.

"Thanks, I would love too."

He flashed a sexy smile. "So, what does a beautiful woman like yourself do?" he asked.

"Well I'm into a little bit of this and that, but more importantly I'm trying to get paid like you." He probably thought I was joking, but little did he know I was serious as a heart attack.

He smiled again. "With beauty like yours, it shouldn't be hard."

"So, I see you're into black chicks," I said boldly.

"I love the sistahs," he admitted.

I admired his honesty. "And why is that?"

"The attitude, the look, everything about a black woman is so exotic and tasteful. Black women are some of the finest women on the planet," he stated gladly.

I smiled. "You probably just like black girls because we have big asses and white girls are flat as ironing boards.

"Actually, I'm a brain over beauty type of guy, but I must say, Dee; you're the most beautiful woman I've ever laid eyes on. So right now you could be dumb as hell and I wouldn't even care."

I began to blush. "You need to stop flirting with me white boy."

He smiled again exposing a set of teeth that looked like they cost a fortune, his smile was contagious. Scottie was certainly a nice piece of eye candy, with his clean shaven face. I also liked the fact that he wasn't too flashy. The only piece of jewelry he wore was a huge diamond studded earring in his left ear. He had class, but definitely had a little thug in him. He was so smooth, that if I closed my eyes, I would've sworn I was talking to a black guy.

We began talking about everything, the business that he was

in, a little bit about himself and even about interracial dating.

Scottie told me all of his old girlfriends were black or Spanish and had been in some form of the entertainment business, whether it was modeling, acting or singing. He also told me that he was originally from New York, and only seemed to date girls who were stuck on themselves, but that I seemed different.

He kept the drinks coming, as we continued to talk, and his money seemed limitless, even though he didn't pull out wads of cash, flashing it for everyone to see. I even saw him give the waitress an American Express black card, which meant he had money and good credit. His style and the way he did things were attractive. *Mya definitely knows how to pick 'em*, I thought to myself. I wondered how she came across this one.

I must've thought her up, because several seconds later, my cell phone began to vibrate. It was Mya calling. "Excuse me, I need to take this," I said to Scottie, lifting myself off the couch.

"Sure no problem. Take your time," he responded.

I walked toward the ladies bathroom and answered the phone in a low tone. I didn't want anybody in my conversation. "What's up?"

"Are you in or what?" Mya asked.

"Yeah, I'm in. I'm having drinks with him in V.I.P as we speak."

"Damn, I taught you well. I told you that he would go for you. So what do you think?"

"He's fine for sure," I replied.

"Look, just make sure you get enough information from him before you start thinkin' about fuckin'."

"No, I think you got me mixed up with you about that shit," I uttered.

Mya giggled. "So, how are you playin' it? Did you get him to open up?" she asked, ready to get his money.

"Definitely. He even invited me to come down to Miami with him," I told her.

"Are you serious? Let's do this," she replied, sounding

extremly hyped and so hood.

"Look we can't rush into this, Mya. I'm gonna have to work this one nice and slow."

"Oh, so you're a professional now? Well let me say this, you work this dude the way you want, but don't take forever."

"Cool. So, where are you now?" I asked.

"I'm actually outside."

I was shocked. "You're outside right now and not coming inside?"

"I might. The problem is, I see so much money and dick out here that I may not even need to come in. I'll probably just stay out here and take a souvenir home," Mya said, always clowning around about dick.

Suddenly, I heard someone coming into the bathroom. "Girl, I gotta go. I'll holla at you later."

"Hit me on my cell, if you need me. I'll be outside chasin' my two favorite things."

I shook my head back and forth. "Bye."

When I hung up, a thin undernourished girl, walked toward one of the stalls. *Damn, it looks like the last time she ate was two months ago.* I laughed to myself all the way out the door. When I returned, Scottie was still sitting in the same spot.

"Is everything okay, Dee?" he asked, sounding concerned.

I almost didn't respond to the name Dee, but quickly remembered that I had temporarily changed my name. "I'm fine."

"Good." He paused for a moment before continuing, "I definitely wanna see more of you."

"And that can be arranged," I said, batting my eyes.

Scottie and I got reacquainted and talked until he invited me to another after party at the Hyatt Regency hotel, and of course I agreed.

As I left the club and walked to my car, I looked around to see if Mya was somewhere acting like a prostitute, but I didn't see her. I thought about calling her when I got in the car, but quickly decided against it. I needed time to think. I wanted to remind myself that I couldn't get caught up in the hype with Scottie, because he was a mark. And if I got too close like I did with Sky, it would surely fuck up our business. I couldn't afford that to happen.

Chapter 4

Mya

Outside of Vision was lookin' like paradise to me with all the ballers and money that was present as I stepped out of my brand new black Yukon Denali. I was hopin' to find the perfect target tonight, so my sexy short Marc Jacobs skirt and three-inch Manolo Blahnik stilettos wouldn't go to waste. I always had to make sure I looked like I'd just stepped off the runway, so I could catch all the men with deep pockets. It took money to make money. If I allowed myself to step out lookin' like some broke ass broad, half the dudes would probably think I was after their paper from the gate, and I couldn't have that. Besides, I was blessed with some well defined legs and loved showin' them off whenever I got the chance. As soon as I hit the button to activate my car alarm, I heard some dumb niggah try his hand with me.

"Damn, shawty…what your fine ass doing comin' out such a big truck. You like 'em big huh. Well if you want, I can give you something big to ride on."

I rolled my eyes and sucked my teeth. I hadn't even made it to the door yet, and somebody was fuckin' wit' me already. "You look like a broke and thirsty niggah, so why waste your time. You can't possibly think you have a chance wit' me?" I asked sarcastically.

"Why the fuck are you so feisty, girl?"

"Niggah, step off!" I shouted. Broke dudes always irritated me. I knew I was rude, but could've cared less. If someone stepped to me, they had to come correct because I wasn't one to lower my standards.

After my remark his boys laughed, which immediately made his facial expression change. I guess I had embarrassed him in front of his friends. "Fuck this trick, she out here lookin' over-rated anyway," he shouted to his friends.

I turned around and gave him the look of death. "What the fuck did you just say to me?"

"You heard what I said, bitch. I didn't stutter," he responded with an evil look.

I guess he felt like he'd redeemed himself in front of his homies with that slick remark toward me. Little did he know who he was fuckin' wit', so I calmly walked over to him. "Don't you ever fuckin' disrespect me again!" I yelled, slappin' him in his face. I was two steps away from knockin' his head off.

He immediately tried to grab me after I had embarrassed him for the second time, but his boys did the right thing and held him back.

"Chill niggah," one of his friends said, grabbing him from behind. He probably had no idea that his friend had just saved his life, because if he would've touched me, it was gonna be on.

"Nah fuck that...ain't no bitch gonna put her hands on me and I can't hit her ass back!" he responded, still tryin' his best to get closer to me.

"Go ahead mutha-fucka, lose your life tonight," I warned. I knew I could easily get to the .45 in my purse. And even if I didn't murder him personally, I would get one of my niggahs to do it for me.

"Yo, chill!" his friend continued.

"You better listen to your boy," I said boldly.

They finally did the right thing and pulled my new enemy away. He continued to throw out threats at me as they led him away. I let out a devilish smile and tried going on wit' my night in peace. All it took was one asshole to bring the ghetto out of me, while I was tryin' to look for a paid dude to get at.

After the small ordeal, I pulled out my money radar again, and walked up to the club entrance. I was surprised to be greeted by Brian, who I used to fuck back in the day. I hadn't seen him since the night I pulled out my whips and chains.

He shook his head at me as I approached him doin' a sexy little dance. "Mya, you ain't even in the club yet and you already starting trouble."

"So tell these clown ass niggahs out here to stop actin' stupid and everything will be okay," I replied.

"What do you want? I know you ain't tryin' to get in?" he asked.

I stood with my hands on my hips. "What do you think I'm tryin' to do, Brian? I'm not standin' out here for my fuckin' health."

"I don't know, Mya. You're already causing a damn scene. Why can't you be classy, like Diamond? I just let her in about an hour ago."

Even though Diamond was my girl, I didn't appreciate anyone tellin' me I needed to be more like her. "Listen, I'm gonna be me, so just deal with it."

Brian let out a slight laugh. "That's just it. I don't wanna deal with that shit."

"Look, why do you have me standin' out here like we don't even know each other?" I asked. He was really startin' to piss me off.

"Cuz, you're still hot-headed right now, and I need for you to calm down before you can even attempt to come up in here."

"Mutha-fucka, I am calm! You think I'm gonna let some clown ass niggah like that upset me," I yelled. "Stop playin' games and move the damn rope!"

He sighed. "See, look at you. I don't need any drama up in the club tonight. Go for a quick walk and cool off. Come back in a few minutes when you can control yourself."

"Brian, you actin' like a real dick right now, but it's cool. Fuck you and this club," I snapped.

"Your ass needs anger management classes or some shit," he replied.

I don't need to be in some club to get money anyway. Besides, Diamond was already inside workin' on a major deal. A deal that would have us set for a while. As I made my way back to my truck, my attention rested on a guy who had just stepped out of a silver CLS 500 Benz coupe with New York tags.

I didn't care for dudes from up north, especially New York, but I was willing to make an exception this time. I could smell money and a big dick a mile away, and I knew he had both talents. He was nice and chocolate like Morris Chestnut and wore a dark blue Yankees fitted hat that was cocked low over his eye He complemented his New York style with a blue and white Sean John button down shirt, baggy denim jeans, and some crisp white Nike Air Force Ones. My eyes were especially drawn to the lengthy diamond and platinum chain that draped down to his abs. He must've known that I was checkin' him out and smiled as we made eye contact.

"Yo, Ma let me holla at you for a minute," he said, in his New York accent, soundin' so sure of himself.

I cut my eye at him trying to play hard to get.

"Damn, luv…it ain't gotta be hostile between us. I ain't a jerk like that last niggah you cursed out. You know how to handle yourself and I like that," he said.

"You saw that?"

"Yeah. I've been watching you since you first stepped out your whip. I even saw them niggahs that fronted on you at the door, but don't sweat that shit. You're too good for that club anyway," he responded.

I guess he thought that comment was gonna make me blush, but it wasn't easy to flatter me. "Yeah whatever, enough with all the chit chat. Are you tryin' to get at me or what? Cuz, I do like what I see," I said, being straight forward.

He smiled. "I like that, you're raw, Ma. I'm definitely feelin' that." I slowly walked up to him so we could get a little closer. "So what's your name, luv?" he asked.

"Precious, and yours?" I never told a dude my real name, just in case he ended up being my next victim.

"I'm Black."

"So Mr. Black, are you out here alone, or what?"

"Nah, I'm wit' my peoples, but they're inside doin' them. I needed a break, so I came out to my whip to smoke."

"You got another cigarette on you?"

"Sure." He reached into his half empty box of Newports and pulled one out.

As he gave me a light, I took a long drag, which was badly needed and exhaled a cloud of smoke into the warm air. "So Black, what are you tryin' to get into tonight?" I asked.

"Whatever you wanna do, I'm down."

I took another pull from the cancer stick. "Is this you, or did you borrow it from someone?" I asked, gesturing toward his Benz.

"Yeah, this me, Ma. Why, you wanna get out of here and go for a ride somewhere?"

I let out a small grin. "That'll work." From the looks of things Black looked like a true hustler, so as usual I had probably hit the jackpot.

As soon as I got in on the passenger side, I fell in love wit' the way my skin felt against his plush leather seats. I gave Black a slight peep when my skirt rose up my thigh as I crossed my legs. He smiled. I knew the sight of my thick thighs made his dick jump.

"So, what brings you down to the dirty south?" I asked, but not really caring.

"I love this city, the ladies, the clubs and I get money down here too," he said.

I knew it. Am I good or what, I thought to myself. "Oh, an entrepreneur just like me. I'm always glad to see a brotha such as yourself tryin' to get ahead."

"Yeah I gotta get that paper, luv," he replied.

So do I, Mr. Black.

As he drove drown Peachtree Street, toward the direction of Buckhead, he blasted *50 Cent's song, In Da Club.* "You want it to be your birthday, boo," I teased. I let my skirt rise a bit more, showin' off more of my smooth sensual skin.

"Ummm, you lookin' good, Ma. I'm feelin' you so much right now. What you workin' with down there anyway?" he said hungrily.

His attention went back and forth from the road to me. He licked his lips and placed his right hand closer to my thigh. I peeped the diamond pinky ring he had on and expressed a lustful smile toward his direction.

"You want to see a sample," I asked, uncrossin' my legs. I spread my legs apart, and exposed my shaved goodies for Black to view. It was a good thing I had on my thongs that looked more like dental floss.

"Damn, Precious you 'bout to make a niggah wreck!" he said excitedly.

I smiled. "Do they have pussy as good as this up in New York?" I moved my hand down to my throbbin' pussy and began rubbin' my clit before lettin' out a wicked moan for his ears to enjoy. I could tell by the smile he gave me that he was extremely pleased.

"Nah, girls in New York be frontin'. I come to ATL just for the women alone cuz y'all be doin' it up with the hips and ass. I guess it's from all that cornbread y'all be eatin' and shit," he joked.

His hand was already situated on my thigh and as he continued to drive, he moved it up a little bit at a time. Soon, his hand rested in between my exposed thighs and he grabbed a handful of my pussy.

"Shit, you're so wet," he said. He quickly inserted two fingers inside my nest and within seconds my juices poured out like an oil spill.

"Mmmm, that feels good," I cried out.

I clamped my thighs around his hand, as he continued to finger me. I could tell he was tryin' to maintain a suitable speed and grip the steering wheel with his other hand at the same time. I felt his fingers thrust in and out with force, and the more he pushed, the wetter my pussy got for him.

"Yo, I'm ready to fuck," he said, lookin' like he couldn't control himself any longer.

"I bet you are," I replied with a huge smile.

I had the situation under my control, and my raw freakiness had him so mesmerized I knew I could get anything I wanted at this point. I learned at an early age, that pussy could make any niggah weak.

The way he worked my walls with his fingers started to remind me of my crazy childhood. At the age of fifteen, I started to develop in all the right areas, and men definitely began to notice. Even my mother started to hate on me. It was probably because I had more of a body than she did. Whenever we went shopping, she would buy me loose fittin' clothing so nothing would fit tight and draw any attention to me. I soon got tired of all the girls in the hood pickin' on my lack of style, so whenever my mother went to work, I would take a pair of scissors to every piece of baggy clothing I had and altered them to fit me extremely tight. In time, whatever whack outfit my mother bought to hurt my sex appeal, I would change into my own sexy style. I was able to change a shapeless church dress into somethin' so provocative that many of my friends started to notice and wanted me to transform their clothes as well. I even made Diamond a pair of jeans from my hood clothing line once.

"Are you okay, Ma?" Black asked. I guess he could tell I was deep in thought, even though he never took his hand out my pussy.

"Yeah, I'm good, baby. Don't stop" I responded and quickly went back into my past.

Soon I started trottin' around the house in skimpy cut up boy shorts or jeans, and wearin' shirts so revealing that sometimes a nipple would pop out for my mother, her boyfriend, Rodney or whoever was around at the time to witness. I liked teasin' Rodney, and would let my skirt ride up my thigh a bit, while we sat on the couch watchin' television. I would always catch him watchin' me from the corner of my eye, so I knew he was no good.

Rodney was a pervert, a horny mutha-fucka who would fuck anythin' breathin'. I used to catch him starin' at me with hunger in his eyes. Even though I was young and still considered a lil' girl, in Rodney's eyes he only saw a sexy girl in a woman's body. When Rodney and my mother would wake me up in the middle of the night from fuckin' I used to get so turned on. I would ease drop by puttin' my ear to the bedroom door and began to wonder what dick felt like. Little did I know I would soon find out.

My mother had a habit of leavin' me home alone wit' Rodney. She would be gone for hours at a time, leaving me with her man. I guess she trusted Rodney, and figured I was only a child and couldn't do any harm to her relationship. But on one particular night, my mother left me at home wit' Rodney, while she went out gamblin' with her friends. However, that night proved to be a huge mistake on her part.

Before that night, I had only messed around, and let a few boys touch my kitty kat, but I never took it to the extreme and had sex. Curiosity was getting the best of me, and even at a young age, I wanted to take it to the next level. That night wit' Rodney, I was bored, and felt like fuckin' with his head, so after walkin' back and forth in front of him with my ass hangin' out of my short jean skirt, it didn't take long for Rodney to grab me and stick his tongue in my mouth. Before long, he had one of his hands inside my pussy and finger fucked me just like Black was doin'. Eventually, he unbuckled his pants and it was on from there. That night I lost my virginity to my mother's boyfriend and loved every minute of it. He fucked me like a grown woman, and didn't even bother to use a condom, but I didn't give a fuck. I just wanted to know what dick felt like.

Thirty minutes, after our encounter, Rodney offered me twenty dollars to keep my mouth shut, and of course I took it. If keepin' a secret was going to get me money, then I was all for it. I guess he started to become addicted to my sex because before I knew it, my hush money was increased to fifty dollars, and weeks later it turned into a hundred. By the time I turned sixteen, I was makin' two hundred dollars every time my mother left us alone. This was my first experience at the game.

In time, I think my mother suspected that Rodney and I were havin' sex wit' each other, but she was so insecure that she didn't even say anythin'. My mother always allowed men to treat her like shit anyway, and she used pussy to try to keep them around and help her with the bills. And I guess since Rodney was payin' our rent, it was best to overlook the things that he did with me. Rodney cheated on my mother with everyone, and sometimes he did it so blatant and openly, that it embarrassed my mother and she would be the talk of the hood. I mean, Rodney had women being so disrespectful that they would call our crib and ask for him knowin' my mother was home. There were even a few times where I had to curse a few bitches out, for disrespectin' my mother like that.

I was young, feisty and didn't give a fuck. I had a fierce reputation around my way as being a badass, and gettin' paper was my specialty. I ran with a female crew that was just as rough and wild as me. We shoplifted, smoked weed and drank all day, and even sold drugs on the side for the local dealers. Even though Diamond and I were friends, her mother and brother kept her on a tight leash, so she couldn't do shit.

By the time I was seventeen, I already had two abortions, got locked up twice, and cut a niggah across his face for callin' me a hoe one night at a club. I was proud of the permanent scare I left on his face to remember me by. Eventually my mother kicked me out of the house, and I had to move out on my own. It wasn't until I met O.C. that I really started makin' what I call real dough.

So do you wanna get a room?" Black asked, interruptin' my trip down memory lane for the second time.

"Oh, yeah sure," I responded. I was gettin' a bit irritated, but I didn't want him to notice. I had to make sure I was sweet and polite until I was able to pull off my plan. Seconds later, I began to think about my money makin' history again.

One night when I went to pick up Diamond from her bullshit job at Body Tap, I met, O.C., the man who changed everythin'. I had thought about strippin' a few times, and even though strippers made a lot of money, I knew I could make more on the streets, so swingin' on poles and grindin' on niggahs for a few dollars wasn't my thing. Besides, I liked to fuck for my money sometimes, and that wasn't a part of the dumb ass club rules. As I waited for Diamond to finish her set, I was head over heels when I saw O.C.'s fine ass enter the building. I knew from the moment he walked in that he had major funds, so I had to have him. Needless to say I kept a close eye on him the entire time. After he received a bullshit lap dance from one of Diamond's co-workers, he gave her some money then stood up to leave. That was my cue to show him what I had, so I followed him to the parkin' lot and made my move. Thirty minutes later, I had him right where I wanted him, and before the night was over, we were fuckin' in his beautiful mansion in Alpharetta. I made sure to suck his dick like a mutha-fuckin' porn-star.

I collected three grand from him that night, and surprisingly he had me open. Not just because of his pockets, but his demeanor too. O.C. was a straight thug and a get money niggah that turned me on, and in time I became his girl. O.C. spoiled me, and I got down with his crew who not only moved kilos, but robbed dudes as well. Sometimes they would use me as their front girl to get at certain niggahs, which always paid well. I learned a lot from O.C. and began applyin' my skills to the streets. Before long, I didn't need O.C. anymore and eventually started my own jackin' business. But soon, the work got to be too much, and that's when I hooked up with Diamond. I needed a fresh face in the game, and she was beautiful. It also didn't hurt that she came from the streets like me, and was about gettin' money. I knew that I needed a partner in this game who was just as good as me to have my back. Now with every score, we keep gettin' better, and I wasn't gonna stop until the streets made me.

"You're my kind of girl, Precious. I'm lovin' you right now," Black said, once again bringin' me back to reality. He still hadn't taken his hand away from my nest.

"Thanks, I have that affect on people," I returned.

I looked over at Black, who had a huge grin. *Too bad this dude doesn't know what he's gotten himself into.* It was clear that he was sprung. Little did he know I was setting his ass up for the steal, and he would soon be my next mark.

Chapter 5

Diamond

The party at the Hyatt was off the hook; almost everyone came through for a good time. The crowd was urban, but classy, and the guys were impressive. If I hadn't been there to scope Scottie out, then I could've easily targeted another one of his friends. They all looked like they had six figures. I had expected Mya to show up, but I guess she got caught up with one of her many special friends.

I continued to get to know Scottie and he loved every minute of my time. He made me laugh even if a lot of things he said were corny, but by three a.m. I was ready to go. Scottie suggested that he pay for a room so I didn't have to drive home, but I politely turned him down, "Maybe next time," I said.

To my surprise he was cool with my response and didn't press the issue. Any other niggah would've practically begged for some pussy. We exchanged phone numbers, and both promised to call each other soon, then ended the night with a soft kiss on my cheek. Scottie seemed like a nice guy, so a part of me was starting to hate that he was another score.

I hadn't even been in my car for a minute when my cell phone started ringing. A smile appeared on my face because at the time I thought it was Scottie calling to check on me, but when I looked at the caller ID the name, *Mya* appeared on the screen.

"What's up, girl?"

"Diamond, I need you right now?" she said, in a desperate tone.

"Why, are you in some kind of trouble?" I began to wonder what she'd gotten herself into while I was in the club.

"Nah, I got a niggah for us to get at right now," she stated.

"What?"

"Yeah, this baller I met outside of Visions. He's from New York, and got plenty of fuckin' money. I can see the bulge in his pocket."

"Mya, it's almost four in the morning, I'm about to head home," I replied. I hadn't had much sleep lately and needed to catch up on some major beauty rest.

"Look, he's goin' back to New York tomorrow, so it's now or never. We can't fuck around and let a perfect hit get away," she replied.

"How you wanna play it?" I asked nonchalantly, finally giving in. She was right; you can never be too tired to get money. I didn't have any kids, so I could catch up on my rest later.

"We about to get a room and do our thing."

I couldn't believe what she'd just said. "So let me get this straight. You're gonna fuck him first?"

"Hell yeah, I ain't tryin' to waste some good dick. Besides, he's been makin' me horny all damn night, so this is how we're gonna do this. When we get to the room, I'm gonna text you the hotel location and our room number. It'll probably be a lil' after four once we get settled in and I start doin' what I do best. Once I text you, come to the hotel exactly thirty minutes after that. I'm gonna slide the cardkey under the door, so when you walk in, you can just point the heat at him and from there it's, payday," Mya said.

"Are you sure about this?"

"Diamond, I'm gonna be fuckin' this niggah so hard, he ain't even gonna know what city he's in after I'm done. Trust me I know what I'm doin'."

"Cool, I'll see you in a little while," I responded.

I hung up and started my car. Even though I didn't have the slightest idea which hotel Mya was gonna be at, I wanted to get away from the Hyatt, just in case I ran into Scottie. I drove to Piedmont Street and decided to wait at that location for Mya's text.

As I waited in my car, I began to think about Scottie. I also began to think about my brother and about my life. I couldn't do this shit forever. It was already starting to become a major inconvenience.

Twenty minutes later, I finally got the text. Mya informed me that she was at the Marriot Atlanta Hotel on Best Road, in room 809. She also informed me not to be late.

I started up my car again and quickly made my way toward my next job. Several moments later, I pulled up at the hotel, parked my car, and headed for the entrance. When I entered the lobby, it was so quiet you could've heard an ant crawling across the floor. I strutted past the front desk like I was on a mission and headed toward the elevator.

I got off at the eighth floor, and started searching for room 809. When I got to the door, I bent down and searched for the key. Just like our plan, the key was right where Mya left it, placed discreetly under the room door, but easy enough to retrieve.

I pulled out my gat and slowly inserted the key into the lock. When the security device changed from red to green, I quietly opened the door. Once in the small foyer, I heard Mya's loud sexual cries along with his loud moans.

"Ummm, fuck me! Yes, give me that dick," I heard Mya cry out.

"Oooh, your pussy is so good, luv," I heard the mark respond.

I slowly made my way into the bedroom, being quiet as a mouse. They both had their backs turned to me, as he fucked Mya in the doggy style position. He was trying to grip her hips but Mya kept backing her ass against him roughly.

As I looked at the clock, it read four forty-five. It was now or never. I sprang into view with the gun pointed at the back of his head, "Can you crawl up out the pussy for a second?"

The guy turned around shocked by my sudden appearance, and immediately stopped. I could see several beads of sweat appear on his forehead.

"Yo, what the fuck is this shit?!" he yelled.

"Sorry to be the one to inform you, but down here, you gotta come out them pockets to play," I replied.

Mya stared at me and smiled. I knew she was proud.

"Bitch, you set me up?" he asked, looking at Mya.

"Black, c'mon baby, why did you stop. You might as well get your nut before you get jacked," she suggested.

"Are you fuckin' serious? Let's just hurry up and do this," I ordered.

"We got time, right Black. You might as well finish fuckin' me," she suggested again. She then stuck her ass out like she was in a music video.

"Mya!" I called out again. Even though, I was disgusted that she'd asked our mark to finish fuckin' her, the moment I called out her real name, I knew I'd messed up.

"Mya?" Black said, with a confused expression. "I thought your name was Precious."

"Well Precious is my middle name, so I like to go by that," Mya responded. She looked over at me, with a face full of disappointment. "Now come on Mr. Black, finish givin' me part of the reason I came here in the first place."

"Fuck y'all bitches, y'all fuckin' crazy down here," he returned.

He tried to be slick and turn around, but I pushed the barrel of the gun into the back of his head. "Don't even try it," I replied.

"Man, I thought, you were a thug. Now I know you're just a pussy," Mya added. She got up off the bed and quickly put her clothes back on. She obviously had an attitude.

After she got herself together, we tied his ass up, and then locked him in the bathroom butt ass naked, with Mya's panties stuffed in his mouth along with duct tape. We then threw his belongings, into an empty pillow case and casually walked out of his room like nothing had ever happened. We left the, *Do not Disturb* sign outside his door and made our exit.

Several minutes later, we were outside the Waffle House parking lot dividing up our earnings inside of Mya's truck. However, after going through everything it turned out to be a pretty lousy score. We only ended up getting fifteen hundred dollars a piece, two platinum chains and a small bag of weed, which I didn't want.

I should've taken my ass home, I thought as I put the lengthy chain and the cash into my purse. "This job wasn't even worth it," I said, looking at Mya count her portion of the money.

"Well, the cash is a lil' light, but at least I got some dick tonight," she replied with a huge smile.

"I can't believe you asked him to keep fuckin' you, and right in front of me at that."

"Well believe it because I was dead serious. As good as that shit was I didn't want you or anybody else to keep me from cumin," she replied.

All I could do was shake my head. Mya was out of control. "I've never met anyone who loves dick more than you."

"But do you know what I love more than dick?" she asked. "Benjamin Frankin, the mutha-fucka on the hundred dollar bill."

I laughed. She didn't even give me a chance to respond to the question, even though I knew the answer. "Well I'm out. I need to go home and catch up on some rest."

"Speaking of money, how did everythin' go wit' the white dude? Did you find a way to get close to him?" she asked, obviously ignoring my statement.

"Well like I said earlier. I need to play this one slow. We can't rush into this thing. It's gonna take some time."

Mya looked at me like she was my mother. "Listen, I don't

wanna wait too long, Diamond. I need for you to handle that."

"You worry too much," I said, patting her hand. "I got this under control."

She gave me another concerned looked before I flashed a smile and hopped out of her truck. *Mya's gonna have to trust me, if she wants me to be a part of this team.* I could feel the softness of my eight hundred thread count sheets as I quickly walked toward my car.

$ $ $

I met up with Scottie several days later at Hodges on Candler Road, in Decatur. Having him pick me up at my place was definitely out of the question. I drove up in my convertible and stepped out in a pair of tight True Religion jeans and a peach colored baby doll t-shirt that looked great against my skin tone. If Scottie liked women with ass then I wanted to show him what I was working with.

Hodges was one of ATL's most well known spots to eat that had the bomb fried chicken and collard greens. I thought it would've been funny to meet Scottie at a place like this because from what I heard white people didn't do greasy food.

I spotted Scottie as he stepped out of his green Range Rover looking better than he did the night at the club. His confident swagger turned me on. I smiled as he entered the restaurant in a white and grey sweat suit with a fresh pair of Nikes. *He even looks good in sweats.* His smile was golden and almost addictive.

"Hey beautiful," he said, giving me a kiss on my cheek.

"You look nice."

"I had to make sure I looked presentable for you."

"Well you passed the test. Even your car looks good. I see you're pushing, a '07 Range already?" I replied, pointing to his car.

"I just drove it off the lot yesterday," he mentioned. "I even paid cash for it."

*If you just bought a 80,000 dollar car in cash, then I know
you got money*, I thought. "It definitely fits your style."

"Thanks. So, why did you want to meet here?" he asked,
looking around like he'd just realized where he was.

"This is one of my favorite places to eat. Why, is there a
problem?"

He smiled. "I'm cool with it. As long as I get to see you, we
can eat near a cliff and if you don't like me, then you can push
me off."

I gave him a strange expression. "That was sort of corny."

"I need to work on it some, huh?"

"Yeah, you do."

We headed over to the counter, and I ordered some chicken,
greens and a large ice-tea. Scottie ordered the same. As we waited for our food, we got a few angry stares from a few people, but
I didn't give a fuck about them, it was 2006. If people were still
bitter about interracial dating, then they needed to get over it.

"You think people hate that you're on a date with a white
guy?" Scottie joked.

I chuckled. "Hey, all I see in front of me is a handsome, well-
mannered man, with style and class, so who cares what other
people think."

"Ditto for me because you're so beautiful," he replied.

"You definitely have some charm with you, Scottie. You must
be like this with all the women?"

"Only the ones that I know will matter to me in time," he
returned.

I couldn't help it, I had to blush. "Can I ask you a personal
question?"

"And what's that?"

"Why do you have a thing for sistahs?"

"Because I think black women are so beautiful," he responded, playing with his car keys. For some reason he seemed nervous.

"What about white women? Don't you date them as well? Or

do you believe in what they say, once you go black, you can't go back," I joked.

He laughed. "I've been dating sistahs since high school. I get excited when I'm around beautiful black women like you. I've been lost in jungle fever forever."

"Still corny," I exclaimed.

He laughed again. "Hey, be nice. I'm trying my best to impress you."

After we got our food, we walked around the crowded restaurant to find a table. Once we finally located one, we immediately sat down to continue our conversation. I was feeling his vibe. I loved the fact that his ego was tamed and that he was quick to compliment me.

"So, I've been wondering, why a beautiful woman like you, doesn't have a boyfriend yet?" Scottie asked, as he put a piece of chicken in his mouth.

"Please, the guys in Atlanta are either gay, or can't handle a woman like myself. I rather be alone, and if I'm alone a little too often, then I have a fully charged vibrator to keep me company," I answered. "And what about you, why don't you have a woman in your life? You're a handsome guy. What's the deal with you?"

He displayed a huge smile at my comment. "Well, I'm very picky when it comes to women," he mentioned. "I don't want to settle down with just anybody. I need a woman with class along with beauty and intelligence. I want a woman that has motivation to do something with her life other than trying to find a rich man and live off his wealth. I date, but I haven't been in a committed relationship in five years. So, I'd rather be alone and date causally, than to be unhappy with the wrong woman in my life."

Damn, that leaves me out. "I hear that, so if you don't mind me asking, how old are you?" I asked.

"I'll be thirty-three in a few months."

"You look younger; I assumed that you were still in your late twenties."

"I believe in taking care of myself, so I workout on a regular.

I have a personal gym in my house, and I love to swim. I also run five miles everyday."

I let out a small laugh. "So I guess you could kill me for bringing you to this place where someone could have a heart attack at any moment," I joked. "Especially since you're really into fitness."

"I told you. You could've asked me to meet you at a place that sells fried lizards, and I would've come. I had to see you again."

I blushed once again. "So you really run five miles a day?" *Maybe I need to start running so I can practice getting away from the cops or the dudes in the street.*

"Everyday, I get up at six in the morning and start running. It's best to run in the morning, so the air can open your lungs, and you don't have the hot sun pounding down on you," he informed.

"Well, listen, you're on your own with the running. A sistah like me is not trying to get up at six in the morning to run any-where unless I'm being chased. Besides, I can think of better things to do at six in the morning, where you can sweat at the same time," I added.

"Hey, I love to sweat," he said with a sexy grin.

For the third time in less than an hour, I blushed.

"So Dee, I have a question…is Dee your real name?"

He had caught me off guard. I wasn't expecting him to ask me that. *Does he know something*? "It's a nickname that I've had since I was a kid."

"So, your real name would be?"

"If you're lucky, you'll find out in due time, but for now, you know me as Dee," I said.

"Dee it is then. And how old is this fine Georgia Peach?"

"Here you go again with the lame jokes. We're definitely gonna have to work on your comedy skills, or get you to watch some Def Comedy Jam or something," I said. "I'm twenty-three."

"Well beautiful, I can't wait to get to know you a little better."

By the end of our meal, his jokes got better and he almost had me in stitches. I began to enjoy his company so much that the time seemed to fly by.

"Would you like to come back to my house," he asked once again catching me off guard with his question.

I couldn't believe how easy it was to get next to him. *I hadn't even planned on going to his house this soon.* "What are you trying to do when we get there? Don't think I'm some type of freak."

"Dee, believe me when I tell you that I think you are a very classy and respectful woman. I'm only trying to get to know you better, so I thought we would drive out to my house and just talk."

After a few more seconds of trying to act like I wasn't sure about his request, I finally answered, "Okay, I'll go to your house, but don't try anything stupid."

"I promise, I'll be on my best behavior," he replied.

Several minutes later, we left Hodges with me following behind my new target. As we headed North on I-85, I started thinking about what it would be like to have sex with him. I'd never fucked a white boy, so I was curious. I started to tingle between my legs and began to think about the numerous dirty positions he could put me in. I hadn't had sex in two months, so my kitty was begging to be touched. I immediately started thinking about my last boyfriend Rashad, who I hadn't heard from in a couple of months. The last time I'd seen him, he told me that he was going to New York for a couple of days and never came back. Since I wasn't the type of girl to welcome every dick that came in my direction like Mya, after Rashad left I used my vibrator almost every night to fill the empty void between my legs. I missed Rashad because even though he was a tough hustler from the streets, he always treated me with respect. But it was no need to dwell on the past because since he'd decided to leave, it was his loss, not mine.

I was in shock when Scottie entered *Greystone Parc,* an upscale neighborhood in Gwinnett County with homes ranging from half a million, up to a million or more. I'd heard Mya mention this neighborhood from time to time, but I never really paid her much attention. Mya was known for talking about fancy places where she wanted to live once she got paid, but as usual I ignored her because she was probably chasing a dream. When we finally arrived at his gated 1.5 million dollar Georgian-style home, I was in awe. I couldn't believe my eyes as I slowly pulled up behind him in the lengthy paved driveway. I'd only seen houses like this on television.

I quickly got out the car with anticipation and walked toward him.

"This is it," he said. "One of my homes. Do you like it?"

"Nice, are you kidding me. You're such a baller," I said.

"When it comes to balling, I invented the shit," he joked.

"Um, mm…right."

"Let me show you around," he said, extending his arm.

"I can't wait."

I followed him into his lavish decorated home that immediately blew me away. When I stepped into the magnificent foyer, it reminded me of one of the celebrity homes on MTV cribs with its exquisite marble floors, curved staircase, and extremely high ceilings.

He then led me into the living room that contained an oversized masonry fire place, and three sets of French doors that led to the backyard.

"Let me show you how I get that exercise I was telling you about," he said, opening up one of the beautiful glass doors.

When we stepped onto the cobblestone walkway that led to the Olympic size pool, jacuzzi and full size basketball court, I felt like a kid at Chuck E. Cheese. Being from the hood, I'd never seen anything so beautiful. *Mya would die if she sees this shit.*

"Damn, this place looks like the Playboy Mansion," I said, admiring the huge stainless steel grill that looked like it could hold a hundred steaks. "Are you sure your name isn't Hugh Hefner?"

He held his head back and laughed. "Of course not. You don't see anybody running around in bunny outfits do you?"

"No, but I haven't seen the rest of the house yet, so it could be a few bunnies around here."

"Well let me show you some place that's really special to me," he replied.

He led me upstairs to his luxurious master suite, with its glass double sided fireplace, sixty inch plasma television, and an Italian Limestone bathtub. *This dude is definitely doing it.*

"So, what do you think of the place so far?" he asked.

I was speechless because it was truly breath-taking. I loved every square inch, but still decided to act like I was used to this type of luxury. "It's okay."

"Okay?" he looked upset at my answer. "Okay is for one bedroom condos; my home is more than okay. I even decorated it myself."

For a minute I thought he sounded a little cocky. Obviously, he was arrogant when it came to his money. *What if I lived in a one bedroom condo*? I sucked my teeth. "Is that supposed to mean something? I mean, you have taste, I'll give you that, but if I lived here, your shit would look like royalty with my touch."

He walked up to me slowly and took my hand into his. "Well, convince me that you're worth staying and we can work something out."

My panties instantly became moist. We stared into each others eyes, with his face just inches from mine. He smelled so good, and his touch felt so inviting.

"You're a beautiful woman, Dee. A woman like you deserves a place like this," he stated.

I felt flattered, but I had to get my head together and think. He was a mark. Both he and his lavish crib were nothing but distractions, and I knew I couldn't get caught up in good looks, a piece of dick and his smooth talking.

Instantly my cell phone began to vibrate. I reached into my purse, pulled it out and slightly shook my head. It was Mya. For some reason, it felt like she knew I was slipping. "I need to take this."

"Cool. I'll be downstairs," he said. When he turned to walk away, I grabbed his arm.

"By the way, I was just joking about your home, it's beautiful."

"Thanks," he said, closing the bedroom door to give me privacy.

I went into his bathroom and closed the door. "Hello."

"So what's goin' on?" Mya asked, getting straight to the point. I'd told her about my date with Scottie, but I'm sure she probably thought I was still at the restaurant.

"You're not gonna believe that I'm at his crib," I whispered just in case he came back in the room.

"Are you serious? So what does it look like?"

"Even more than you could imagine. You would be sick to your stomach."

"What did I tell you, can I pick 'em or what," Mya screamed into the phone.

"Yeah, you definitely got a gift when it comes to sniffing money."

"Shit Diamond, after this score, we're gonna be good for a minute," she said.

I thought I heard a noise in the bedroom, so I quickly turned on the faucet. "I gotta go. I think he's coming." I quickly hung up when I heard a knock at the door.

"Dee, are you okay in there?" Scottie asked.

"Yes, I'll be out soon," I replied. I decided to turn my cell phone off so I wouldn't be disturbed anymore. I knew Mya would be calling back. I looked at myself in the mirror, played with my hair, and opened the door.

An hour later, we were in the backyard enjoying some bar-b-que chicken, potato salad and baked beans that Scottie had whipped up, and to my surprise it was very good.

"Does everything taste okay?" he asked.

"Yeah, you can definitely burn for a white boy," I responded.

He smiled. "I learned from the best. I grew up with a lot of black friends and their mothers use to cook for us all the time. I love soul food."

"I couldn't be around you if you cook like this all the time. I would be big as a house," I said, rubbing my stomach.

"I don't think that's possible. You have a wonderful body...definitely thick in all the right places."

"Look at you, lusting over some brown sugar," I teased.

"Hey, the darker the berry...."

"The sweeter the juice," I interjected his statement.

He smiled. "So how sweet is your juice?"

"Oooh, are you trying to get fresh with me, Scottie?" I teased.

"Only if you get fresh back," he commented, showing off a devilish grin.

"Well, put your hormones on hold for now. I came here to chill, not to do anything else."

"I'm sorry if I offended you. I guess I got caught up in the moment. I love your company, so we can talk all night if you want."

During the rest of the day and into the evening, Scottie had my undivided attention. We talked about his family, Atlanta, kids, and even his business. He wouldn't tell me his net worth, but I already had my own idea.

The more we continued to talk, the more I felt comfortable around him. Despite what I had been taught by Mya, I began to tell Scottie about my real life. I told him about my love for hair and how I wanted to own a salon one day when I saved enough money. I knew Mya would've disapproved.

"So how long have you been doing hair?" he asked.

"Almost six years now."

"Wow, so when are you getting your license?"

"After I finish school in a few more months. I've been doing hair in my kitchen for a while, so I've got a pretty decent clientele," I replied.

"Hey with some luck and your skills, pretty soon you'll have a house bigger than mine," he said.

"You've got jokes, huh?"

"No, I'm serious. I see a beautiful, gifted and well rounded woman, and if she puts her mind to it, she can do whatever she wants. You are your dream, Dee, and you'll get there someday. Don't let anyone tell you any different," he said.

I was shocked. "That's the nicest thing anyone has ever said to me. You don't even know me, and you believe in me so strongly," I said, blushing by his words.

"I know your character, and I see me in you, so don't let any obstacles stand in your fuckin' way."

"Thank you," I returned. His words were so motivational he had me smiling for the rest of the evening.

I got quiet for a minute because different sets of emotions were going through my head. *Fuck it! I haven't had sex in two months.* Suddenly my pussy began to throb and all I could think about was his dick.

I stood up and walked over to him seductively. He looked up at me with his beautiful green eyes and then sat his drink down next to him.

"You ready for me?" I asked in a seductive tone. Before he could answer, I decided to straddle him, and instantly felt his dick getting hard. "Mmmm, it feels like you're a big boy," I teased, grinding my pussy against his crotch.

He grabbed my hips and enjoyed the slight lap dance I performed. He leaned in for a kiss, and I didn't resist. Once our lips connected, our tongues deeply entwined with each other. Our kiss became intense, passionate, and suddenly we couldn't keep our hands off each other. Bit by bit, he gradually started taking my clothes off. I saw his eyes widen when he unbuttoned my

Victoria Secret's bra and my large breasts stood at attention. He slowly began to lick each nipple and they instantly became hard. His tongue felt so good against my skin. Seconds later, the only thing that I had on were my four-inch heels.

Scottie quickly took off his sweatpants and then his boxers. He was pretty big for a white guy. I looked at him and displayed a huge smile. I was glad he had plenty of dick to work with.

"Don't believe the myth," he joked.

His body looked even better, with a washboard stomach, firm thighs and nice biceps. I stood and looked at him as he put a Magnum condom over his shaft. It had been too long since I felt a man's touch, so I couldn't wait to feel him inside of me.

"It looks like you're ready," I said, walking up to him. I slowly positioned myself on top and didn't waste anytime inserting his dick into my dripping pussy. I instantly felt the penetration opening me up.

"Mmmm," I moaned, as he began thrusting into me. I wrapped my arms around his neck to get a better grip, and began gyrating my hips against his lap.

"You feel so good," he said between thrusts.

"You do too," I cried out. As he pushed himself deeper inside, I dug my manicured nails into his back, leaving scratches.

I continued to move my hips back and forth, taking his entire dick, until I felt my legs quiver, and my clit tightening. I was about to cum.

"Don't stop...ooh, right there...right there," I chanted. It felt like my whole body was on fire. I dug my nails deeper into his skin and held my head back.

When his thrusts became faster and harder, I instantly felt myself cumin'. He clutched my ass firmly, feeling the juices of my pussy all over him.

"Damn, you feel so fuckin' good," he shouted.

The sex seemed to get better every time he pushed himself further inside. I moved my ass back and forth until I saw his eyes roll into the back of his head. I knew he was about to explode.

Suddenly, he let out a loud moan and immediately began to quiver. I wasn't sure about him, but my two month itch had definitely been scratched, and it felt damn good.

I climbed off of Scottie's lap and looked at him as his chest moved up and down at a rapid pace. My pussy felt so damp, but so fulfilled.

"Are you okay?" he asked in between deep breaths.

I nodded.

As he stood up, I took another look at his thick long dick. Staring at his manly figure made me instantly want a second round.

"We need to cool off," he said, and with that, he took a dive into his pool.

"You're crazy," I said, as he came up out of the water.

"C'mon on in, it's the best feeling after sex," he replied.

"So I take it you've done this before."

"Maybe, once or twice."

I smiled, took off my heels, and then jumped into the pool after him. I dived in head first, not giving a fuck about my hair. I hadn't had this much fun in a while, so I wanted to enjoy every minute.

Later that night, we ended up in his bedroom and fucked until we were both exhausted. I knew Mya was gonna kill me for getting too close to another mark, but at the moment I didn't care. If she could have pleasure before business, then so could I.

Chapter 6

Diamond

The next morning I woke up with Scottie between my legs and loved every minute of it. I guess one myth was true, white boys really did know how to eat pussy. I held his head into place and loved how he devoured me with strength and authority. I was so loud that I thought I was gonna shatter the glass in his bathroom.

Later that morning, I walked downstairs and found him flipping pancakes butt-naked. Scottie had no shame in his game. Even though we had sex, I was still a little uncomfortable being around him in my birthday suit, and had decided to throw on one of his t-shirts.

"I know you're not insecure about having the perfect body," he said, handing me a plate of eggs and sausage.

"No, I'm not insecure about my body. I'm just a little uncomfortable walking around naked," I replied, looking down at the oversized Miami Dolphins shirt.

"How can you be uncomfortable when your ass has been in the air all morning," he joked.

I looked at him and laughed. "Where are we eating this?" I asked referring to the food.

"Oh, let's go out by the pool."

"Please put some clothes on," I replied, as I walked out the kitchen.

During breakfast, we stared at each so much we could barely eat. I was glad he had taken my advice and put on a navy blue robe that looked expensive.

"I need to leave soon," I said, taking a sip of orange juice.

"Well, what if I say I don't want you to go?"

I blushed for the tenth time since I'd met him. "That's sweet, but I need to go home. I have a few things to take care of."

Scottie took a deep breath. "I like you a lot, Dee, so you know what I'm gonna do. I'm gonna help you open up that hair salon."

I looked at him like he was crazy. I knew his offer had to come with a catch. I'd never even thought about having a partner. "Why would you wanna do somethin' like that? You barely even know me," I asked.

"Because I'm a businessman, so let's call this an investment on my behalf. I can front you the money, and you do whatever you want with the shop. I'll just be a silent partner," he explained.

His offer was tempting, but I didn't want to rush into it. I needed time to think, and that's exactly what I told him, I had to think about it. He agreed and didn't push the proposal any further.

As the morning progressed we went for another dip in the pool, then took a shower together where he fucked the shit out of me in the doggy style position.

$ $ $

It was late in the evening by the time I got back home. I needed a nap badly, because I hadn't gotten much sleep with Scottie around. He was a sexual tyrant and couldn't get enough of my lovin'. *And I thought black guys loved sex.*

I was in the comfort of my bed, enjoying the tranquility of

home, when someone knocked on my door like the police.

"I need to fuckin' move." I cursed at the sound of the constant knocks.

I got up sluggishly, put on my robe and made my way toward the door. When I looked through the peep hole, I shook my head. It was Mya. *She always has the worst timing.* I wasn't in the mood to be grilled. Mya of all people should know how tired you are after a long night of fuckin'. When I opened the door, she walked in with a serious attitude.

"So, what's the run down on this dude?" she asked, storming inside like she was being chased. "I see you turned off your fuckin' phone."

"Damn, I can't get a hello or anything."

"Hey...so what's the deal since you didn't come home last night. Did you fuck him?"

Mya wasn't known to beat around the bush, so it didn't surprise me that she was so direct. "Well, let's just say I got to know him," I responded with a smile.

"So, in other words you fucked him. Well since you decided to have fun instead of take care of business, I hope you at least scoped out his stash spot or something."

She got some nerve. Doesn't she have sex with marks all the time? What makes her so uptight about Scottie? "Damn Mya, you need to chill for a minute. You're sounding desperate and shit. I told you, it's gonna take time."

"Fuck that, Diamond. This dude got money, real fuckin' money. Not that lil' ass shit we've been gettin' from them other niggahs. I'm not about to keep waitin' like this!"

I wasn't in the mood to argue with her, so I put up with her bullshit for the moment. I wanted to chill, and I hated the fact that she'd shown up unannounced. I watched as she sat on my couch in her tight fitting jeans and continued to plead her case about Scottie. I was sick of hearing about it already.

Truth was, I was starting to have feelings for Scottie, especially since he offered to put up money for my shop which I was definitely considering. I would be one of a few girls to come straight out of school with my own shop to hold down. I didn't have to worry about booth-rent and taking bullshit from other females. And even more important, I would be my own boss. It couldn't get any better than that.

I kept that information from Mya because I knew she would've gone off the deep end. In her eyes, we were supposed to be taking his money, not forming a partnership. Even though Mya knew I loved doing hair, she'd always been against me getting my own salon and becoming legit. I guess she wanted me to be in the game forever, but those were her goals, not mine.

Mya continued to talk non-stop for almost an hour about getting Scottie's money. I started yawning thinking that she would get the hint, and luckily for me she picked right up on it.

"Do you want me to leave or somethin'? Don't be over there throwin' out no fuckin' hints," she snapped.

"I'm sorry, girl. It's just that I didn't get much sleep last night."

"Yeah, I bet you didn't. Well since he obviously knows how to sling dick around, pass him over to me when you're done," she said, sounding extremely ghetto.

I wasn't sure if she was joking or not, but I didn't think it was funny. I wasn't into sharing my men. I didn't reply to her remark. I just looked at her like she was on crack.

Suddenly, her cell phone soon rung and she picked up, while I went into the kitchen to make myself something to drink. I knew it was probably some dude calling her for a booty call.

A short moment later, Mya came into the kitchen smiling, "Well you got yours last night, now it's time for me to get mine."

"Another one of your sex toys on the phone, huh?" I asked, not really caring.

"Yeah, I wanna see what this one is about. I met him a few days ago in the mall. Can you believe his ass was pushin' a brand new Porsche? He got to have money," she stated.

"Is he a mark?" I asked, pouring some lemonade into my

glass.

"We'll see. If the dick is good, then I'm gonna hold off for a minute. But eventually he's gonna have to go down. I'm just gonna enjoy his company 'till I get tired of him," she explained.

"Well, go ahead and have fun, but be careful."

"Always. Oh and since you're handin' out advice now, don't lose focus anymore. Stay on Scottie's ass, and I don't mean on his dick either."

I nodded.

She quickly turned around and walked out the kitchen. Several seconds later, I heard the front door close, finally leaving me in peace. I went to my room with my fresh lemonade to relax and watch some television, but I was in my room less than five minutes when my cell phone rang. It was Scottie. He asked to see me later, but I declined. I really did need some rest. My body as well as my mind was completely exhausted. Instead, we spent hours on the phone talking and laughing. When I finally hung up, it was three in the morning.

$ $ $

Over the next two weeks, Scottie and I couldn't get enough of each other, and I'd spent almost every night at his house. We took long drives throughout the city, enjoying the warm spring air and tranquil scenery, and ate at all the exclusive restaurants throughout Atlanta. I especially enjoyed the long walks through Neiman Marcus where he bought me everything I touched. It felt good to be spoiled again. A feeling I hadn't experienced since my brother got locked up.

Even the sex was the bomb. I quickly learned that white guys were totally different in bed because they believed in pleasing their woman first. I loved that about him. He always made sure that I got mine before he got his. I also loved the way he went down on me. He deserved an award for that shit. He always ate my pussy like it was a delicate piece of chocolate. I also returned the favor, giving him head regularly, especially in the car. For us, having sex in the riskiest places was a complete rush.

One night, I fucked him in his truck while we sat in traffic. I rode his dick forcefully with my eyes closed, not even giving a fuck about getting caught by onlookers or the police. The crazy thing is Scottie didn't even have tint on the windows of his truck, which made it even more exciting.

We even fucked in a men's public bathroom, which proved to be quite a challenge in the small stall. All of Atlanta was becoming our personal playground. We'd become two freaks enjoying each others company a little too much, where we painted the town red leaving our marks every where. I guess my two months of abstinence had turned me into a complete nympho.

Three weeks after meeting Scottie, Mya really started to get pissed off at me. She would ask me at least twice a day when we were going to get Scottie, but my excuse was always the same, "I need more time." For some reason, I couldn't bring myself to set Scottie up. He was starting to become off limits. I knew I couldn't keep telling her that forever. I was surprised she'd waited this long.

In the meantime, Mya continued to set up small jobs for us to keep our income flowing. After our scores, I would drive to Scottie's house in the middle of the night so I could wake up next to him in the morning. He would often ask me why I was out at such late hours, and I always told him that I had late hair appointments. I knew those excuses were stupid, but I had to come up with something. I felt bad about lying to Mya and Scottie, two people I cared about.

I was breaking our number one rule about the game, *never fall in love with your mark*, but I couldn't help it. Scottie treated me like a queen. After Rashad, I didn't think any man would ever come into my life and steal my heart again, but Scottie had managed to do that and even more. He was a white boy, but when I looked at him, I didn't see color. I only saw a man that I loved being with, and I loved giving him my time and my body.

Eventually, Mya got tired of playing my games and decided that enough was enough. One day, when I arrived home from school, she was waiting in front of my door. When I saw her pacing back and forth like a mental patient, I knew things were not good.

"Mya, what's up girl, why you here?" I asked with a confused expression.

"We need to have a fuckin' talk," she said, in a stern voice.

"About what?" I had to act dumb even though I knew where the conversation was headed.

"I don't want to talk out here, open the door."

When I opened the door, Mya rushed past, bumping my arm in the process. At that point, I knew she needed to calm down before things got out of hand. Before I could ask what her problem was, she gave me the look of death. "You in love wit' that white boy, ain't you?"

Fuck it no more excuses, it's now or never. "It just happened, Mya and…."

"What do you mean it just happened? He's a fuckin' mark, Diamond. Our biggest mark at that. We are supposed to be about money, and now you fuckin' that up. I don't like it when people fuck wit' my money. This dude needs to be taken down now!" she barked.

"It's not happening, Mya. Scottie doesn't deserve that," I said.

I could almost see steam comin' out of her ears. "What…he doesn't deserve it! Are you fuckin' serious?! You gonna protect that white boy, after all the brothas we robbed. You mean to tell me you wanna protect this cracker mutha-fucka! You gonna keep us from gettin' this money, because he probably told you he loved you after gettin' himself some dark pussy!"

"It's not about color, Mya," I whined.

"Then what the fuck is it about? You don't know this dude. He could be playing your ass. Trust me, all men got game."

"He' different," I said in Scottie's defense.

"Ain't shit different about any of our marks! What's wrong wit' you Diamond? Did you let this mutha-fucka get into your head? I thought I taught you better than that!" she yelled. "What did he promise you, huh? Money...cars. You know we can get that shit on our own once we get his paper," Mya yelled loudly.

I was still reluctant. She didn't know Scottie. He'd promised to help me open up my own salon, which was information that I still decided to keep from her. She didn't need to know everything.

When Mya looked at me, I guess she saw the reluctance in my face. "If you won't help me get Scottie, then I'm gonna call a few niggahs and get at him on my own," she threatened.

"It ain't gotta be like this. I feel different about this one."

"Sorry, it's gotta go down like this. I've been waitin' a long time, so with or without you, I'm gettin' that paper. What you need to do is get your head out your ass and get wit' the fuckin' program, like we been doing, cuz it's on either way," she warned.

Without saying another word she quickly turned around and slammed my front door. I knew Mya meant business, and I couldn't let it happen. Now she was interfering with my life and my business. I finally had a chance to go legit, but she wanted to throw a monkey wrench in my plans. Mya was straight hood, and could be ruthless at any given moment. We were cool, having the same short term goals, but I had goals and wanted something better for myself. It seemed as if we were heading in two separate directions.

I quickly showered, changed clothes, and rushed over to see Scottie. When I finally got to his place, I wanted to warn him, but at the same time, I didn't want him to know what my first intentions were when we met. I didn't want to fuck up the relationship that we were building. I needed Scottie to leave town for a while, for his own safety. I would miss him, but at least I knew he would be safe and come back to me in one piece.

When I arrived at his house, he was waiting for me at the door with two dozen of white roses. I got out my car and ran up to him, hugging him tightly.

"Is everything okay, baby?" he asked, sitting the vases on the floor.

"Yes, I just wanted to hold you," I responded.

He held me in his arms, squeezing me tighter. I didn't want to let him go.

"Are you hungry? I was just about to make something to eat."

I nodded and followed him inside. As we walked toward the kitchen, I began to think about Mya. *How can I protect him from her crazy ass?* Mya didn't have his address, but she had her ways and when she wanted something, she went for it at full force. If she found him once she could find him again.

As we dined by the pool, indulging in some grilled shrimp, and fine red wine, I felt so comfortable that I didn't want the evening to end. The meal was delicious. Scottie had prepared everything himself. He had proved to be a wonderful chef.

"You look beautiful tonight," Scottie complimented me, staring at me with a lustful look in his eyes.

I smiled playing with my hair that I'd pulled up into a long ponytail. "Thanks."

Scottie poured himself another glass of wine, took a sip, and then stared at me again. "Do you love me, Dee?"

I was so shocked by his question that I almost choked on my food, but something in my heart told me to be honest. "Yes, I believe I do. I mean everything about you just warms my heart and I love spending time with you."

"I love you too, and want us to be together," he replied, grabbing my hand.

He then reached under the table and pulled out a long black velvet case. My heart started racing. I knew the box was too long to contain a ring, but coming from him it had to be expensive.

"This is a small gift from me to you, for all the love you've brought to me over the past few weeks," he said, passing me the box.

I was overwhelmed. I slowly opened the long velvet casing as my heart began to beat faster than a race car. I gasped as my hands quickly covered my mouth in shocked. His small gift to me was a diamond necklace that almost blinded me. The fine chain was iced out in round brilliant-cut diamonds.

"Oh my goodness, Scottie, this is beautiful," I said, feeling flushed.

"You like it?"

"I love it."

He smiled. "I'm glad you like it, it's something for you to wear and remember me by when I'm gone."

"What? What are you talkin' about, Scottie?" I asked, shocked by his statement.

"I'm leaving for Miami in two days. I travel back and forth between Atlanta, Miami and New York on business. I want you to come along, but I understand that you have to finish school first," he stated.

I was surprised, but at the same time relieved that he was leaving. His unexpected trip had saved me the trouble of telling him the truth.

"How long will you be gone?" I asked.

"I'll be in Miami for a few months, and then I'm flying up to New York," he informed me. "But I'll be back for you, Dee. I promise you that."

I felt sad that he was leaving, but I knew it was best. I thought about Rashad for a quick moment. He promised that he would return to me, and it'd been over three months since I've heard from him.

Scottie noticed the troubled look on my face and grabbed my hand again. "I have an idea." He picked me up out of my chair and embraced me. "I know you'll miss me when I'm gone, but when you finish school, I want you to fly down to Miami to come see me. You'll love it down there, believe me. I wanna get you out of Atlanta for a while. I'll pay for your trip, first class on any airline you want. And then from there, we can fly to New York. Have you ever been there?" he asked.

"No," I answered, feeling a little embarrassed. I'd never been outside of Georgia.

"Well, now you will. Is that okay with you?"

"Yes," I replied, and hugged him tightly.

"Okay, so once you finish school, you holla at me and then we're gonna get it poppin," he said.

I was so glad that he was leaving without me having to expose myself. It had been a while since I'd felt this happy. It seemed like everything was finally falling into place for me I couldn't wait to finish school and then fly down to Miami.

Scottie held me in his arms for a moment, making me feel so loved, so comfortable, and so safe. "Ummm, baby, you smell so damn good," Scottie said, softly in my ear.

"I do, huh."

"Yes you do," he replied.

I felt his hands slowly moving down my back and soon rested firmly on my ass. We gave each other a deep kiss and within seconds we were all over each other. Our actions traveled to the bedroom where I slowly stripped for him as he watched from his plush king size bed. I wanted to show him all the moves that got me paid at Body Tap and what he would miss when he was gone.

When he couldn't take anymore, I climbed onto the bed, mounted his erection and rode him like I was in a rodeo. We made love for hours with the night ending with my body nestled against him, on his expensive wrinkled sheets.

Chapter 7

Mya

Yo, Mya, what's up wit' your girl? Is she close to gettin' at that dude or what?" Donte asked.

He was becoming frustrated that it was takin' Diamond so long to get on her fuckin' job. Donte wanted to get at Scottie bad, and wasn't goin' to let up until his mission was complete. Donte and his crew were straight thugs out of my old neighborhood, Kimberly Court. Their reputation was fierce and they pushed kilos of hard white throughout Atlanta and murdered any niggah that went against them or fucked up their money.

I got down with Donte and his crew a while back, after O.C. got locked up. Donte was O.C.'s cousin, who looked out for me, in and out of the bedroom. He wasn't blessed in the dick area like his cousin, but he was all about gettin' money which substituted for anything that was slackin'. He loved pleasin' me. If I had a beef wit' niggahs, Donte took care of it wit' one phone call, and in return, I put him and his crew on to some of our scores, and gave them a percentage of our earnings. I also helped move drugs for them, and always got information from dudes they were skeptical about, which quickly made me the first lady of their crew.

Donte was very intimidating, with his six three muscular frame and loads of battle scars that covered his body. His whole life didn't exist of anythin' but drugs, guns, murder and any other type of criminal activity that he refused to speak about.

"She's on it, Donte," I said, soundin' sure of myself. But deep inside, I knew Diamond was frontin' on me, and was playin' a dangerous game.

"Mya, you know we gotta murder Scottie when we get at him," he said coldly.

I knew he was serious. Donte and his crew wanted to set Scottie up, because little did Diamond know Scottie was a major cocaine and ecstasy distributor throughout the city. Donte had been beefing wit' the white boy over money and territory for months, and wanted him dead by any means necessary. Donte was even the one who'd put me on to Scottie in the first place. We trusted Diamond to set it up for us, having her think it would be nothin' more than our usual robbery, and then carry it out from there. But now the plan had backfired on us. We never expected her fuckin' feelings to get involved. Somethin' I told her to never do.

Donte knew somethin' was up, but he was unaware that Diamond had actually fallen in love wit' Scottie. I tried to keep that information on the down low to save her life, but even though she was my home girl, I couldn't protect her much longer. If shit didn't pop off soon for my crew, it would be out of my hands and even her blood was going to spill.

"Mya, come here," Donte said, pattin' his leg.

He was seated on his plush leather couch, watchin' the Lakers lose to the Knicks by ten points with a .357 lying next to him.

As I walked over and took a seat on his lap, he wrapped his arms around me, and began massagin' my thigh gently. "You know, ever since my cousin got locked up, I been takin' care of you, right?" he said.

"Yeah, I know."

"You down for anything, and I trust you. And usually I don't trust any bitch." He stared at me before continuing. "Because we're so much alike, I know we can run this mutha-fuckin' city.

But your girl, Diamond, I don't trust her. It's takin' her too long to set that white boy up. So if she don't do her job, then I'm gonna have to do her," he said.

"She's goin' through some issues, baby. You know wit' school and all," I replied, in Diamond's defense.

"Fuck that bitch and school! She should be about this money like you, and wit' Scottie out the way, that's gonna leave the whole ATL market wide open. That's when we step up and become the number one distributor in this fuckin' city, and really start gettin' paper. Are you ready to ride or die for your niggah?"

"You know it," I responded.

"Cool, so if your girl fucks it up, are you ready to kill her and prove your loyalty to this crew?" he asked.

I hesitated for a moment. I was down to shoot anyone, but Diamond and I grew up together and went back like bell bottom pants. I wasn't sure if I could do that.

"You gettin' quiet on me, Mya. You good wit' that?" Donte asked.

"I don't know. Even though she's been actin' funny…"

"Fuck dat bitch. If she's slippin' on her game, then you know what we gotta do," Donte interrupted. He pressed his fingers firmly into my thighs. "Now I need that white boy to disappear before that mutha-fucka gets a chance to leave town again, so your girl needs to handle that."

"She will," I assured.

He looked at me like I was lyin', and then picked up the .357 from his side. "You see this gun right here? Ain't no escaping from this shit. It'll lay down a mutha-fuckin' elephant," he said, passing me the gun.

I looked at the piece of steel like it was my favorite pair of shoes. I gripped the huge cannon with both hands and pointed it at the television. I watched Stephon Marbury go for a lay up past two guards and sink the basket. I aimed at Mr. Marbury and followed his every move up and down the court.

"You like the way it feels in your hands, don't you baby," he said.

"Is it loaded?"

"Come on. You know I don't keep empty guns around me. I'm ready for anythin' that comes my way," he replied.

As I continued to grip the gun in my hands, I felt his hand travel further between my thighs until he reached my treasure.

"I know you ready to pop off wit' that, but be careful. You might need some trainin'," he said.

"Niggah, you know I like 'em big. I can definitely handle this."

The gun was heavy, but I knew how to get down. I felt Donte's fingers penetratin' me slowly and I let out a blissful moan. He then lifted me up and placed me on the couch. As Donte removed my panties and began to devour my kitty, I let out another loud moan. If it was one thing he had over his cousin, it was his ability to eat pussy.

My legs were wrapped around his neck while I pressed the cold hard steel against my breasts. "Do that shit, baby, it's all yours," I said.

His warm long tongue went deep inside of me and lightly brushed against my clit. I was in heaven as I placed my hand under his wife beater, and made long scratches down his back. He nibbled on me for almost an hour until I had reached a record of four orgasms.

As Donte went to the bathroom, I thought about what he said to me, about us runnin' ATL together. I then thought about Diamond and even though she was my home girl, I knew I couldn't let her get in my way of makin' money and becomin' that bitch in the dirty south. *She's gotta go,* I thought, because I definitely wanted to show my loyalty to the crew.

$ $ $

The next day I went to visit my baby, O.C. at the federal prison on McDonough Blvd, who was doin' a twenty-five to life year bid for several murder cases. As I entered the visitor's entrance in my tight low rise jeans that accentuated my thin waist line and low cut shirt, all the guard's eyes were directed toward me. But out of all the men, I messed wit', I didn't fuck cops or anybody representing one. I went through countless security searches and metal detectors, and literally got harassed by men who wanted my number. When I looked at my watch, I realized that it had taken me over half an hour to go through security. *Damn, they act like they've never seen a fine woman in here before.*

When I finally made it into the visitin' room, I looked around at all the women who were talkin' to their family members. *By the looks of these women, no wonder the guards were all up on me.* As I sat down, O.C. walked into the visitin' room, escorted by a husky Correctional Officer. The guard pointed over in my direction and O.C. made his way toward me with a huge smile.

He looked good in his green overalls and freshly braided hair. Almost as good as the day we first met. His dark skin shimmered behind the partition as he took a seat and picked up the phone.

"How you been, beautiful?" he asked.

"I'm good. How they treatin' you up in here, baby?"

"You know I'm good. I'm livin'," he replied. "Damn, you look good. My cousin takin' care of you, right?"

"Yeah, he 'bout to have Atlanta in a chokehold soon," I boasted.

O.C. nodded, like he approved Donte's hustle. "Is he takin' care of your body too?"

"Now you know Donte can't fuck wit' you in the bed, but you got twenty five to life baby, and even though your dick was good to me, I need mine," I replied.

"Yeah I know how you roll, Mya. I ain't mad at you. I'm gonna be on hold for a long time, probably life up in this bitch, so I don't even blame you. But you still need to come see a niggah."

"Of course, you know I'll never stop doin' that," I responded.

"No doubt," he said, lickin' his lips. "What you got on?" I knew my outfit would keep his interest.

"You know I had to come correct for you." I stood up and did a little twirl, showin' him how phat my ass looked in my jeans. "You like?"

"Hell yeah. Damn, I wish I wasn't behind this fuckin' glass. It's drivin' me crazy not to be able to touch you," he responded.

"You and me both. Why aren't you in a regular visitin' room?" I asked.

"Because these mutha-fucka's think I'm a threat. They tryin' their best to break me, but you know that's not gonna happen."

"Yeah you're one hard nut to crack," I joked.

"So, what's my cousin talkin' about these days?"

"Well, he wants me and my girl, Diamond to get at someone," I mentioned.

"Who?"

"The white boy, Scottie," I informed.

"Damn Donte's going after a big dog this time, huh? Scottie got connections, and he's not someone you wanna play wit'. If you go at him, you better come correct."

I was surprised to hear him say that. It had never occurred to me that Scottie could be that much of a threat. "What do you think about it?"

"You need to be careful wit' that dude. We did business once, and he's very subtle, but he can hold his own. He's been in the game for a long time, so just watch your back." He noticed a guard walkin' past and decided to change the subject. "So, how's Diamond doin' anyway?"

"She's okay I guess. Still goin' to hair school and talkin' about ownin' her own shop someday," I replied nonchalantly.

O.C. smiled. "Diamond always had dreams."

"Yeah, but now her dreams might fuck around and get her caught up."

"Well, you just be careful out there yourself. You know if I wasn't up in here, I would be holding you down right now," he said.

"I know." His comment immediately made me blush. O.C. always had a way of makin' me feel special.

"But right now, I need for you to hold me down."

I nodded. "What do you need from me, baby?"

"I got a few problems, so I want you to handle a few things on the outside for me. I need you to reach a few niggahs that I can't reach and do business the way I would handle it if I was home right now," he replied. "Can you do that for your niggah?"

"You know I'm down, baby."

He gave me a huge smile like he was proud of me. "My niggah, Ace is gonna get at you and give you the run down. It's certain niggahs we're tryin' to touch that can only be done by you."

I nodded. I understood what O.C. was gettin' at. He couldn't say too much over the phone, so he kept it short and simple.

"You're my number one, Mya. Make it happen for me and my crew," he said.

"I will."

"There's money to be made out there, and you could be sittin' on sumthin' sweet, baby."

"Don't worry, you know how grimy I can get, boo," I said with a smirk on my face.

O.C. let out a wicked laugh and nodded his head, like he approved of my remark. "Damn, I wanna throw you across that table and fuck the shit outta you. You know I always loved it when you got rough wit' a niggah."

"You know I can't fuck wit' no weak niggahs, O.C. You the only dude I think about all the time. Even wit' you in here, you still got my heart," I replied.

"Hold me down out there, Mya. And get that money, ayyite," he said. "Oh, and watch your back, baby. I don't need anymore bad news reaching me behind these walls. Anything pops off wit' you, and I'll go fuckin' crazy."

"I will."

At that moment, the Correctional Officer stood behind O.C.

and tapped him on his shoulder, indicating that his time was up.

"I hate these fuckin' guards!" he shouted angrily.

I was sad to see O.C. go, but there wasn't anythin' I could do about it. "Don't sweat it, baby, I'll send you somthin' nice to remember me by."

He smiled, knowin' what I was talkin' about. He then blew me a kiss, and I blew one back. I continued to sit there and watched the C.O. escort him back into lock up. His back was broad and looked so good, that my pussy began to drip.

I hated to see my boo caged like that, but I knew what I had to do. I walked out of there with a cold attitude.

$ $ $

Several days later, I met up with Ace at the bar inside of Justin's Restaurant. I hadn't seen him in months. The last time we'd seen each other was when I saw him beatin' some dude down for his money in a club parkin' lot. Ace was one of O.C.'s right hand men, and a stone cold killer. He had a thick scar lining his cheek bone, and sported long well-kept dreads that crawled down his back. His arms were thick and well defined, and displayed a huge tattoo of a Mac-10. Ever since the day we met, I wanted to fuck Ace, but that was O.C.'s boy, so I kept my hands to myself. But the sight of that sexy thuggish, hardcore mutha-fucka made my pussy wet every time he came around.

Ace was a hard-core niggah from Chicago, who'd come down south a few years back. He was also a big-time gambler, who was known to bet thousands of dollars on everything from sports to card games. I guess that's how he got the name. O.C. was also a gambler, which is how they met and became boys in the first place.

I sat by the bar and watched as Ace strolled in alone and scanned the bar for me. He had an evil stare, and his dreads were tied into one long pony-tail. He looked sexy in his oversized white t-shirt, baggy jeans, timberlands, and a long chain which hung from his neck. He had thug written all over his mocha colored face.

Every time I was in his presence, my pussy smiled and got excited. I wanted to look extra sexy for Ace tonight, so I came to the bar dressed in my sexy black off the shoulder dress and my brand new Jimmy Choo sandals that made my ass sit up even higher.

As I worked on my second Belvedere and Cranberry, Ace spotted me and forced his way through the crowd not givin' a fuck. But no one said a word or tried to step to him, because he looked like he was ready to kill someone.

"What's up, Mya, it's been a long time," he said. His voice was thick and deep, like a baritone Barry White.

"Hey Ace," I replied. I tried flirtin' wit' him by crossin' my legs in his direction. I wanted him to see that I didn't have any panties on under my dress.

"Yo, it's too crowded in here, we need to talk somewhere else," he ordered.

"You don't want a drink?"

He looked at me for a short moment. "No, let's talk outside."

I placed a twenty on the bar and followed Ace outside like a little puppy. I felt everyone watchin' us as we walked toward the exit. I knew niggahs wanted to get at me, but I was in the company of a beast, and I knew everyone sensed that.

I walked out into the cool night air, and my pussy began to tingle. I loved the fact that Ace towered over me like a tree. Without saying a word, he made his way toward a burgundy Hummer H2 that was parked across the street indicating that I should follow behind, and I did. *Not bad*, I thought as I walked quickly in order to keep up.

As we climbed into the truck, Ace sat quietly for a minute. He leaned back in his seat, and peered out the windshield, staring at nothing in particular. Being the hoochie that I am, I purposely raised my dress a bit, showin' off my smooth thighs and perfect legs.

"Cat got your tongue, Ace or does it need to be busy doin' somthin' else," I hinted.

He cut his eyes at me.

"Okay…why am I here?" I asked with a slight attitude.

"I need for you to lay it thick on a niggah, and give him some room to fuck up," he mentioned.

"Who?"

"We're moving in on a Washington Road, niggah named, Praise who runs shit out there. He doesn't trust anyone, and he's never alone. His territory is money, and we want that. His crew is weak without him, so if we drop that fool, we can move in."

It was the most I'd ever heard him say. I guess with O.C. being locked down, and Donte not around, he had to open his mouth and talk.

"So you need pussy to make this niggah's knees buckle, right?"

"Mya, just do what you do…and do it quick," he stated sternly.

Damn this dude is a fuckin' rock. I was literally throwin' the pussy at him, and he wouldn't take the bait. All he was concerned about was business, but I respected that.

We talked for a short moment and Ace gave me a brief description of Praise and informed me of places he went to. And with that, I got out of his Hummer and he drove off, leavin' me behind horny and thirsty for a piece of dick. *Shit, I put on this outfit for nothin'.*

Chapter 8

Mya

A week passed and I was finally able to catch up to Praise in club 112, a well known hip-hop club on Peachtree Street. I'd been in the club waitin' for him to show up for over an hour which pissed me off. I hated waitin' for anybody, so once he arrived, I was more than ready to start my performance. As he made his way through the crowd, I watched as he sent one of his flunkies to the bar, and continued to the V.I.P. area. Usually the weakest members of the crew went on bar runs, so this was the perfect opportunity for me to make my move. I had to find a way to get into V.I.P. and the weakest link was gonna be my ticket.

As I approached the bar, I made sure to stand right next to him, so he could smell the sweet fragrance of my Hanae Mori perfume. "Excuse me, can I get a Belvedere and Cranberry," I said to the bartender.

The weak link immediately looked at me and smiled. "What's up, gorgeous? Can I buy that drink for you?"

"Sure," I responded. I batted my eyes and licked my lips. Weak guys always fell for that shit.

"Yo, bartender, let me get two bottles of Cristal and put that Vodka and Cran on my tab," he ordered.

"You a baller huh," I said, standin' so close he could probably smell what I had for dinner two days ago.

He turned to look at me, like he was fuckin' speechless. "Um...um...yeah, me and my niggahs always get down up in here. You know how we do, beautiful."

I smiled, and definitely played him so close, that I felt his hard-on pressing against me. The weak link loved every bit of me and instantly invited me back to the V.I.P section with his boys as soon as the drinks arrived. *That was too easy*, I thought.

Clutchin' two bottles of Cristal in his hands and navigating his way through the thick dance floor, I followed behind the link closely. When we reached the roped off V.I.P area, the link passed through easily, but the bouncer looked at me reluctantly.

"Yo, she wit' me," he said, reachin' for my hand.

The bouncer nodded and let me though with ease. I followed the weak link up a few short steps and entered the V.I.P area where Praise and his entourage were seated around a large circular table that was cluttered with several more bottles of champagne.

As soon as I was in full view, all eyes were on me. I wasn't the only woman in their presence, but I was the most remarkable.

"Damn, niggah, we send you to the bar to get two bottles of Cris, and you come back wit' her? Yo, we need to send this mutha-fucka to the bar more often," Praise joked.

"You know me, Praise," the weak link bragged.

"Yeah whatever niggah, you must've paid her about two g's to follow your ass in here," Praise continued.

Shit, for two g's I would've taken him outside and gave up a nice piece of ass.

"What's your name, beautiful?" Praise asked me.

I knew it was time to get a new name, but it was all I could think of at that moment. "Precious."

"And that you are," he responded. "My name is Praise, please have a seat."

I saw the other women cut their eyes at me as I sat down, but I didn't care. I knew they were probably threatened by my sudden presence, but I was only there to do a job, not clown around with these seven gram niggahs.

I sat in between the weak link and Praise, who couldn't stop staring at me. I knew he liked what he saw. He was seated next to some high yellow bimbo with big breasts, but she didn't have anything on me. I had sex appeal and style.

His entire crew were loud, obnoxious show offs, who flashed lots of money, got high and were probably thirsty for some ass. Being around them was startin' to get on my nerves, so I wanted to hurry up and get the show on the road.

Suddenly, I felt the weak link's hand wander under the table and it soon found a place on my uncovered thigh. I let it be, he was cute, and his touch excited me. While the link molested me under the table, Praise still couldn't take his eyes off of me. His eyes seemed to talk to me, so I returned his gaze and licked my lips.

"Bitch, you got a problem with your fuckin' eyes," the high yellow bimbo shouted.

"I know this bitch ain't talkin' to me," I loudly returned.

"Yes, I'm talkin' to you. Don't be starin' at my man like that!"

I chuckled. I was tired of runnin' into fake ass broads who wanted to be gangstas. "Yo, you better check your girl before she finds herself fucked up," I replied, lookin' at Praise.

"Fuck you!" she shouted.

"Meeka, chill. Look, take her to the bar and get her a drink," Praise ordered to the weak link.

"But Praise, I just came from the bar," the link responded.

"And…" Praise shouted. "Just go niggah, and take your time."

The link looked unpleased by Praise's order to go back to the bar, but held his composure. Besides, Praise was the boss. His cheap fills off of me were gettin' him hard, and gettin' me somewhat excited, but now Praise had my attention.

"Praise, don't even go there!" Meeka yelled.

"What? Look, just get your ass up and go wit' that niggah to the bar to get a few drinks," Praise said, more like command than a suggestion.

The weak link and Meeka reluctantly got up. Meeka stared at me for a few seconds, and I returned her glare with a nasty smirk. That bitch knew what was about to go down with Praise, so to throw salt on her wound, I said, "Hey, can you tell her to bring me back a Belvedere and Cranberry."

"Bitch, fuck you!" Meeka cursed and stormed off.

As soon as the two losers left the V.I. P. area, Praise didn't waste anytime gettin' to know me a little better. "Precious, come sit next to your boy."

Praise made some room for me next to him, and told the rest of the bitches at the table to get up and leave. *Damn, I guess he got more than one weak link.* As they followed his orders, I sat next to him like a magnet.

"So why are you alone, beautiful?" he asked.

"I choose to be."

"Well, it's good you came alone because I don't want to fuck some niggah up tonight," Praise replied. "Yo, I'm ready to roll out. Are you rollin' wit' a niggah for the night?"

"I'm down for whatever," I responded with a sexy grin.

We both got up and made our way toward the exit, when the weak link and Meeka walked back into the area. The link had two drinks in his hands, and Meeka just had an attitude.

"Where do you think you're goin' wit' this bitch!" Meeka barked, twisting her neck and rollin' her eyes at me.

"Look, you seriously need to watch your mouth!" I spat back.

"Is that a fuckin' threat? This is my man, I'm tired of your tri-fling ass!" she shouted.

I sighed. This girl was askin' for a beat down. "Praise, check this stupid bitch before I hurt her," I said, ballin' up my fist. She was lucky I couldn't pull out my gun. Luckily Ace had set it up where I didn't have to get searched at the door when I first arrived, so I could get my gun inside. *Maybe he knew somethin' might pop off.*

"Meeka, we gonna go talk for a minute, so stop actin' jealous," Praise said to her.

"You're full of shit. You can't talk to a hoe. You should've left this hoe where you found her," she yelled to the weak link.

I was tired of her talkin' shit. She'd come at me wrong too many times in one night, so I slowly walked away and went back to the table.

"Yeah you better step the fuck off!" I heard her yell.

I picked up an empty champagne bottle, and gripped it tightly in my hand. I then walked back over to her, with a casual expression even though I was heated. "Disrespect me again, and you gonna see what's up."

"Shut the fuck up, hoe...."

Before she could say another word, that empty bottle quickly smashed against her head, and she instantly stumbled back.

"I told you to stop disrespectin' me!" I shouted.

Meeka dropped to the floor, clutching her head. She was bleeding badly, but that didn't stop me from whooping her ass. I caught her with a hard right, and then stomped the shit out of her. The crowd around us was in awe, and for the first few minutes, no one attempted to stop me.

"Yo, Precious, chill," I heard Praise say, as he and his boys pulled me off of her.

"Fuck that, I warned her," I screamed.

Praise held me tightly in his arms. He looked over at one of his boys and said, "Handle this shit. I'm out."

With that, he led me to a back exit before security came on the scene. I wanted to continue beatin' that bitch down, but then I remembered what I was there for in the first place, and decided to calm down. I was finally alone with Praise as we walked to his ride.

Praise led me by my hand as we made our way to the front of the club where he was parked. I walked beside him like everything was all good. We looked like a couple who was ignoring all the drama that was happening around us. Once we reached the front entrance, there was still a small crowd waitin' to get inside even though security had shut everythin' down. Within minutes, the flashing police lights lit up the night. Several minutes later, I was safely inside the passenger's seat of Praise's pearl Escalade.

"Yo, Precious, you a wild girl," he said, speedin' off. "I mean, I've never seen anyone come at Meeka like that."

"That bitch bit off more than she could chew. I ain't the one to fuck wit," I replied.

"I see this," he said.

As we drove past, several policemen jumped out of their cars like they were ready for war. "Damn, you definitely do make a scene. It looks like four police cars have rolled up for your ass," he said.

I knew O.C. and Ace would've been pissed if the plan had gone sour, so I was happy that Praise decided to get me out of there.

Several minutes later, I was in Praise's lavish apartment in Duluth. As soon we walked in Praise picked up his cordless phone and dialed a number.

"Yo, I'm back at the crib. Is Meeka okay?" I heard him say. He then laughed and glanced at me. "Yeah, she's a wild one. Nah, I'm good…you know what I'm already about….Oh yeah I got my heat, but y'all niggahs play it close just in case."

While he was talkin', I started examinin' his place. It screamed out money for sure, with the marble bathroom floors, a fifty-two inch plasma television and imported paintings that lined the walls. The boy definitely had taste.

As I continued to check out his crib, my phone vibrated. It was a text message from Ace. *You good? We're outside….followed you from the club.*

I quickly sent him a message back statin' that I was good and had everything under control. Soon Praise was off the phone and he approached me with raw hunger in his eyes.

"I'm definitely feelin' that sexy ass body," he said.

His approach toward me was calm, but also aggressive. He pulled me into his arms and his hands rose up the back of my skirt, exposin' my voluptuous ass. His grip on me was firm as he lifted me slightly in the air, with my breasts pressed against his face.

"Um...you feel so good, Precious. I'm gonna fuck the shit outta you tonight," he said in a boastful tone.

"You are, huh. You think you can handle a girl like me?" I teased him by rubbin' my hand against his crotch. I instantly felt an erection growin' in his jeans. I wanted to know the size, width, and what he could do with it.

His breath reeked of alcohol, but his body felt so masculine. He began nibblin' at my neck, with his hands still planted on my ass. I let out a slight moan, feelin' his tongue molest me from my neck, down to my collarbone.

"Umm, you feel so good," he said again.

While he kissed me, I reached down for his crotch area again, and felt for his zipper. I wanted the dick out and in my view. I hated wastin' my time with lil' ass dicks. I slowly unzipped his jeans, and dug my hand inside his pants feelin' around for his dick. When I finally found it, my eyes widened. It felt like a monster. I slowly pulled it out and began strokin' him, while he was preoccupied with my neck and ass.

"Suck my dick," Praise said, in a commanding tone. He began forcin' me down on my knees by pushin' the top of my head.

He was dominant, but I didn't have a problem with it. I got down on my knees, and slowly took him into my mouth. I began lickin' and suckin' on the tip of his head very slowly, causin' Praise to moan with his hands tangled in my hair.

"Yeah...do that shit, girl. Umm!"

After playin' wit' the tip for a short moment, I swallowed him whole, and moved my head back and forth. He gripped the back of my head tightly, which was pissing me off.

I pulled back. "I don't like when you grab the back of my head like that."

"What?" he answered with a confused expression.

"Don't do that shit. I'm only gonna give you one warnin'," I said, very sternly.

He looked at me like I was stupid. "Yo, I ain't Meeka, so don't fuckin' come at me like that. Now finish suckin' my dick, bitch, before you get hurt!"

I looked up at him, keepin' my composure, but thinkin', *why mutha-fuckas gotta act stupid, especially in a vulnerable state?*

"What the fuck are you waitin' for? Finish that shit!" he yelled, scowling down at me.

"No problem big daddy." I sounded submissive. I leaned forward and took him into my mouth again. I wrapped my lips around his thick long dick and coiled my tongue around his shaft. He moaned, and ignored my previous warnin' about grabbing the back of my head. This time he grabbed the back of my head tighter, with his fingers knotted in my hair, and tried forcing his dick down my throat like he wanted me to choke.

I was pissed, but I didn't show it. I continued to suck his dick, being passive. I soon had him in a zone. I reached my hand up and cupped his nuts gently, and massaged them with my fingertips.

"Oh shit….Oh shit," he cried out.

Praise gripped my head tighter, and began pullin' my hair even harder. It began to hurt. It seemed like he was being spiteful. *Maybe he's pissed off that I fucked up his girl.* I gagged a few times, with him tryin' to thrust his dick down my throat. I'd had enough. When I felt he was in the zone again, that's when I struck. Simultaneously, my gentle hold on his nuts transformed into a tight squeeze, and then I bit down. My teeth bit into the thickness of his dick, and I felt his skin breakin' inside of my mouth.

Praise let out a loud piercing scream, "Aaahhh!!!" He collapsed on the floor, clutchin' his family jewels. His dick was covered in blood, and so was my mouth.

"You bit my dick," he cried out, rollin' around on the floor.

"I warned you niggah," I barked.

"Ah shit…you fuckin' bitch!"

I wiped the blood from my mouth with the back of my hand and stood over him. He looked so pathetic, but I didn't give a fuck.

"I need help, please…I'll give you anything," he begged.

"Niggah, all I want is your fuckin' life."

I knew the pain had to be excruciating. I took pleasure in watchin' Praise squirm around on the floor, whimperin' like a lil' girl.

"Just like your ugly ass girlfriend, I told you not to fuckin' disrespect me. But both of you had to learn the hard way tonight." I spit on him and then kicked him in the balls with my heels.

I went over to my purse and pulled out my nine, but I knew the gun would be too loud. In this area, a neighbor hearin' gun-shots were sure to call the police. So that option was out the door. I went into the kitchen and got a large knife.

"What you gotta say now, niggah!" I taunted him by wavin' the knife around in his face.

"You better kill me, because if not, consider yourself dead," he said, in a low voice.

"You were too easy to get at…so smart, but yet so fuckin' dumb," I stated, as I towered over him in his weakened condition.

"Fuck you!" he cried out, still clutchin' what was left of his manhood.

"I know you wanted to baby." I then stood behind him, put-ting him in a chokehold, and pressed the sharp knife to his throat.

He tried to fight me off, but it was no use. I slowly carved open his throat, slicin' his jugular and sprayin' the walls with his blood as it squirted out like a fountain.

He gagged and then choked off his own blood. I watched him die slowly and painfully. I watched his breath slowly fade.

My hands were drenched with his blood. I stood over his lifeless body with a scowl on my face. It was done. I took the initiative and did the dirty deed myself, without having a bit of remorse in me. I'd known Praise for a short moment, and knew he was an asshole, so I did his crew and everyone else a favor by endin' his life.

I went into the kitchen to wash my hands, dropped the knife in the sink and stared at it for a moment. For some strange reason, I felt good about what I'd just done. After washin' my hands. I walked back into the livin' room and took out my cellphone and called Ace. He answered on the first ring.

"It's done," I said.

"What you talkin' about?" he asked.

"He's gone."

"Not over the phone. We coming up," he said, and then hung up.

The plan was to set him up, not murder him myself. But I couldn't resist. He pissed me off, and I had to let my crew know that I could get down just like the fellas.

I needed a cigarette. I looked down at Praise's dead body sprawled out on the bloody blemished carpet. I went into his pockets to see if he had any cigarettes and pulled out a huge knot of money. *This turned out to be a pretty good night after all*, I thought as I took the stack of money that was in his pocket.

Soon there was a loud knock at the door. I looked through the peephole just to make sure, it wasn't Praise's boys. When I realized it was Ace and two other men, I opened the door. As they walked in their eyes looked down at the body, admirin' the murder I'd just committed for them.

"Damn, that niggah really is dead," one of his goons said, standin' over Praise's body.

"Yo, she bit that niggah dick off or somthing," the other thuggish goon said.

Praise was not a pretty sight. His pants were still positioned around his ankles with his mutilated gentiles still exposed, and his throat was covered in blood coating the thick cream carpet underneath.

Ace looked down at Praise and then stared up at me. As he held a cold stare, I wasn't sure if that meant he was happy or upset.

"Yo, remind me never to piss you off, Mya," one of his thugs said.

"What you want us to do, Ace?" the other one asked.

"Leave dat niggah for his boys to find. What did you touch up in here?" Ace asked.

"The knife in the kitchen, maybe the sink….and, him," I replied.

He continued to look at me for a moment. I was so turned on by his strong presence, and the way he took control. His wife-beater hugged his body like a young child to its mother. "Y'all two niggah's know what to do….clean this place up, and do it good. C'mon, Mya," he instructed.

I didn't think twice. I gathered my things and left with him as his two goons stayed behind to clean up any evidence. They must've been good at whatever they did if Ace fucked with them.

I followed Ace out of the building tryin' to keep up with him as he walked three steps ahead of me the entire time. This time we got into a polished black Lincoln Navigator. He started up the engine, put the vehicle in drive and drove off. I sat there wondering where he was takin' me, and why he was still quiet, even at a time like this.

I ended up in a two bedroom apartment in Conyers that I assumed was his place. It was simple, nothing extravagant and only contained a few pieces of furniture, a thirty-two inch television and dusty hardwood floors. Nothing stood out.

"Why did you bring me here?" I asked, lookin' around the unfamiliar place.

"You need to take a shower. It's clean," he replied.

"I could've gone home," I said. I hid my excitement about being alone with him because at the moment it didn't seem like the time, but it was definitely the place.

"No, I want you here wit' me. You need to be on the low for a minute."

"Niggah, I can handle myself. Didn't I prove that to you and your boys tonight? I don't need protection."

"Has anybody ever told you that you talk too fuckin' much? Now shut the hell up and go take a shower. I'm done talkin'." He walked away from me without a second thought of what he'd just said.

I stood there dumbfounded. Ace disappeared into another room and closed the door behind him.

"Niggah, you need to let me give you some pussy, then maybe you wouldn't be so fuckin' uptight," I said to myself.

I shrugged off his attitude toward me and then went into the bathroom. I peeled off the little clothin' I had on and got into the shower. As the hot water ran down my back, I closed my eyes and tried to collect my thoughts. I felt so horny. I began playin' with myself as thoughts of Ace fuckin' me from behind filled my head. I wanted to feel heaven between my legs.

But my quick attempt to reach an orgasm was unsuccessful, because Ace actually had me stressed. Here I was naked in his shower and he was in the next room doin' God knows what. I was throwin' my pussy at him, and he ignored me every time. *Niggahs don't ignore me, they chase me. Maybe he doesn't like women*, I thought. *Or maybe it's because I'm O.C.'s girl, and also fuckin' his cousin Donte.* He probably didn't get down like that. I hated the niggah, because he was a fuckin' mystery that I couldn't solve. He intrigued me so much, that just bein' around him was tearing me apart.

After my shower, I stood in front of the mirror and wrapped myself in a large blue towel. I'd seen better bathrooms, but I couldn't complain. It wasn't my place.

I need to leave, fuck Ace and his crazy ass, I told myself, staring at my reflection. But it was a crazy thought; I knew I wasn't going anywhere.

I stood over the sink with my head down, when I heard, "You

did ayyite, tonight."

I turned around to see Ace standin' in the doorway with his shirt off. His abs looked so fuckin' good. It felt like my pussy was about to explode.

"Fuck you!" I barked slightly.

"Really," he said. He walked into the bathroom and came close to me. With each step he took toward me, my pussy became almost intolerable.

As he approached me, he wrapped his arms around my waist, pressin' my face against his bare chest. I felt his lips near my ear, and his breath felt so warm against my skin. "You did good tonight, but you also fucked up."

"What?" He had me confused.

"I just got off the phone with Donte. Word on the street is, Scottie left for Miami, and Diamond ain't wit' the program," he said, in a calm manner.

Hearing that, I didn't know what to say or do.

"You proved yourself tonight, but your girl, Diamond, she needs to go." He turned around and left the room, leaving me alone to think about my next move.

Chapter 9

Diamond

As I drove home from my weekly shopping trip to Saks Fifth Avenue in Phipps Plaza, I began to think about my new man. It had only been a week since Scottie's departure to Miami, and I was already missing him like crazy. I missed his touch, his sincere compliments and sexy smile. I couldn't wait until I finished school in a few weeks, so I could take the trip down to Miami just to be near him again. Besides, things between Mya and I were slowly turning sour. I'd been leaving her messages over the last few days to see if she was still upset, but she hadn't returned any of my calls. I didn't like to be ignored, but at the same time, I wanted to give her space so she could cool off.

Thirty minutes later, I parked my car in front of my building and grabbed the huge shopping bag from the trunk. As I activated the car alarm and walked toward my door, I heard someone call out my name. When I turned around, I saw Mya in a dusty black Suburban that was filled with dudes.

"Diamond, let me holla at you for a minute!" Mya yelled from the passenger's seat.

When I looked at her, a funny feeling came over me. As I watched Mya hop out the truck in her usual skimpy attire, I couldn't help but think how my childhood friend felt more like a stranger now. In my heart, I knew something was different about her and I was beginning to feel like my life was in danger.

"Hey girl," I greeted nonchalantly.

"So what happened to your little boyfriend, I heard that mutha-fucka left town and went back to Miami. Are you responsible for that? Did you tell him that we were tryin' to get at him!" she shouted.

"I didn't tell him shit, he just left," I replied.

"I don't believe you, bitch! You violated my money. We could've been livin' large, but you let a piece of dick fuck up a good thing for us."

"Look who's talking," I returned. "I'm tryin' to get my business poppin' and all you care about is robbing niggahs and being a damn gangsta! Well now you can have that job all to yourself because I'm out. I don't wanna do that dumb shit anymore," I said.

"Oh, so it's like that! You didn't think the shit was dumb, when you were out at the fuckin' mall," she responded. She looked at the shopping bag in my hand and smiled. "You probably bought that shit with money from one of our scores."

"Actually I didn't, if you really wanna know."

"Oh, so now you got yourself a rich white boy and actin' brand fuckin' new. Well, do you think that white boy gives a fuck about you! You are such a naïve bitch, Diamond," she said.

I always knew that Mya loved money, but I never thought in a million years, that our friendship would be based on it. She was starting to piss me off, and had one more time to call me out my name, before I let her see my other side. "Say what the fuck you want. I got goals in life, which obviously are not gonna include you, so just do me a favor and get back in that dirty ass truck with all those niggahs and go fuck somebody like you always do!"

I could tell I'd pinched a nerve by the way she clinched her jaw. "Bitch, let me tell you somethin', you lucky to be alive right now, and if you ever get in the way of my money again, I'm gonna fuck you up!" she threatened.

I had never heard Mya come at me like that. *Did she forget that I'm from the same hood she's from? I will fuck her up if she puts her hands on me.* "Mya, just move on to another dude because Scottie is off limits. Damn, is he the only paid white dude in fuckin' Atlanta?"

"You still don't get it do you? You fucked up by lettin' him go to Miami. You lucky my niggahs in the car don't put a bullet in your ass because you fucked up their money too. But since we're girls, I saved you from death, but this is the last favor you're gettin' from me."

My eyes widened. I couldn't believe what she'd just said. *She saved me from my death? Who would want to kill me?* "So, you know people who want me dead, Mya?" I asked.

"Look, I'm about this money, and I'm gonna get mine with or without you," she replied. She took a long look at the necklace Scottie gave to me before he left. I'm sure the flawless color diamonds almost blinded her. "I see you still got somethin' out the deal before he bounced." She held the necklace on her fingertips and smirked. "Yeah, you really came out on top of the deal," she continued. "How much, fifteen, twenty thousand? You lucky I don't snatch this shit from around your neck!"

I took a couple of steps back. If Mya thought she was gonna break my necklace, then she was truly insane. "I think it's time for you to leave," I said to her sternly.

"Yeah, whatever. I can see you ain't really about the hustle anymore. You too caught up in tryin' to find love and romance than makin' this money, but it's all good. I'll see you around," Mya said. She turned around and walked back to her waiting entourage.

As she opened the door, I noticed her crew of niggahs staring at me with cold eyes, which immediately made me uncomfortable.

Before they pulled off, Mya stuck her head out the window and mouthed, "Watch your back, bitch."

At that point, I knew our friendship had reached an end, and that there was something more to the story about Scottie than she was willing to tell. The last thing I needed was beef with someone, especially since I was so close to getting out of school. *I need to move*, I thought. Mya had always told me not to stay in the same place long, so I was finally gonna take her advice.

During the next few weeks, I stayed to myself and only went out when it was necessary. I even only let a select number of clients come to my house to get their hair done. I didn't trust anyone. For all I knew Mya could've sent someone to set me up. After I had enough, I decided to move to an apartment in College Park so I could finally feel a little more comfortable in my own home. I was tired of sleeping with my heat under the pillow.

Scottie would call once or twice a week, to make sure he kept in touch. I tried not to show him how unhappy I was when we talked, but the truth was I wanted to cry on his shoulder like a baby. I couldn't wait to see him again.

I would often hear about Mya through one of my gossiping clients, and what they said wasn't surprising to me. Apparently she'd hooked up with a notorious drug crew from Kimberly Court and her name was buzzing all throughout Atlanta. They were into everything from guns, prostitution, auto theft and fake I.D.'s.

After hearing that Mya was still playing a dangerous game, I was glad that I wasn't going down that road anymore. I wonder why she hadn't realized that people in that life didn't have retirement parties. If she wasn't careful, she was gonna end up being somebody's bitch in prison or dead.

$ $ $

On Saturday June 23rd, 2006 I finally graduated from Arnold Patrick's Hair School, and finally got my license. Three well known shops in Atlanta wanted to hire me instantly, but I turned all of them down. I had bigger dreams for myself.

The day I got my license, I called Scottie and told him the good news. He was ecstatic and said that my first class ticket to Miami would be ready whenever I wanted to come. That was all I needed to hear. I told him that I was gonna take a first class flight the next day, and that he could pay me back ounce I arrived. I had to do it that way because he still didn't know my real name, and I couldn't let him find out. Besides, I didn't see the point in wasting anymore time. Not only did I need to see my man, but I also needed to feel him.

That same night I packed all of my best outfits and put them into three Gucci suitcases. With all the excitement that consumed my body, I could barely sleep. As I waited for the sun to come up, I couldn't stop smiling. It was almost as if I could feel the sun sweeping across my face.

The next day, I got out my car and strutted to the entrance of the Hartsfield-Jackson International Airport with the same smile from the night before.

Chapter 10

Mya

"Fuck Diamond," I said, to myself as I got dressed for the day. The more I thought about how my friend had played me the angrier I got. I couldn't believe she'd chosen a dude over me, and a white one at that. I looked at myself in the mirror and admired my perfect body. *I should've been the front girl on that score. My dumb ass had to give it to her.* Little did Diamond know, she owed me her life. Even in broad daylight, Donte and Ace wanted to murder her, the day we were in front of her building, but I'd talked to O.C. and luckily he gave her a pass. Even though O.C. was locked down, he was still runnin' things, and being that I was his boo, he let Diamond live. But if she crossed the crew again, there was nothin' I could do the next time. From here on out she would have to save her own ass.

Not being able to set Scottie up, took its toll on Donte, and he decided to take his frustration out on me. He was also pissed that I'd gone to visit O.C. without tellin' him first. I felt his quick wrath one day, when he slapped me upside my head, slightly bruisin' my cheek. No man had ever put their hands on me, and if I'd had a gun, his mother would be pickin' out a black dress. It wasn't my fault O.C. still ran shit, even on the inside.

Donte hated playin' second to his cousin, but I loved O.C. He was my first love, and even though Donte knew this, it still got

under his skin. I might've been fuckin' Donte, but he still could-
n't compare to O.C.

But my fight with Donte was the least of my problems.
Praise's body was found the day after I smoked him, and his
boys instantly swore revenge on me and the crew I ran with.
Word on the street was that there was a hit on my head, because I
was the one who left with Praise at the club. Plus, my altercation
with Meeka didn't help either. My head was probably on a platter
in the street.

After givin' myself one last look in the mirror, I grabbed my
purse and headed out the door. I had plans on scopin' out another
niggah today, and I was already behind schedule. As I walked to
my truck, I saw two unfamiliar men comin' in my direction. I
laughed to myself and shook my head. I could smell a cop from
two miles away.

"Mya Robinson, my name is Detective Holmes and this is
Detective Fry," he said, pointin' to his skinny partner. "We need
for you to come down to the station so we can ask you a few
questions."

How the fuck did they know who I was? "For what? I ain't do
nothin' and don't know nobody who did," I responded.

"Listen, don't make this hard. We just wanna talk to you
about the murder of Christopher Roberts," the skinny detective
stated.

I looked at both of them with a confused expression. "I don't
know no damn, Christopher Roberts."

"Well, I'm sure the name, Praise rings a bell," the skinny
detective replied.

After several minutes of going back and forth, I finally agreed
to go with the annoying detectives to the police station. I'd talked
to them long enough out in the open and in front of my crib. The
last thing I wanted was for people to think I was snitchin' on
somebody. Besides, I didn't have anything to worry about. If
Ace's goons did their job correctly and made sure that there were
no traces of me being at Praise's spot, then I knew everything

was good.

But I was still a little nervous because I'd actually fucked up. I knew by givin' him a blowjob and biting his dick, that high tech forensics and DNA could be traced straight to me.

An hour later, I was sittin' in an interrogation room with the two cops as they constantly blew coffee breath in my face. "You know that's some sick shit you did. I can't believe you almost bit his dick off," the skinny detective said.

"Like I told y'all dumb asses before, I don't know what you're talkin' about."

"So you think this is a joke! We know you were there. We know you set him up," Detective Holmes shouted at me.

I looked at his salt and pepper hair and he immediately reminded me of Bill Cosby. "Whatever, I already told y'all, I fucked him in his car, and after that he took me home," I lied.

"Bullshit, you expect us to believe that? Come on, Mya, make it easy on yourself, just tell us the truth, and maybe we can work out a deal with you. Just tell us what really happened, and we can tell the judge to be lenient toward your case. We may even be able to say it was self defense. We know Praise wasn't a boy scout, shit, he probably deserved it, but we need to bring in this case," the skinny detective said.

He was shorter than his partner, and rocked a small fro. He stared at me with hard eyes and gripped his cup of coffee tightly, while he paced back and forth.

"Look, I already told y'all my fuckin' story. We left the club, fucked, and then I went home. So if y'all gonna charge me, then lock me up. But if not, then I don't have shit else to say. I need to talk to my lawyer," I shouted.

Detective Holmes looked at me and smirked. "You're not going anywhere where until the truth comes out."

I sighed and returned his smirk. "Well, I'll be sittin' here all night because I told your dumb ass the truth. You know what I think, both of ya'll could use some pussy. Maybe then, y'all can loosen the fuck up."

"If you're saying that we should have sex with you, then don't flatter yourself. We don't fuck hoe's like...," the skinny detective replied.

I quickly rose out of my chair before he could finish his statement. I wanted to fuck his skinny ass up. I was at the point where I didn't give a damn if he was a cop or not.

He laughed hysterically. "You better sit down, before you give me a reason to lock your ass up."

"Everybody just calm down and you, Mya sit down," Detective Holmes said to me.

The anorexic cop and I exchanged hard stares at each other as I slowly sat back down in my seat. I'm sure they thought since I was a woman that they could easily get a confession out of me, but they had no idea who they were fuckin' with. I don't back down easily.

They questioned me for several more hours before they had to let me go. They didn't have anything on me anyway. I'd admitted that I left with Praise, but they couldn't put me at the crime scene. The building did have cameras, but the footage from that night was missin'.

I walked out the station a free woman and had Ace to thank for that. Whatever his goons did that night worked, and was obviously professional. They covered my tracks like I was the invisible woman. Now I knew why Ace kept them around. They were worth it.

$ $ $

After my ordeal with the two detectives I needed a hot shower and to chill for a moment. I made it back to my apartment only to see Ace and one of his thugs parked outside my building.

Ace got out of the passenger's side with his trademark evil look. He looked good in his wife beater, baggy jeans and black Nike boots.

"Mya, everything good wit' you?" he asked.

"Nothin' that I can't handle."

"We heard that the police picked you up a few hours ago."

Damn, news travels fast in the hood. "Don't worry. I ain't a snitch, so take that bullshit somewhere else. Your people did a good job, so I don't have nothin' to worry about, right?" I asked.

He just looked at me and ignored my question, which pissed me off. I wasn't in the mood for his usual silent treatment. "Look, I need a fuckin' shower. If you're comin' up cool, if not, just bounce. I had a stressful day, and if you ain't tryin' to break me off, then I don't need this shit right now." I was blunt and stern, but I didn't care.

If Ace didn't want to fuck me, then I had plenty of other niggahs to call who would happily give me what I wanted. I looked at him for a moment and sucked my teeth. He still hadn't said a word. I was fed up with his nonchalant cocky attitude. He was fine, but his attitude was gettin' played out with me. I turned around and left him standin' there alone.

I walked into my apartment and began takin' off my clothes, leaving a small trial from the door to my bathroom. I turned on the shower and sighed from the stressful day. I knew the streets would be talkin', so from here on out, it was game time. Killing Praise was bringing down a lot of heat on me, so I had to watch my back now more than ever.

The shower calmed me down, as the runnin' warm water smacked against my breasts. The force of the water on my tender nipples was startin' to make me extremely horny. I needed some dick, and immediately thought of a few niggahs that were worth my time and would be able to please me the way I needed to be please.

As I gathered my thoughts, I heard a strange noise from the living room. I became suspicious and quickly turned the water off. I stepped out the shower drippin' wet and went for my gun that was stashed under my sink. I kept it loaded at all times, just in case somethin' popped off.

I picked up the gun and quietly walked into the living room

naked. Whoever was in my house was about to see a show in more ways than one. I had an itchy trigger finger, and didn't take too kindly to someone creepin' around my crib.

As I entered the room, I crept around corners like I was one of the members of Charlie's Angels. After lookin' around for a few minutes, everything seemed to be in order. *Maybe my nerves are getting to me. Yeah, I need some dick so I can calm down.* I relaxed a bit, bringin' the gun down to my side, but as soon as I did, a dark figure quickly loomed out of nowhere. Before I could raise my weapon, someone pushed me against the wall, causin' the gun to fall out of my hand.

"Chill Mya, it's no need for that." I heard his voice and immediately knew who it was.

At that point, I didn't know if he was a friend or foe. Everybody was probably tryin' to kill me, so I didn't trust anyone. I knew Ace and Donte were mad because I'd vouched for Diamond and that she'd fucked up the hit. I'd gone behind their backs to spare her life. If he was here to kill me, I wish he would stop tauntin' me and get the shit over with.

"Get da fuck off me!" I shouted.

Ace's hold on me was strong. "Chill, girl I ain't here to hurt you," he said.

"So what you here for!" I barked.

Of course he didn't say a word. He kept his hold on me and stared into my eyes, not givin' me any indication what was gonna happen next.

"For the second time, you need to chill," he commanded.

"No!" I shouted, standing my ground. "Why you in my place sneakin' around?"

"It ain't like that. I don't have any beef wit' you, Mya. I'm just here to watch your back. Meeka put a twenty thousand dollar hit on your head for killing Praise," he informed.

"That bitch!"

"So do you wanna chill and trust me, or do I gotta get real ugly," he said, in a demandin' tone. His eyes never left mine.

I was pissed that Praise's dumb ass girl, Meeka had the fuckin' nerve to come at me. It was only right for her to lash out at me to gain her respect and credibility back after the way I embarrassed her at the club the other night, but I was still upset.

"Now go put some fuckin' clothes on," he ordered. "We need to go take care of somethin'."

I hated the way he treated me. Here I was standin' in front of him in my birthday suit and he hadn't even bothered to look. *Yeah, this mutha-fucka is gay*, I thought. It was no way a straight dude could stand in front of a drippin' pussy and not get hard.

I watched as Ace moved away from me and bent down to pick up the gun. He took a seat on my couch and stared at me like I was a fuckin' clown. "Do you not like pussy?" I asked with my hands on my hips.

He continued to look at me and never said a word.

"Whatever!" I uttered with an attitude and walked into my bedroom to get dressed.

$ $ $

A few hours later, I was sittin' in the back of a rented minivan holding a Glock in my hand. I had on a short platinum blond wig and dark shades to disguise my identity. I was hyped and ready to prove myself to my crew once again. This wasn't my first murder and certainly not my last.

Ace sat up front in the passenger seat while another one of his goons, drove us around. It was quiet as we all waited for the victim to loom from out the shadows and into our view for the slaughter. Ace turned around and looked at me. The shades that covered my eyes hid the coldness I'd formed.

"You did good wit' that Praise thing, so I know this shouldn't be a problem for you," he said.

I stared back at him and remained silent. I kept my hand planted firmly around the cold steel, trying to get familiar with the gun. I'd never shot a Glock before, and couldn't wait to see what kind of mess it could make with my victim. I tried to bring my own gun when we left my apartment, but Ace informed me I would be crazy to use my own.

"That weapon right there is fresh, no bodies are on it," his goon pointed out. "Make sure you get up close, so you can see what that mutha-fuckin' steel can do."

"She's a soldier," Ace responded.

His comment made me smile. Hearing him speak so proudly of me, made me want to carry out the hit like a true professional, assassin style. For me, this was personal. I wanted to see the whites in my victim's eyes, before I spilled their brains out on the pavement.

We sat in the van for another half hour, watching all the activity around us, especially who came and went. The less people that were around to witness what was about to go down, the better. I was starting to get antsy and needed the target to make an appearance.

Suddenly, out of nowhere the mark strutted out the building. "Bingo," I said.

I watched as Meeka walked down the street, with a small poodle on a leash. We all observed the area around us one more time, just to make sure nobody was around. When the coast was clear, Ace's goon slowly pulled up to the sidewalk and positioned the vehicle near a bunch of thick shrubberies in the direction she was walkin' her dog. I cocked the gun and stepped out the van with a stern look on my face.

With my disguise on, and my victim in view, I moved forward. As I quietly walked toward her, she had her back to me, which was her first mistake. I could hear her on the phone cursing someone out as her poodle trotted around the bushes, tryin' to find a place to pee. Meeka was so distracted on her cell-phone, that she never saw me comin'.

Dumb bitch, I thought. *Always watch your back.*

I raised the gat and aimed it at the back of her head, but for some reason I wanted to see her eyes when I fired the hot slugs into her. Suddenly, the dog noticed me and began barkin'. I guess the lil' mutha-fucka knew Meeka was in danger.

Meeka instantly turned around with the cell-phone still clutched to her ear, but when she saw me, she dropped the phone like it was on fire.

"Yeah bitch, now what!" I yelled.

She was in shock. She stared at me as the dog continued to bark. "Please don't....I'll give you whatever...."

Bang! The first shot went into her skull and her forehead exploded. The force from the gun pushed her back a few feet, and she hit the ground like a fallin' tree.

I didn't care what she had to say, I just wanted to see the look on her face when she knew death was near. I walked up to her body, and stared at her. The bullet had hit her inches from her right eye. The dog continued to bark at me from a distance but dared not to come forward.

I fired another round, strikin' her in the chest just to make sure there was no comin' back. I looked down at the barkin' dog, which was annoying the fuck outta me, and fired again.

Ace's goon pulled the van up and shouted for me to get in. I quickly followed his command without hesitation. I knew the gun was loud and messy, but I loved what it did. The bitch tried to challenge me by puttin' out a hit, but she was the one who'd fallen on the tip of my sword. I had no regrets on layin' her ass down.

"Damn Mya, you a cold bitch, you shot the dog too," the goon said, as he drove the van toward the expressway at top speed.

I just sat in the back with the gun still gripped in my hand and stared out the window. The last expression that Meeka had on her face when she saw me, was so fuckin' priceless.

Of course Ace was distant and acted as if he could care less about the hit. He just sat in the van like I didn't even exist. One minute the niggah was giving me props and the next minute you couldn't pay him to talk.

I wasn't going to let him ruin my excitement. As I continued to stare out the window, I thought about what it would feel like to be a chick that nobody fucked wit' in ATL. I wanted my name and reputation to be feared, because I had plans to show this city how hard I could truly get. And if Ace couldn't give me the respect that I deserved, then he could lay down too. I just didn't give a fuck.

Chapter 11

Diamond

I arrived at Miami International Airport smiling from ear to ear. I strutted through the airport in my Rock and Republic skinny jeans, sexy halter top and new Gucci bag that matched my luggage. All the men stared as I made my way through the terminal.

It was my first time in Miami and I couldn't wait to hit South Beach with my bikini. As I began to think about the clubs, the people and the atmosphere, I could barely hold back my excitement.

Once in the baggage claim area, I removed all three pieces of my luggage off the conveyer belt with the help of a male sky cap who either liked what he saw, or wanted a big tip. He was a nice looking guy with a dreamy pair of eyes.

"You here alone, beautiful?" he asked me, in his strong Cuban accent.

I smiled. "Actually no, I'm waiting for my boyfriend to pick me up."

"I knew you were gonna tell me that disappointing news. Well, if you ever get tired of that man of yours, give me a call."

I couldn't help but laugh at the fact that he already had his number written down on a piece of paper. "Thanks for the help with my bags, but I see my boyfriend," I replied.

Scottie walked into the terminal wearing a blue Polo sweat

suit, along with a diamond encrusted Presidential Rolex that could be seen from miles away. Seeing his thuggish style immediately turned me on.

I ran up to him and jumped into his arms, causing everyone to stare at us. I gave him a deep kiss that seemed to last forever.

"You miss me, baby," Scottie asked, with his hands on my ass.

"Yes, can't you tell? I'm so glad to be here in your arms right now." At that moment, I realized that he looked different. He'd shaved his head and now rocked a goatee. "Why did you cut your hair?" I asked.

"I just wanted a different look. What's wrong, you don't like it?" he asked, putting me back on the floor.

I rubbed his head. "No, it's fine. I just have to get used to it."

"Good, where are your bags?"

"By the conveyer belt," I said, pointing to the huge pieces of luggage. I'm sure by the way I'd packed, Scottie probably thought I was never going home.

As Scottie and I walked over to my bags, I saw the cute sky cap helping another woman. He looked at me and smiled. *Another ones bites the dust*, I thought.

Scottie called over another sky cap to come get my bags, and all three of us headed out the door with me nestled against my man's chest.

As we walked out the terminal hand in hand, the fresh air and beautiful Miami sun instantly hit me in the face. "Oh my God, I know I'm going to love it out here," I stated, staring up at the sky.

"I'm sure you will. It's pretty addictive," Scottie responded.

I kept looking up at the cloudless sky as Scottie led me to one of the most beautiful things I'd ever seen. When he hit the button to unlock the doors to his shinny silver convertible Bentley Continental GTC, I almost fainted. You could tell from the look on everyone's face that passed by that the car was stupendous.

Scottie displayed a huge smile. "You're not a baller in Miami if you're not pushing something like this. You have to do it real big down here, Dee." He walked over to a guy in an airport security uniform and reached in his pocket. "Thanks for keeping my baby safe," Scottie said, pulling out a hundred dollar bill.

"No problem, anytime," the security guy replied.

I could tell by the way the sky cap beamed that he was happy he had my bags. He couldn't stop smiling and staring at the car, as he placed my bags into the trunk. When he was done, Scottie gave him a hundred dollar bill as well.

"Thank you so much, Sir…thank you," the sky cap responded.

When we finally got in the car I was in awe at the beautiful cream interior. I started visualizing myself in the driver's seat with the top down and the wind dancing through my hair. I loved a convertible car. Before driving off, Scottie leaned toward me and planted a huge kiss on my lips.

"I'm so glad to see you, beautiful," he said.

"I'm so glad I'm here." *Especially in this bad ass car.*

"Well, are you ready to see what Miami has to offer?"

"Hell yeah, let's roll," I replied, pulling out my favorite Chanel sunglasses.

He dropped the top down as we pulled off, headed toward paradise. I felt like royalty. He took me straight to Ocean Drive, so I could see Versace's mansion and all the beautiful art deco hotels that lined the famous street. I immediately fell in love with the atmosphere along with the numerous restaurants and boutiques. Everyone walking around looked happy. I guess the intoxicating sun had that affect on everybody.

After touring the Bayside and Bal Harbour areas, we decided to head to Scottie's place. As he drove, his right hand rested on my thigh and he massaged my leg soothingly, making my pussy moist. I loved riding in his Bentley, it felt like I belonged. This was definitely a come up from living in the projects of Atlanta, Georgia.

When we entered the lavish section of Biscayne Point, it took my breath away. You could tell by all the million dollar homes and luxury cars that there was nothing shabby about this part of Miami.

As soon as we pulled into the gated driveway of Scottie's 2.8 million dollar waterfront home, my eyes almost popped out of my head. This house even made the one he owned in Atlanta look like shit.

"You like?" he asked, getting out the car.

"So far, I'm kinda impressed," I replied. I knew comments like that got under his skin.

"Kind of." He laughed. "Well, you haven't seen anything yet." He grabbed my luggage out the trunk. "Damn, Dee what do you have in these things, dead bodies?" Scottie asked pulling two of the rolling suitcases onto the smooth driveway.

I laughed. "Just a few items," I replied grabbing the third suitcase.

Once I stepped inside his house, I was overwhelmed by the beauty and structure of his all white palace. I immediately walked over to the huge floor to ceiling window in the living room and looked out onto the breathtaking view of the water. I also admired the infinity pool that was surrounded by several swaying palm trees.

"So what do you think of my place now?" he asked with a smile on his face.

"I'm speechless."

"I thought you would be," he replied. "Well, enjoy and relax yourself. This is your place too."

I almost fell out on the floor after he made that comment. The thought of me living in a place like this was like a dream. I took his advice and stepped out onto deck and stared at the water. This was heaven. A girl like me could get used to this.

I felt that gentle breeze brush against my face, and I thought about how it would feel to make love out here, under the warm blue sky, or under the stars. I closed my eyes, enjoying my life for the moment.

The view was so beautiful it immediately put me in a short daze. I became hypnotized by what Miami had to offer. I didn't think about Atlanta, Mya, or the bullshit that was going on back home. I felt so peaceful and relaxed, it was a new world for me.

Scottie stepped out onto the deck and embraced me into his arms, with my back pressed against his chest. He stared out at the water with me. "It's beautiful, just like you."

He always had a way to make me feel special. "I love it out here."

"Well, if you think this is nice, you definitely have to come out here at night. I come out just to think sometimes."

"I could never get tired of this," I said.

"Like I could never get tired of you," he returned, turning me around to face him.

"How much did you miss my kitty?" I teased, rubbing my hand gently across his crotch.

"I thought about it everyday." He leaned in and gave me a passionate kiss while he began to unzip my jeans.

"You wanna do it out here?" I asked even though I knew the answer. We were known to have sex everywhere except the bedroom.

"Hell yeah," Scottie replied. He began pulling my jeans and panties down a bit until they reached my thighs. "I want it from the back."

My pussy began to throb uncontrollably at the thought of Scottie entering me from behind. We walked over to his expensive patio furniture and I placed my body over the back of a chair. Scottie quickly pulled down his pants and boxers exposing his rock hard dick. Soon I felt his big shaft thrust into me and I gasped, trying to hold onto the chair for support.

"Mmmm…" I cried out.

Scottie gripped my hips and starting fuckin' me at a rapid pace. He cupped my breasts as he plunged in and out of me, making my juices pour out. I pushed my ass back against him, feeling the full affects of the dick. My body began to quiver, as I

grinded my ass against his pelvis. I wanted to show him how
much he was missed.

"I'm about to cum, baby," Scottie cried out.

Fuck me harder!" I shouted.

I felt his nails pressing into my back, and his legs wobbling
as he released himself into me. A few seconds later, my legs
began to quiver and I let out a huge moan. The orgasm felt so
good that I wanted to collapse onto the concrete. We stayed in
that position for a few minutes, panting like two dogs in heat.

"I definitely needed that," I said, out of breath.

Scottie nodded his head in agreement.

After a few more minutes of getting ourselves together,
Scottie finally spoke. "So, what do you want to do? You know
there's more of Miami too see."

"I know, but it's your town so you decide," I replied.

He flashed a sexy smile and rubbed my cheek softly. "Cool, I
got something set up for tonight."

$ $ $

As the evening came, Scottie and I got back into his Bentley
and headed for a club called *Macarena Tavern* on Washington
Avenue. It was a sizzling late-night, hot spot known for salsa
dancing, and was mostly populated by a young Latin crowd.

The night life in South Beach was exciting. We pulled up
to the club, and I stepped out in my white strapless mini dress
and Giuseppe Zanotti sandals. Scottie complemented me in his
gray Hugo Boss shirt and black slacks. We looked like the perfect couple.

The valet took Scottie's keys and we approached the club in
style and class. There was quite a crowd outside, but Scottie was
obviously a V.I.P because we passed security and the extremely
long line with ease.

"Hola, Mr. Morales," a Latin worker greeted Scottie as we
walked in.

"Hola, Hector," Scottie responded.

"What did he just call you?" I asked.

"It's what they call me here in Miami…Mr. Morales, that's my last name, my father was Cuban, but my mother was white," he informed me.

"Wow, I had no idea. And you speak Spanish too?"

"Si, mi nombre es Senor Morales," he said.

I smiled. "What did you just say?"

"I said, Yes, my name is Mr. Morales."

I was so turned on by his flow of Spanish that my panties were heating up. He kept me intrigued and I loved it. *That's why Mya said he likes Spanish looking girls.*

Scottie held his head up high and was greeted by so many people that you would've thought he was the President. Everybody wanted to speak to him or get his attention. But he remained calm and casual as we paraded through the crowded club and headed toward the V.I.P section.

"I need to meet with some business associates of mine," Scottie mentioned. "Do you want to hang around on the dance floor?"

"No, that can wait," I replied.

We walked to the V.I.P that was roped off with two huge bouncers standing guard out front. When Scottie appeared, they nodded their heads with respect and immediately let us through. I followed Scottie into the dimly lit room that had it's own bar, and was decorated in comfortable white suede sofas that lined the walls. Everybody in the room looked important and paid.

Scottie walked up to a group of men, who were all in expensive looking suits, and had champagne glasses in their hands. "Scottie, como estás?" one of the men said. He stood up and hugged Scottie then kissed him on his cheek. He was a burly looking man with a cigar clutched between his fingers, and sported a trimmed dark beard.

"Bien…muy bien," Scottie greeted with a smile.

"Good, my friend. And who is this lovely lady with you?" his friend asked of me.

"Dee, I would like for you to meet, Juan, a very good friend of mine."

"Nice to meet you, Dee. You are a raving beauty sent down from the heavens," Juan said.

I smiled and thanked him. Scottie then went on to introduce me to his other friends or associates that were also seated at the table. They were all handsome, charming, and very respectful. They were also accompanied by three beautiful ladies who had on skirts and dresses just as short as mine. *See, if Mya wasn't so stupid, she could be here with me right now. All these Spanish dudes are paid.*

I took a seat next to my man, and listened to all of them talk in their language. I was clueless to what they were saying, so I just sat around looking cute.

"You want a drink?" Scottie asked me.

"Yes, I would love one."

He called a waitress over to our table. "Bring us four of your best bottles of champagne." The waitress didn't even see if we wanted anything else before she dashed off to fulfill Scottie's request.

As the night continued, I got tipsy with the other three girls, as Scottie continued discussing business with his friends. The girls and I all decided to hit the dance floor and have a good time, while our men did their thing. I wanted to have some fun. I told Scottie where I would be, and he nodded, saying it was cool.

The club was packed, but it was a beautiful crowd, majority Latino and all of them were dancing to the hot salsa that blasted throughout the club. Everyone was twirling, twisting and moving around like they were performing at a show. The ladies looked beautiful in their slinky or ruffled salsa dresses. I loved Miami.

I soon joined in on the dance floor, moving and twirling around with the other ladies. The beat was up-tempo, and you had to be fast. The men were also good on their feet. They grinded their hips against the ladies, and moved across the dance floor

looking as light as air itself. I moved to the beat just as good anyone else, and about a half-hour later, I felt a pair of arms grab me
from behind. I was about to catch an attitude until I noticed that
it was Scottie coming to join me.

He pressed himself against me and swayed his hips with mine
to the music.

"You done with business?" I asked.

"Si, mi bonito flor," he said, all smooth.

"You know I don't understand," I replied.

"I said yes, my beautiful flower." So, how's everything going
out here?"

"I'm good, but even better now that you're here."

We continued to dance together, and for a white boy, he definitely had rhythm. I guess that was the Cuban side in him. He
danced salsa like it was in his blood. He twirled me around and
caught me in his grip, and glided across the dance floor like he
was Ricky Martin. I smiled and moved along with his every
move.

After we finished tearing up the dance floor, we headed back
to V.I.P, but his friends were gone. We had a few more drinks,
talked, flirted, and then decided to call it a night.

Outside, the valet pulled his car around to the front of the
club, and I was escorted into the passenger's seat like the queen
that I was. The night was so alive, warm, and South Beach was
so animated. The clubs and bars had tons of people outside; the
traffic was dense with exotic looking cars, and pedestrians just
having a good time. We drove down Collins Avenue taking in the
sights.

"Miami looks like it could be the town for you," he said.

"I love it out here, Scottie. I needed this. Thank you so much
for bringing me out here."

"Anything for you my love," he replied. He picked up my
hand and kissed the back.

We were definitely drawing attention in his Bentley as we
strolled down Collins. It showed everyone in town that we were

balling for sure, and I wasn't complaining. I loved the attention.

As we continued to drive his cell phone rang. He looked at the caller I.D and picked up saying, "Speak."

"Que!" I heard him shout out in Spanish.

He continued his conversation in Spanish, while I tried to mind my business, but it sounded like he was upset with the person on the other end of the phone. I just stared out into the night and enjoyed the scenery as he cruised at about 30mph down the busy street.

"No, mismo importa," I heard him say, and then he hung up.

"Everything okay?" I asked.

"Just business," he returned.

Soon we ended up in a part of town referred to as, Palmetto Bay. It was a rich and classy area with palm trees lining the streets. Scottie drove up to a beautiful two story home that was structured so beautifully, with manicured lawns, a stucco roof top and a red Ferrari parked in the driveway.

"Come inside with me," Scottie instructed, stepping out of the car.

"Who lives here?" I asked opening the passenger door. At first, I thought it was another one of his homes until we walked up to the front door and rang the bell.

"A friend that I need to see at the moment," he answered nonchalantly.

Moments later, a petite blond hair white woman answered the door, and my eyes got big. She was a beautiful woman, but was also topless and only wore a red thong.

"Hey Scottie, I didn't know you were coming by," she said. She looked high, holding a cigarette in her hand, as she leaned sluggishly against the door.

"Hey, sweetie. Is Carlos in?" Scottie asked.

"Yeah, he's in the back, by the pool," she told him.

Scottie walked past her, as she moved out the way and I followed right behind him. The inside of the house was lovely. It had Italian décor in every room we passed, with a large skylight in the living room and dozens of antique paintings cluttering the walls.

We walked through the house and emerged out back to the pool area that was illuminated with blue lightening. I immediately noticed a man and another woman seated by the jacuzzi.

"Scottie, my main man, what's going on? Why didn't you tell me that you were stopping by," the man shouted. He wore a big gold chain around his neck and was also Spanish with a thick moustache.

The woman he was with was lounging on a chair in a pair of pink panties and was also topless. She looked high, too. I then noticed the four lines of cocaine sprawled out on one of the glass tables, with a small straw like instrument and a bottle of Moet. It was obvious that they were having a really good time.

"Carlos, you fuckin' up business," Scottie said.

"Scottie, there was a problem, but I can fix it," he responded.

"Fix it, it seems to me that you're too busy fixing your addiction and fuckin' these hoes than taking care of business."

"No, it's not like that," Carlos replied. He looked terrified. "I fucked up this once, Scottie, but you know me. I take care of my own."

"Joder ese mierda!" Scottie shouted out in Spanish.

I stood off to the side so I wouldn't get in Scottie's way. He looked so serious and extremely determined. He stepped to Carlos, turned over the table and the glass shattered to the ground. The woman sitting by the pool looked like she'd seen a ghost when all the lines of cocaine spilled over.

"Don't fucking play with me, Carlos. I'm here with my woman tonight and you're messing that up!"

"But Scottie, c'mon, it wasn't my fault, shit happens," Carlos responded with fear in his eyes.

The woman went into the house like this was her normal routine. Seeing Scottie like this didn't actually shock me, but it did come as a surprise. He grabbed Carlos and dragged him to the pool then pushed his face into the water and held him underneath for a short moment.

Carlos squirmed and wiggled, trying to free himself from drowning in Scottie's grip. Scottie then turned to me, with him still holding Carlos' head underwater and said in a nonchalant tone, "Don't worry baby, we'll be out of here soon. Let me just finish talking to this punk and then we can go."

He pulled Carlos' head out of the water, but could care less that he was choking and trying desperately to catch his breath.

"Scottie, c'mon man... It doesn't... have to be like this...It wasn't on me... I didn't fuck it up!" Carlos shouted in between deep breaths.

"Then who did?!" Scottie screamed.

Carlos said something in Spanish, but it seemed like Scottie didn't like what he had to say in return, so he pushed his head back under the water. He held him underneath a bit longer this time, and once again, he looked over at me and smiled. "You okay, baby?"

I nodded.

I knew Scottie was in the drug game as soon as I saw his car earlier today. Something told me that the restaurant business wasn't paying that fuckin' well. After arriving in Miami and seeing his house, car, and how established he was, I knew he was a major player here. It intrigued me that he seemed so at home beating up on Carlos with me standing and watching like I was at a boxing match.

Scottie pulled Carlos' head out the water again, but this time he was coughing and gagging a little bit harder.

"Scottie, don't kill me man...I'll make it up to you... I promise...it won't happen again," he begged.

"Too many chances with you, Carlos, too fuckin' many!" Scottie still had his hand gripped around his friend's neck. "This is the last time with you," he continued and then banged his head against the ground, splitting his forehead open. At that moment, Carlos seemed to slip into unconsciousness.

Scottie stood up and smiled at me. I remained nonchalant. I

wasn't a stranger to this kind of violence. Shit, I'd seen worse growing up with my brother. But Scottie was definitely a gangster with his. He walked over to me casually and embraced me into his arms.

"I'm sorry you had to witness that side of me, but I figure better sooner than later," he said. "You're not scared, are you?"

"You think seeing you smash a man's head against the ground is going to scare me off. I grew up around worse."

"Maybe one day, you'll tell me about that because I don't know much about your past. Shit, you won't even give me your real name, Dee."

At that moment, I wanted to confess because I was tired of lying, but I was afraid of what he would think of me. I loved Scottie, and didn't want him to leave me because of a stupid ass decision I made with a friend, who was now my enemy. If he was willing to let me see a different side of him, then it was only right that I do the same, but I just couldn't do it. "I don't like my name, so I like people to call me, Dee."

"Well, I'll accept that for now, but not for long," he replied and kissed me softly on the lips.

We left the pool and walked back into the house. The two white girls were hiding out in the great room and when they saw us walk through, panic spread across their faces.

"Scottie, is Carlos dead?" one of them asked.

"Y'all bitches better shut the fuck up about this, and when that mutha-fucka wakes up, you tell him to call me," he demanded with a stern voice.

They both nodded timidly

We walked out the house, got into Scottie's car and drove off. *I'm glad that I went with my heart and didn't try to set him up*, I thought. Scottie was definitely connected and who knows what would've happened if Mya and I had robbed him.

As we rode north up Pinecrest Parkway, I wanted to ask him what Carlos did to fuck up, but I decided to stay in my place. Besides, it wasn't my business.

"So, you're a gangster?" I asked breaking the silence.

He smiled. "I'm a business man, Dee. Gangsters end up in prison," he replied.

I smiled at his remark. "After tonight, you could've fooled me."

He laughed. "I have to admit, that sometimes my temper does get in the way of me doing business."

"So how deadly can your temper be?"

"Why, are you turned on by me?" he asked.

"Maybe," I teased.

"Maybe, huh….maybe you need a spanking tonight, for being turned on by bad boys. Didn't your mom tell you about men like me?"

"She did, and she told me if they get rough, just get rough right back, and you already know I can get pretty rough," I said seductively.

"You keep talking like that and we're not gonna make it back to my place."

I smiled.

We got back to his house around three in the morning. Once inside, both Scottie and I walked straight out onto the deck.

"I told you that you would love it out here," Scottie said.

He embraced me into his arms as I continued to stare out at the water. "You turn me on, Dee and I love the fact that you keep it real. What I did tonight was a test, and you passed," he explained.

"A test?" I looked at him with a confused expression.

"Yes, I wanted to see your reaction. I wanted to see how you would react witnessing a man almost murdered by my hands, and you played it cool. You're not emotional, and I like that," he said.

"Why did you want to test me?"

For some reason he didn't answer, so I decided not to push the issue. A part of me wasn't sure if he was really telling me the whole story, but again I didn't want to open up a can of worms. We were having a nice time enjoying each other's company, and

I didn't want to ruin that. I hadn't been this happy in months.

$ $ $

I woke up the next morning with the beautiful bright morning sun peeking through the bedroom window. It was a beautiful day, and I couldn't wait to see what Scottie had planned. If it was anything like the night before, I was in for a treat. When I rolled over, I noticed that he wasn't in bed, so I got up and put on my favorite Victoria Secret's robe and went to see what he was doing. When I found him, he was on the deck naked sipping a glass of orange juice. He turned around and gave me a warm smile.

"Buenos días, beautiful. Did you sleep well?"

"Yes." I walked out onto the deck and gave him a huge hug. "Why are you always naked at the oddest times?" My thoughts went back to the first time I stayed over his house and he was cooking my breakfast in his birthday suit.

"I don't know. I guess it just feels like I'm free," Scottie responded. He gave me a kiss and asked if I wanted some breakfast, and I gladly accepted. I was starving. We talked and chilled on the deck for a moment and then got dressed and went out to get something to eat.

Scottie wanted to take me to his favorite restaurant for breakfast called *Wish* on Collins Avenue and 8th street. The place was classy and apparently had the best omelette's and home fries in town. After we ate, Scottie and I talked so long that by the time we finally got up, lunch time had came and gone.

My first week in Miami went extremely well. Every where Scottie and I went we were treated with top notch service, so I felt like a celebrity, or even a queen when I was with him. He made Miami my personal playground when it came to shopping and partying, and spent countless money on me. My favorite place was the Bal Harbour Shops that made our mall in Atlanta look like a flea market. The Shops had every top designer from A to Z. Luckily, Scottie had dropped ten thousand for me to shop with, so I put a serious dent in my favorite stores. My baby was definitely spoiling me.

At night, we hit up clubs like, Opium Garden, Rain and Prive. But our favorite place to hang out was the Rose Bar inside the Delano Hotel. It was a sophisticated place where we could have nice quiet conversations or even start up a game of pool. Wherever we went, it was always the same V.I.P treatment for us, no lines, quick valet parking, and endless bottles of champagne. Scottie had even informed me that he had a few partnerships in some local clubs and restaurants, but he wouldn't go into detail about it, and once again I didn't press the issue.

My time in Miami was going by so quickly, that I found myself never wanting to go back home. What was the point anyway? The people I knew in Atlanta, were always about drama and chaos and I wanted more for my life. It was time for me to finally get out the hood, the legal way and start making better decisions. I was having the time of my life with Scottie, and even if it took everything I had, I was gonna make sure it stayed that way.

Chapter 12

Mya

After I murdered Meeka, what was left of Praise's crew tried to go hard and retaliate against us, but we quickly cut 'em down like the weeds they were. I had blood on my hands, and my name was beginning to run through the streets like a track star. I'd become the first female enforcer for O.C. and Donte's crew, and was damn proud of it. I didn't take shit from anyone, and everyone stayed clear of me, knowin' what I was all about.

The money started comin' in lovely after we took over Praise's territory. I'd stepped up my game by tradin' in my Denali for a brand new artic white CLK550 Benz. My wardrobe had also been upgraded since our Washington Road takeover. After our lil' war with Praise's crew, we became untouchable and no one in Atlanta wanted to fuck wit' us. I began to live my life like a diva. I no longer needed to rob niggahs. That became petty shit for my status.

Two weeks after my last shootout, I walked into Donte's house ready to have some fun. Once a month, he hosted a gamblin' party where guys came from all over Atlanta and the surrounding areas to play craps, blackjack, Georgia skins, or whatever else you were into. The parties normally started on Friday nights and wouldn't end until Sunday mornin' dependin' on how much money was being made. I'd known for Donte and Ace to be at the party for the entire two days without even stoppin' to take a damn bath. Now that was serious gamblin'. Normally at these parties, Donte invited several girls to come and work the room, and in return they would get loads of cash in tips. I always worked these parties because even if I went and got a niggah a soda, when I returned I would have a fifty dollar tip. Sometimes even a hundred, if I had on an extremely tight outfit.

I strolled into the spot in my short red BCBG wrapped dress and three inch stilettos. I topped off the outfit with some bright red lipstick that made my lips beg for attention. Normally, I did-n't wear red because it reminded me of a prostitute, but tonight that was the look I was going for. I wanted to be a hoe as long as I was a paid one. I concealed my nine millimeter in my Fendi bag, and moved through the apartment with a grim stare. I saw several people bobbin' their heads to an old Eric B. and Rakeim song as I made my way through the small group of gamblers. I noticed the stares from a few men as I made my way toward Donte's bedroom to meet up with my crew. During the parties, Donte always had a high rollers room for people who really wanted to get down. The minimum bet on any game was normal-ly five-thousand, so they kept the bedroom door locked at all times and had someone guard the door. This way nobody could get in, but also no one could get out, just in case they didn't want to pay up. I guess Donte had him a regular fuckin' Caesar's Palace.

Before I reached the bedroom door, I noticed a girl with a honey colored complexion keepin' this one gentlemen company. I had to look twice because she looked a lot like Diamond, and I knew that couldn't be true. I'd heard she went down to Miami to chill with her bitch ass boyfriend, Scottie. I was sure she'd prob-ably gotten scared knowin' what was about to go down and moved down there for safety. I'd gone by her crib in the middle of the night a few times, and noticed that her old apartment was completely empty, so that bitch was officially, M.I.A. But didn't she know that if I wanted to find her down there I could. Obviously Diamond was underestimating me and more impor-tantly, my skills. Before I could walk over and confirm if the girl really was Diamond, the look-alike turned around. *Oh, shit that's not her*, I thought. Besides, I knew she couldn't be that dumb. Damn near everybody in the house was a part of my crew, and wanted her ass dead.

I walked over to the high rollers entrance where one of Donte's goons was standin' guard tryin' to look intimidating for the crowd. I laughed because the niggah looked like he was tryin' to protect the President.

I eyed him down, and he glared back at me like I was a fuckin' pain in the ass.

"You got a problem wit' me?" I asked.

"Nah, Mya, I ain't got no beef wit' you," he said, in a very stern tone.

"So why you lookin' at me like that?"

"Hey, I'm a man so I'm just lookin'….that's all," he replied.

I didn't like his attitude toward me.

"You like what you see?" I walked closer to him and placed my hand gently on his chest, then slowly moved it down until my hand rested on his crotch.

He tried to tense up, but I felt the excitement spread throughout his body as I squeezed his dick tenderly; caressin' the small bulge he had growin' in his jeans.

"Go ahead, and say it. I know you wanna fuck me, and I can probably make it happen for you," I teased.

He tried to keep his thuggish composure, as he allowed me to fondle him for everyone to see. I began caressin' him, and he reluctantly let a slight moan escape from his mouth.

I wanted to see how far, I could go with this dude, so I continued with my lil' game. Besides, if I ever needed a niggah to help me bring Donte's ass down he might be the one. "Imagine my thick lips wrapped around your dick," I whispered in his ear.

I suddenly felt his erection on the rise.

"Mya, please stop. You belong to Donte," he said softly.

My eyebrows began to wrinkle. "What? I don't belong to no one. Donte's name ain't engraved on my pussy. I'm wit' whoever

I want."

He just stood there. I knew he was contemplatin' the sexual offer. I knew I had him so excited that he was willin' to betray his loyalty to Donte just to get a taste of me. I knew he was weak, and the thought of that, turned me the fuck on. My pussy and my gun could bring any niggah to his knees. I got a rush by flirtin' with the weakest ones in the crew.

Lookin' into his eyes, I had him in a frenzy, so to fuck with him even more, I took his hand and moved it up my thighs underneath my short dress and rested it against my manicured treasure. I'd given myself a Brazilian wax that mornin', so I was bald as a baby's ass. As usual, I didn't have any panties on. With one of my lovers in the next room, I was takin' a risk, but risks always turned me on.

"Now doesn't that feel good? Go ahead; stick your fingers in, she won't bite." I gripped his wrist tighter and tried to force him to do it. I knew he wanted to. We had onlookers around, but no one dared to say a word to us.

"I can't, Mya. Donte's in the next room," he said, tryin' to fight the urges he had for me.

I gave a disapprovin' stare and quickly removed his hand from underneath my dress. "Next time don't look at me so fuckin' hard if you too scared to take risks. If I were you, I wouldn't give a damn about Donte because he sure as hell don't care about you. Next time you see me, show me some damn respect," I responded.

I walked past him, probably takin' away a few points from his manhood. I loved fuckin' wit niggahs that doubted me. "Now use the secret knock, so I can get in,"

He had a look of death in his face, as he used the code for the door. After waitin' for a few seconds, someone finally opened it. As I walked into the high roller section, all I could smell was smoke and ass. *Damn, it stinks in here.* I looked around at all the young women who were barely dressed. "I'm the only woman in this room wit' clothes on," I mumbled to myself. *That's odd.*

I looked at Donte who really seemed to be into his card game. I didn't want to disturb him, because it looked like he was betting tons of money, so after the hand was over I cleared my throat to get his attention. Donte, Ace, and two other strange men were seated around a large round table that was cluttered wit' bottles of Grey Goose, ashtrays, and a few lines of coke.

"There's our girl right there," Donte pointed out.

He stood up and gestured for me to come and give them some company. I strutted over and sat next to my lover in my sexiest walk. Donte placed his arm around my neck and began introducing me to the two men who were unknown.

"Mya, these are my two niggahs from up top," Donte said. "They came down here to do some business wit' us…so we can make some money."

After the introduction, Donte snorted up a quick long line of coke off the table; which disappeared up his nose like a vacuum. Ace just sat there and watched. I guess like myself, he was disgusted with Donte's daily drug use. He was using his own product, and that was one fatal mistake in the game.

One of the up top dudes looked at me wit' some contempt, and instantly put a bad taste in my mouth. He was a high yellow niggah who sported long braids and a fitted Yankees hat.

His partner, was a cutie, but had a fierce image about him; one like Ace carried around. He was quiet, and also had long braids that looked like thin little ropes. It didn't hurt that his hazel colored eyes were hypnotic.

Off the break I wanted to get at him, but Donte knew how I felt about dudes from New York. I hate 'em. They had New York written all over them, especially wit' their fitted baseball caps, northern accent, and ignorant personality. *Why is everybody in New York so fuckin' up tight?*

"Is this your bitch?" the light skinned New Yorker asked Donte.

"What da fuck did you say?" I barked. I was ready to get in his ass.

He looked fiercely at me. "She looks nice, but I don't do business wit' hoes sittin' at the table, they talk too fuckin' much."

I couldn't believe what that fool had just said. Didn't he realize that he was in a room full of killers? Ace cut his eyes over at him, but kept his cool. "Watch how you talk to our women down here."

"Yo, this is business, and when I do business, I don't want a bitch around me," the New Yorker stated boldly. He looked at me. "Now, shorty, take your fine ass away from this table and make you some money dancing on niggahs or some shit. You look like you need it."

I'd had enough. "Mutha-fucka!" I shouted, jumpin' up. I was about to charge at him, but Donte pulled me back down.

"Mya, take a walk for a minute." Donte ordered.

"What! A walk, please tell me you jokin'?"

"I said go for a walk, let me talk to my people for a minute," he said. I knew he was high.

I cut my eyes at Donte. I was ready to murder his ass too just for allowing that bum ass niggah to talk to me like that. If it was O.C., that niggah would've been down on the floor after he said the word bitch to me the second time. He usually only gave people one warnin'. At least Ace tried to stand up for me.

I looked at Donte for a minute, disgusted with his decision to have me leave the table. Ace seemed appalled by Donte's action, but why did he just sit there and let that niggah talk shit to me. *Wasn't I part of the fuckin' crew?*

"Fuck you, Donte! And you, whatever the fuck they call you, I'll see around. Don't leave town so soon," I warned the high yellow dude.

"Don't come at me wit' no threats. I don't give a fuck who you fuckin'!" he shot back.

Rage burned through my entire body. I was more than ready to take his ass out. I stared at him so long and hard, that I could've put a hole through his chest.

"Mya, this is business, so bounce and let us talk," Donte continued takin' his boy's side.

"Fuck you!" I shouted and stormed off.

"Yo, man, excuse my bitch, she can fly off the handle some-times," I overheard Donte say as I headed out the door.

"No problem, but I like to keep my bitches on a short leash. Looks like you need to do the same," the New Yorker replied.

I briskly walked past Donte's bodyguard, and headed for the bar that Donte had set up in the kitchen. I needed a drink to calm me down before I did somethin' stupid. And once my mind had murder bounchin' around, it was gonna take a miracle for some-one to calm me down. Just knowin' his bitch ass was only a few feet away, had me in a burnin' frenzy.

I fixed a Grand Marnier with lemon and instantly took it to the head. Minutes later, I lit a cigarette and inhaled deeply and then exhaled a large cloud of smoke with my eyes glued to the entrance of the high roller area.

Just do it, Mya, just fuckin' do it, my mind kept racin'. I took a few more pulls from the cancer stick then put it out under my shoe. *What am I doin'? Just go home, Mya."*

I ended up leavin' Donte's apartment a few minutes later and walked outside to my car. I knew I should've gone home, but I felt stuck to the ground. I couldn't stop thinkin' about that high yellow mutha-fucka. *Couldn't they see he was a problem?* I did-n't give a fuck what kind of business Donte was doin' wit' him, he was gonna pay one way or the other.

It was around three in the mornin' when I dozed off in the dri-ver's seat of my car with my gun still in hand. It felt like I was only sleep for five minutes before I heard a sudden tap on the driver's side window. I jumped, pointin' my nine millimeter at the target. I was startled a bit, and almost shot Ace.

Realizing it was him, I lowered my gun and rolled down my window. "Why are you scarin' me like that, I almost shot your ass," I said.

"You okay?" he asked.

"I'm fine, but I'll be even better if you go and pick out that niggah's casket."

"Chill," he said, wit' a stern look.

"Fuck being chill, you heard how that niggah disrespected me in there. I'm gonna fuck him up, Ace. How y 'all gonna let a New York niggah come up in here and talk shit like that to me! He's in ATL now, far from up north!" I shouted.

He looked at me wit' that same trademark straight-faced look of his, and replied, "Mya, just chill."

"What did I tell you before, huh..."

Ace reached into the car and strongly grabbed me by my chin, and then stared at me wit' the coldest pair of eyes, I'd ever seen. "For the last time, you need to chill."

I stared angrily back at him, but kept my mouth shut. I placed the gun next to me on the passenger seat, and told him that I was cool. He looked at me for a short moment and then walked off. I watched as he got into his Hummer and drove off.

"Fuck you too," I uttered.

I had such a strong yearnin' for Ace, but I was fuckin' pissed off at how he was handlin' the situation. I began to wonder why Ace was the only one who'd said somethin' in the first place. Now I knew Donte was a bitch ass niggah who only cared about business. I wanted to tell O.C., but it wasn't a need, I could handle myself.

I put in a CD and was about to drive off, when I looked to my left and saw the two New York dudes exit Donte's house. The sight of the high yellow dude instantly sent me into rage. I picked up my gun, and was ready to step to the niggah, but gun shots would've brought Donte out the house faster than I could blink.

So, I remained calm and watched their every movement. Minutes later, they got in a champagne Cadillac STS, it looked like they didn't have a care in the world. They both were smilin' and laughin' like they'd just won the lottery. I hated to see him have a good time, and couldn't wait to wipe the smile off his high yellow face.

As I began to follow, I drove two cars behind them the entire ride. They got on I-85 and headed south, toward the city. I tried to be discreet, but I knew they didn't know my car, and besides, the high yellow one was actin' as if he was untouchable. But little did he know, he was gonna learn the hard way and pay wit' his life for underestimating me.

They ended up pullin' into the parkin' lot of a twenty-four hour convenient store near Morningside. I parked in the dark and watched both of them get out and walk into the store. For a Friday night, it was unusually quiet.

At that moment, I didn't give a fuck if I was makin' a mistake or not. He had to be dealt wit' so I cocked my gun, ready for war. The only thing on my mind was that he'd disrespected me in front of my crew, which was unacceptable. I got out my car and waited for the right moment to strike. I ignored Ace's advice to chill and lingered in the dark, like a predator waitin' for its prey.

Ten minutes passed before they walked out of the store and back to their car. The cutie was carryin' a plastic bag, while high yellow was talkin' on his cell-phone, makin' the same mistake Meeka did. I narrowed in on them and moved forward with my nine gripped tightly in my hand. Luckily, the parkin' lot was empty, leavin' no witnesses to the murder I was about to commit.

I quickly loomed out from darkness raisin' my weapon. I wanted the loud mouth asshole to see me comin', so I dropped his boy first, which I hated to do, because he was cool, but any acquaintances had to go.

His head exploded when I shot him in the temple at point blank range, and he dropped like a large sack of potatoes on the cold ground.

"Oh shit!" I heard loud mouth say.

I quickly shot him in his knee cap, cripplin' him before he could reach for any weapon. His phone flew out of his hand, as he dropped and clutched his bloody knee. "You fuckin' trick!" he cursed, looking fiercely up at me.

I stood over him with a grim stare and pointed my gun directly at his forehead. "Welcome to ATL, you stupid mutha-fucka!" Blam! Blam! Blam! Blam!

I put three shots into his head and one in his big fuckin' mouth. After lookin' around to see if anyone was watchin' me, I quickly retreated to my ride and drove off. I didn't regret my actions, but I was worried about Ace because I'd disobeyed an order. *Nah, fuck that! I did what I had to do. Nobody disrespects me like that.*

I drove hastily back to the city at top speed. I knew word would get out soon about the murders, so I contemplated about going back home but decided to go away. Minutes later, wit' the murder weapon still concealed in my purse, I made it back to my place safely. I went into my bedroom, hid the gun under the mattress and crashed on my bed. "Wait a minute, somebody might try and come at me tonight," I said out loud. I snatched the gun from under my mattress and put it under my pillow instead. If somebody wanted to play rough, then I was the perfect opponent.

Chapter 13

Mya

I woke up the next mornin', and slowly opened my eyes only to see, Ace towerin' over me like the Empire State Building. I jumped up, startled by his sudden presence. *How in the fuck does he keep gettin' in here?* Without a seconds notice, he lunged toward me, as I tried to scramble to the other side of my king sized bed to grab my gun. But he was quick; he grabbed me by my shirt, and pulled me back in his direction like a rubber band. He tightly clutched his hand over my neck, and then body slammed me back on the bed. With Ace's different mood swings, I was really startin' to think that something was wrong wit' him mentally. If I was gonna continue to be around him, I needed to protect myself.

He was strong, and so hostile. The veins in his arm flexed as his fingertips began to lunge into my skin. As a woman, I should've been terrified, but I wasn't. In my line of work, it would've been stupid to run from death, so I welcomed it.

"What da fuck did I tell you!" he yelled. His eyes were burnin' into me wit' rage. "You never wanna fuckin' listen to anybody, Mya."

"Fuck them niggahs," I retorted.

"Do you have any idea what you just did?" he yelled. "I should kill you for being so fuckin' stupid."

"So do it then, Ace because I'm not afraid to die. Actually, I don't even give a fuck!" I snapped. His grip around my neck never budged. I returned the same hostile stare. "What are you waitin' for? Go ahead and get the shit over with, but I'll be damned if I was gonna let that niggah live after last night," I said. "So do it...the gun I used is under the pillow."

Suddenly, I noticed the rage and his tense stare slowly disappear from his eyes. His grip around my neck became looser, and then disappeared all together. I stayed on my back like a dead bug, and looked up at him in shock. I still couldn't believe what had just happened.

"Who the fuck was he anyway?" I asked.

"A high profile niggah from New York with a lot of connections," he explained.

"So, who gives a fuck? Connects come and go, we'll live."

Ace looked at me with a blank expression. I wasn't sure if it was because of my lack of remorse. The fire he had in his eyes a moment ago was completely gone. Suddenly, I noticed a Glock he had concealed in a leather holster under his left armpit. I guess it was meant for me.

"You fucked up, Mya!" he shouted.

"So if I fucked up, then shoot me. I know you gotta handle your business. I ain't scared to die."

I continued to lay on my bed as I watched Ace with a close eye. He stood next to my nightstand like he was contemplating somethin'. I was beginnin' to wonder, why he hadn't reached for his gun yet. When he couldn't look me in the eyes, that's when I realized, he couldn't do it. Ace was a stone cold killer, a murder with no remorse, but with me he just couldn't pull the trigger. I'd fucked up last night, so I should've never been able to open my eyes this mornin'. In our crew, those who fucked up and disobeyed orders like that had to see the other end of his smokin' gun. In this game, there were no room for mistakes, and I'd already made two.

I knew at that moment, that if he couldn't kill me then he must've had feelings for me. It was hard to read him, but I felt some kind of connection between us.

"Does Donte know about the murders?" I asked.

"He's the one who sent me," he informed.

That bitch ass mutha-fucka. I guess he won't be gettin' anymore pussy. "So why am I still alive?"

I knew he didn't want to respond to the question, but I needed an answer. Even though, Ace's eyes were cold, and his expressions were meaningless, he had to be feelin' somethin' inside.

I stared at Ace and boldly asked him, "Do you want to fuck me, Ace? Is that the reason why I'm still here?"

He quickly displayed a deranged expression with his eyes, pulled out his Glock and charged forward. He began to choke me and put the gun to the back of my head. "Do you want me to do it, you stupid bitch!"

I'd obviously hit a nerve. After a quick struggle, he quickly released his grip.

"Can I ask you somthin'," I said, waitin' for his reply. I'd wanted to fuck him for a long time now, so it would be perfect if he felt the same way.

He looked at me, but never said a word.

"Can I ask you somthin'," I repeated again. This time I didn't wait for a response. "Why are you such a mystery? I practically throw myself at you, and all you do is fuckin' ignore me."

"Because you belong to Donte."

I sat up in the bed, "Please, do you think I give a fuck about him at this point. That mutha-fucka means nothin' to me."

"Well, It means somthin' to me," he countered.

I had to laugh. "Are you serious? You don't wanna fuck me because you think I'm his girl?"

He remained quiet, with that same deranged stare he was so known for.

"Look, Donte may be good at other areas, but in the bedroom, he's definitely slackin'. He can eat some pussy, but his dick game is lackin', if you know what I mean," I said wit' a smirk.

Ace just stood there not amused by my comment. He was a cold blooded killer and a drug-dealer with morals. I laughed to myself.

"You're different, cuz any other niggah would've been fuckin' me as we speak. But you, you have a code, and a certain type of respect. You don't like to get involved with other men's affairs, and I like that."

"Donte wants you dead, he thinks you're a risk," was his only reply.

"Fuck Donte, and fuck you too, if you think y'all gonna put fear in my heart!" I shouted.

Ace just stood in front of me wit' his Glock to his side, pointed toward the floor.

"Donte has changed, Ace. I know you see it. He's too paranoid. He's the one that's becoming a risk," I said.

Ace stood there, probably listenin' to what I had to say, but didn't respond.

"You saw what happened last night. He was high and let them fools talk to a member of this crew anyway they wanted. He's becoming hooked on his own product, and now he's paranoid and wants to have me killed for what, those two fools?" I asked. "C'mon, Ace, I know you see it too. He's fuckin' up. He's the one becomin' a risk. There's no tellin' what he's out there doing when we ain't around," I continued.

"What you gettin' at?" he asked.

"You're not stupid, niggah. You and Donte are the only ones who know I killed them two fools last night. Y'all are also the ones who know I had a dispute wit' that one high yellow niggah. Besides that, anyone could've killed them. With that fools mouth, I know he had plenty of enemies. So the blame can't be placed on me, but with Donte, he needs to go."

"So you're sayin' we should kill him?"

"Yeah, Donte's not the same; he's becomin' a coke head. He's running his mouth like a bitch, and could easily get us *all* killed or locked up," I responded.

I stood up and stepped to Ace with a soft approach, and my eyes fixated on his body. I stood an inch from him and said,

"With Donte out the way, we can take over and become larger than anything ATL has ever seen. We can become like fuckin', Bonnie and Clyde. You're smart, you're ruthless, and you show a sign of respect. Niggahs respect you on these streets, more than they respect Donte. Believe me, I hear things, and the consequences of killing Donte won't be as severe as you think. He might have a few loyal soldiers by his side, but once we cut them down and show them who's in charge, those niggahs that come against us, will become your personal bitches to deal with."

I knew Ace was takin' in the proposal. He stood erect with his gat still gripped in his hand. "And what about O.C.?"

"Let me handle O.C. He can be a very understandin' man, but if he's not on board, then we'll put the green light out on him, too," I informed.

Ace was quiet. I still didn't get the reaction I wanted. But I knew he had to see the bigger picture with us takin' over the drug trade in Atlanta. It was our time, I felt it. I wanted to be that girl no one could touch. My reputation was already becomin' fiercer. And with Ace by my side, we could become the supreme team.

Ace stood in front of me lookin' the way a man should look, tall, muscular and handsome.

I was horny and a bit frustrated. After the night I'd just had, I needed a niggah to break me off wit' some dick, and Ace was the perfect candidate. I didn't give a fuck about his morals, I just wanted to fuck.

"So you feel me on this proposal?" I asked.

He returned my gaze. "I need to think about it."

"That's understandable," I lied. Truthfully, I was tired of playin' games.

I gently grabbed Ace by his tank-top and said to him, "With Donte out the way, I can be your woman. And you can have the best of both worlds, a good business partner and some sweet pussy." I took off the small teddy I had on and tossed it to the side. Because I hardly ever wore panties, for the second time I was completely naked in front of the man I desperately wanted inside of my body.

I ran my hands across his chest, touchin' his muscular pecks, and feelin' his abs through his tank-top. I then placed my hand on the prize, which was the bulge between his legs. It felt so nice in my hand that I wanted to molest him. "You and me, baby...think about it," I continued.

I lifted his shirt, exposing the raw six-pack he had underneath. I slowly ran my hands across his stomach touchin' every inch of his skin. I squatted in front of him a bit, and ran my tongue across his body, tastin' every last inch. Even though his personality was a little crazy, he was still a man, and a man needs pussy. He couldn't resist me forever.

Ace's dick was stiff as a board, so I had to get to work. I fondled him with one hand while I tried to undress him with the other. He placed his gun on the nightstand, and then I pulled his wife-beater over his head, exposin' his chiseled body. I began kissin' every inch of him, and, he finally started to come alive and show some interest. He took his index finger and made small circles around my nipples, which instantly made them hard. Once they were pointin' at him, he sucked wit' gentle tugs, and then began to suck wit' force. This was the first time, I'd ever been this close to him without him turnin' away and it felt wonderful. My pussy began to throb.

I went for his pants and quickly unbuckled them. I needed to see what he was working with. From what I felt in my hands, I definitely wasn't gonna be disappointed. My body began to ache with lust, and my pussy juices poured out like hot liquid from an explodin' volcano. Every touch from him on my bare skin made my body shake.

As I pulled his boxers down, my eyes said it all. I was in complete awe when I stared at his thick penis. It had to be at least ten inches, and felt like a pipe. I stroked it back and forth, feelin' the veins pulsate in my hand. The more I stroked him, the hornier I got.

Within seconds, I jumped up and pushed him on the bed. I

couldn't take it anymore. I had to climb up and straddle that
horse. Even in the heat of the moment, Ace was quiet. He didn't
talk shit to me like every other niggah I'd been wit' which was
odd for me. Right before I was about ride his dick, he grabbed
me by the waist and flipped me over.

"Wow, you're rough, but I like that. Get rough with me,
daddy," I said, in my sexy child like voice.

I fell on my back against the mattress with Ace's big frame on
top of me. I spread my legs apart and opened then as widely as I
could, waitin' for him to dive in. I looked up at him with a strong
hunger in my stare, yearnin' for him to take me.

He gripped my leg and positioned himself close to the pussy.
He then gripped his large hard dick and only put the tip of the
head in, then pulled it back out.

"No, don't tease me," I begged. "Please put it back in."

He looked at me like I was lying. "Do you want it?" he asked.

I almost fell off the bed because I couldn't believe that he'd
finally said something. "Yes, I want it, can't you tell?"

"Well, I don't think I should give it to you since you've been
bad."

I looked at him with concern. If he was gonna get me horny
as hell, then take away the dick, there was gonna be a problem. I
decided not to jump to any conclusions. "I'm sorry I've been
bad, please give it to me."

As I was prepared to hear another question, he thrust his dick
inside of me, which caught me off guard. I let out a loud scream.
His thickness had opened me up like no one had ever done
before. *Damn, have I been messing wit' lil' dick niggahs all my
life*? He grabbed both of my legs and spread them so far apart, I
almost did a split. Wit' my legs lookin' like a cheerleader, he continued to thrust his massive dick inside my pussy, causin' my
screams to turn into moans. I clutched the bed sheets as the feeling of ecstasy overcame my body. He was fuckin' the shit outta
me.

He continued to pound into me like he was literally tryin' to

kill my pussy. I hoped he wasn't tryin' to have a murderous reputation in the bedroom too. But I loved it rough. He fucked me for
twenty minutes straight until I felt a nut beginning to brew. His
dick began to swell, so I knew he was about to explode. It felt so
good, that I clawed his back and nibbled on his ear as he continued to pound my pussy. He gripped my thighs and his thrusts
became even more intense.

"Cum for me, baby," I moaned.

His pace became rapid, I felt his body tensin' up and soon he
began to jerk out of control. I grabbed him in my arms and held
him close as he continued to get the last bit of semen out.

I love to see a niggah cum, because they lose all control and
no matter how hard and dangerous they are, at the moment of cli-
max, they are all the same, weak and helpless. It was like lettin'
the air out of a balloon and watching it deflate.

I couldn't believe after having that explosive sex, Ace was
still quiet. A few minutes later, he got up and immediately began
to get dressed. As I laid there and watched him put on his pants, I
couldn't help but to think how satisfied I was. He reached for his
gun and placed it back in the holster.

"Are you gonna leave me a tip?" I joked.

"We'll talk," was his only reply before he turned around and
walked out my door.

That was the first time I'd ever had sex with someone and he
left before me, this felt strange.

Chapter 14

Diamond

It was my last day in Miami and I didn't want to leave, but I needed to take care of some business back at home. I'd spent four weeks living in a fantasy world, but now things had to get back to normal. It was hard giving up this life, even though I knew it was only temporary.

I was already packed and decided to go out on the deck to take in one last bit of sun, while I drank some of Scottie's famous Ice Tea. Scottie had been gone for a few hours, and I wasn't quite sure where he'd gone, and wouldn't dare ask.

During the weeks that passed, I'd gotten to know a little bit more about him and his life. I learned that he was a major cocaine and ecstasy supplier throughout Miami and majority of the south, reaching up to Atlanta and New York. The man was a multi-millionaire, who laundered his money through so many legit businesses, that he was damn near untraceable. He was a smart business man. The guy, Juan who I'd met at the salsa club when I first arrived was his number one partner, and the two of them had Miami and other parts of the south on lock.

Together, they moved tons of cocaine and ecstasy through the borders of Florida and disturbed the products wholesale to dozens of dealers throughout the southeastern seaboard. I began to wonder if Mya knew about Scotie's real job all along, and that's why she'd sent me to set him up in the first place. It was just like her to be sneaky and conniving.

An hour later, Scottie arrived back at home with a pleasant look on his face. I walked up to my man and greeted him with a hug and a passionate kiss.

"Are you packed baby?" he asked.

I held my head down like a sad little puppy. It took me a few seconds before I answered. "Yes."

"You sure you don't want to stay a few more weeks with me?"

"I really want to, but I need to get back home and handle some business," I responded.

"Well, when it comes to business, I understand." He went in his pocket and pulled out a black, square box. I smiled and instantly thought of jewelry.

"It's my going away gift to you," he said.

"Scottie, you're spoiling me." I replied, trying to play it off. I actually enjoyed it.

When I opened the box, I was stunned to see a platinum bangle with four rows of sparkling princess cut diamonds. "Oh my God, Scottie, you didn't have to do this." I lied. Inside, I was jumping up and down.

"I wanted to get you something to match the necklace, but when I saw this I had to get it."

My hands shook slightly as I picked up the beautiful piece of bling and placed it around my wrist. "This is so beautiful, Scottie. I love it and I love you," I replied giving him a huge kiss.

After watching me admire my new gift for a moment, Scottie cleared his throat. "Are you ready to open up that hair salon when you get back to Atlanta?"

I looked at him in shock. "Of course," I replied.

"Well, good because I'm gonna help you, but you're gonna have to get a loan," he stated.

Is this dude crazy? Why should I get a loan when he's paid? "A loan...I thought you just said you were gonna help me out."

"I am, but the money can't come from me directly. I don't

want anything to be traced back to me, so it's better if you go to the bank and apply for a loan," he replied.

"But I don't have any collateral. A bank is not gonna give me a huge loan. Besides, I barely have any credit, and I just got out of school."

"Listen, the first thing you do when you get back home, is head down to Trust Bank and apply for a loan. When you get there I want you to ask for Mr. Jonathan Frazier," he informed. He passed me a card with the man's name and address. "You give him my name, and everything will be taken care of."

"But Scottie...."

"Listen Dee, everything is under control. All you have to do is show up, sign the paperwork and play your part. You cool with that?"

I nodded reluctantly.

"Okay, Mr. Frazier will walk you through your application step by step, and tell you what to write down. All you have to do is listen. But here's another thing I want you to do; I want you to put the loan in your mother's name."

"My mother?" I looked at him like he was crazy.

"I know you haven't talked to her in years, but her name needs to be on the paperwork. We can make it happen, she'll never even know," he responded.

"How do you know this?"

"I just know," he replied nonchalantly.

I was shocked that he knew about my mother, but then again, Scottie always intrigued me with the information he was able to attain about people. He had all types of people on his payroll; from judges to cops, and even federal agents.

"Are you surprised that I know about your mother, Diamond?"

I was speechless and just stood there like a deer caught in headlights. He knew my real name and even information about my mother. If he'd found out all that then I was sure he knew about everything else.

"Yes, I know your government name, Ms. Diamond Pierce. With every woman I meet, I always do my research. I like to know who I'm getting into bed with. And I like you, Diamond, that's why I brought you down here to spend some time with me, and shower you with lavish gifts. You're smart. You don't get emotional, and you're crafty, I love that in a woman," he said. He went over to the bar and began fixing himself a drink. "An emotional woman can cause too many problems, Diamond, don't you agree?"

"What else do you know about me, Scottie?" I asked casually.

He looked at me and flashed a sexy smile. Something told me that he knew a lot more than I thought. "Do you trust me, baby?"

"It depends, do you trust me," I returned.

"Answering a question with a question. You don't like revealing too much about yourself, which is another fine quality that I like about you."

He finished fixing his drink and then walked back over to me. "I know you're thinking that this is a set up, but I can assure you, that it's not. One of my rules is, never get too involved with a woman because it can complicate things, and fuck shit up. You know throughout history, a woman has been the downfall for many great kings and leaders."

"Cut to the point, Scottie, where are you going with all this? I learned my history in high school. I don't need for you to repeat it to me."

He smiled. I was more than sure that he knew the truth about me, and I wanted him to get it over with.

"Back in Atlanta, you could've been my downfall, but you fell back on me, why is that?" he asked.

"So you know."

"I've known since the night we met," he admitted.

I sighed. "So why did you continue to see me if you knew?"

"Like I said, I wanted to test you."

"So is this relationship with us nothing but a test for you, a fuckin' lie, or do you really feel something for me?" I asked. I needed to know the truth because I was in love with him.

"Baby, I love you," he said, staring dead into my eyes. "Are you sure you want the truth?"

I shook my head. "Yeah, I can handle it."

"I could've had you and your wild ass girl, Mya killed a long time ago, but I held back. I was so intrigued by your boldness and how you came at me, that I wanted to know a little more about you. Plus it didn't help that you were the most beautiful woman that I've ever seen. I wanted to see what you were truly about, so I played along. And I like you, Diamond. You get money by any means necessary, but don't you feel it's time for a change? First you were stripping in front of horny ass men, and then it got worse. I mean setting up men, and putting yourself out there is a bit too risky, don't you agree?"

"It's what I do best," I answered.

He smiled. "And that's why you're the one for me. Listen, I have a proposition for you. It's a chance for you to finally make some real money."

Scottie walked over to the pool and looked out into the ocean, holding his Rum and Coke. "You like this lifestyle that I live, right, baby?" he asked. "The money, the cars, the fly ass houses. Don't you want this for yourself? You're the kind of woman that wants to hold her own and you can. If you deal with me, I'll make you a rich woman."

What in the hell is he talking about? "How?" I asked walking toward him.

"Answer this one question, Diamond. You were obviously setting up dudes for one reason and that's to get money, so how rich do you want to be?" he asked.

I couldn't believe he asked me that question, but I wasn't gonna lie. I'd done enough of that already. "Very rich. Why do you think I went after you, Scottie?"

He smiled. "Cool. So this is what I want you to do for me. When you open up your salon, I'll supply you with ten kilos of cocaine and ten thousand ecstasy pills to push for me. Atlanta is a huge market and I need someone I can trust to operate a business for me in that city. I'll become your connect. You can put together your own crew of people that you trust and before long, all of you will make more money than you can count. If you ever run into any problems, then you call me, okay?"

I couldn't believe what I was hearing. *I thought he was trying to help me become legit, not get me deeper in the game.* If he knew me like he said, then he should've known that I didn't fuck with drugs, especially since my brother got locked up for the very same thing.

"Can I trust you, Diamond?" he asked interrupting my thoughts.

After a few seconds, I finally nodded my head. Even though I was skeptical about Scottie's plans, I knew I had to do it. I was willing to do anything to make him happy.

"No, I need to hear you say it," he ordered.

"You can trust me, baby. I'm ready for this," I replied.

"Good, that's what I need to hear from you."

"Can I ask you a question?" I said.

He downed the rest of his drink. "What's that?"

"Are you really sure about this because I've never done anything on this scale before?"

He turned to me and embraced me in his arms. "You need to ask yourself that, but I do believe in you. I see a woman that's about her business, and together you and me, we'll own these cities. Even move your girl, Mya and her weak ass crew to the side. Now you get on that plane, fly home, and do what you gotta do to make this money for the both of us. I got mine and I want you to get yours. Do you hear what I'm saying? Protect what's yours, and when the time comes if you need to murder a man or woman, do it without hesitation. You need to be sharp, fair, and at the same time, ruthless. I look in your eyes and know that I got the right woman on my side. It's your turn, Diamond, make it happen for yourself."

Even though I'd always told myself that I would never get involved with drugs, I knew I couldn't let my man down, and just like with Mya, I wanted his respect. "I'm in."

Three hours later I was walking through the terminal getting ready to board my flight back to Atlanta. When I stopped off at a store to pick up something to read, I noticed the news paper that read, *THREE BODIES FOUND BUTCHERED AND MUR-DERED IN THE PALMETTO BAY AREA OF MIAMI.*

I was shocked to see Carlos' name and picture under the headline. And I knew the other two bodies that were found were the two high looking white women he was with. Scottie instantly came to my mind. I put the paper back down and walked to my gate. Like my brother, I'd entered a dangerous world where it was easy to get rich, and just as easy to die in the process. *Damn, just when I thought I was getting out of the game, now I'm being pulled right back in.*

Chapter 15

Mya

The murders of two New York dudes were heard throughout the city. Apparently both men worked for a drug Cartel out of the Bronx, and were huge money makers for the organization. The loud mouth was supposed to be Donte's new connect, but I'd cut that deal real short. Now word was on the street was that several people from the Cartel were lookin' for the person responsible for their deaths.

I knew the only way for me to step up in the game was to take the responsibility for the deaths of the two men. It was risky, but I had a plan. I told Ace to put the word out that I wanted to meet the people in the Bronx, who loud mouth worked for. Even though I'd killed off two of their lieutenants, I saw a big business opportunity ahead of me.

Several days later, Ace told me that one of the men in the Cartel, named Mr. G. was flyin' into Atlanta in a few days, and he wanted to meet up with us. I was ready for him, but knew it could be a life or death situation. I'd murdered two on his top earners, so the meeting could very well be a set up, but that was the chance I was willin' to take. Money moved me, and if it was a set-up, then whatever way the chips fell, I was ready.

Since the murders, Donte hadn't been seen out in the street, which I knew was a problem. He was a serious risk. If I didn't know any better he was probably somewhere gettin' high and tryin' to figure out a way to kill me and Ace, since he didn't carry out the hit. Donte needed to go, before he had a chance to get to me first.

Donte was a fuck up and had only stepped up as boss of the crew because he was O.C.'s cousin, not because he was puttin' in work. I'd always thought that Ace should've filled that position a long time ago, but now with a plan in place, new management was on the way. There was tension within the ranks, but that problem would soon be solved.

$ $ $

Two days before my meetin' with Mr. G., I decided to pay a visit to O.C. I needed to talk to him about the crew and see how he felt about a new chief, even though I knew he was always gonna be on my side. It was early on a Thursday mornin' when O.C. walked into the visitin' room escorted by two muscular Correction Officers. He looked fine as always, even though his braids needed to be touched up a bit.

O.C. stared at me, but he wasn't smilin' like he usually did when I went to visit him. I still knew he was happy to see me. *Maybe he got into a fight wit' another inmate or somethin'*, I thought. I sat in front of him in a short denim jean skirt, and a pink sheer top that made my breasts look delicious.

O.C.'s presence always excited me; even behind bars, he was sexy. But I was here to see him on business, and to talk about the crew's future. I picked up the phone and used my sexiest voice. "Hey, boo? You look good."

"What's good, Mya? What brings you back down here?" he asked, being straight up.

"I know you've been hearin' things, baby, but…"

"Things like what?" he asked interrupting me.

I sighed, with the phone still to my ear. I leaned forward with my elbows on the table, and stared at him through the thick partition. "I know you heard that things ain't been going so well between me and Donte. Can you believe he tried to have me killed?"

"Well, I heard you makin' plans of your own. I heard that you cut down two weeds that didn't belong in the garden," he stated.

Thank goodness I was from the street and knew what he was talkin' about. "I did what I had to do. Donte's fuckin' up. That niggah's gettin' high and sloppy."

"He's my cousin, Mya and runs the show while I'm in here. You, you're just our head bitch."

I was speechless and looked at him in shock.

"I like you, Mya, and looked out for you, but you need to do as you're told. I tolerated you these past few months, cuz you always bring in good money. But Donte's my fuckin' cousin, and I don't want anything happening to him," O.C. instructed.

"You're makin' a mistake. With Donte still in charge, it's a risk. I told you he's gettin' high," I responded agitated by his request.

"It's a risk that I'm willin' to take. If you and Ace are promoted, how is it gonna look if I put down family for some hoe and a niggah that acts like a fuckin' mute most of the time," he said, in a stern tone. "No matter what you say, Donte has respect on the street, he gets shit done. I might not approve of some of his methods, but that's him and his ways."

I couldn't believe he was talkin' to me like that. After all this time, I'd been messin' with him, he never called me out of my name. "So what about me, O.C.? I've been loyal to you since we met. Am I supposed to let Donte disrespect me and let it be? He tried to have me killed."

"You'll get over it."

"Excuse me." I replied.

"Look, I'll talk to him, but you need to stay out the politics of the game and do what you do best, being our bitch and doing what you're told. Just go fuck a few niggahs tonight like you normally do, and forget all about it," he responded.

I'd never felt so insulted. Hate began to brew inside me, as I sat there and listened to O.C. disrespect me in a way he'd never done before. My expression toward him changed. I didn't see the man that I was in love wit' anymore. I saw a man that was against me and my rise to power. But it was all good, because he wasn't understandin' me, and not understandin' me could become a fatal mistake.

"I set up a meetin' wit', Mr. G. from New York," I informed him.

He looked shocked. "You did what?"

"You heard me, niggah. I meet with him in two days."

"Mya, are you fuckin' crazy! You're gonna meet with the man after you took out two of his weeds?"

At that moment, the same heavy Correctional Officer that escorted him in walked over to show his authority. "You need to calm down, inmate!" the officer demanded.

O.C. looked back at him, and then sucked his teeth. I waited for the officer to leave before I continued.

"It's a risk that I'm willin' to take," I said, being sarcastic with him.

"Do you think you're fuckin' funny? I made you. I protected you, and now you wanna go behind my back and do that? Don't get it twisted, just because I'm in here; don't think I can't catch up wit' you. I still have plenty of pull in the street. You of all people should know this, Mya!" he snarled at me through clenched teeth.

I shook my head. "I love you, O.C., but you're not under-standing me."

"Understand this, Mya, if anything jumps off, you're gonna pay for it wit' somethin' that you cherish the most." He looked at me and mouthed the words, YOUR LIFE, just in case the prison was tappin' his conversation. "I fuckin' made you in this city, so don't cross me, because you'll be sorry," he warned.

I wasn't the least but scared of his threats. Things were already happenin' and O.C. was losin' control. He called the shots behind bars because he still thought that he had Ace under his wing, but now his boy was fuckin' me. Ace had my back and no one else's. He was pure muscle in this town and O.C., Donte and the entire crew knew that.

I kept my affair with Ace quiet. I didn't need niggahs knowing what was going on between us. Ace had told Donte that I wasn't at my apartment the day he was supposed to kill me and that I'd disappeared. Luckily, his pipe-head ass believed it. That gave me some time to think, but now playtime was over. This city was gonna become my playground.

"Fuck your threats, O.C., I'm my own woman, and more gangsta than any niggah you ever had in your bitch ass crew. I can handle mine, so if you get a niggah to come at me, then he better come hard. If he don't, then when I'm done with him, best believe I'll be comin' for you," I warned.

He chuckled, "You run with men and now you think a dick swings between your legs. Without me, Donte and Ace havin' your back, these niggahs will eat you alive."

That's just it niggah, Ace does have my back. "Well you never had a problem wit' eatin' me alive huh, O.C. Being that you were always on your knees tryin' to please me," I remarked. Fuck you, asshole!" I shouted.

I slammed the phone down, stood up, and walked off without givin' O.C. a second glance or look. I was done with him. The partnership was terminated.

"Fuck you, bitch! You gonna see!" I heard him shout as he banged the phone against the glass partition. I knew the C.O's were gonna snatch his ass up for bangin' on the glass before I even walked out the door. *I hope they fuck his ass up.*

$ $ $

Two days later my meetin' wit' Mr. G. finally arrived. Ace had set it up through his New York connection and assured me that everything was legit and that I would be in good hands. But I didn't underestimate O.C. and what he could do, so I hired a team of hood snipers to watch my back in case anything went wrong.

I had my shooters posted up outside in discreet locations and told them if I didn't come out at a certain time, then they were to shoot up the place without leavin' a single witness.

The meeting happened on the outskirts of the city, in a motel room not to far off of I-85. The location was open, not too congested with traffic or people and was close to a main road in case somethin' jumped off.

It was ten o'clock when Ace, myself and one of his soldiers pulled up into the parkin' lot. But unaware to Ace, I had three more men hidden in different areas armed with Mack 10's if I didn't come out in one piece.

Mr. G. was on time and already waitin' for our arrival inside. We noticed a man in a long black trench coat posted outside of room 125, and knew he was packin'. Besides, it wasn't like the huge bulge in his coat was a bouquet of flowers.

"Mr. G. has been waiting on you," the man said, as he stared at us.

"Open the door then," I snapped.

The guard insisted that we be checked for weapons, but Ace's goon refused. I didn't want any trouble so early, so I told him to stay outside and keep an eye out for anything funny. Ace passed the goon his loaded Glock, and then we walked inside.

"Are you the bitch that killed my men?" Mr. G. asked me in a firm tone.

He didn't waste anytime wit' the interrogation. He was seated at the raggedy desk the motel provided with his legs crossed, in a sharp dark gray suit that looked custom made. Dark sunglasses covered his eyes, and he held a straight cold face. He had gangsta written all over him with his diamond pinky ring, and tan skin.

Two armed men stood on either side of him, with one clutching a Glock 17 and the other holdin' onto a .357.

"Tell me why I shouldn't have my men kill you right now?" he said. "Those two soldiers made me good money down here."

"With all due respect, one of your men was a damn fool. I

only met him for a brief moment, but he was a disaster waitin' to happen," I remarked. "Plus, the guy you were gettin' ready to deal with would've given you problems as well."

"And what makes you so sure?"

"Because he's gettin' high everyday and sloppy wit' his work. And from what I've been hearin' one of your men was makin' a lot of enemies down here. If it wasn't me, then someone else would've gotten to him real soon, and you don't need that kind of heat on you. But me, I'm careful. I'm respected, and I have a team ready to move some serious weight for you," I explained.

"And I'm supposed to trust some bitch just because she knows how to shoot her daddy's gun," he retorted.

"I've been in this game since I was fifteen. I've robbed, killed, and fucked for cash all my life. Money moves me, Mr. G. I know what I'm doing, I've made it this far. And even after I killed your men, how am I still able to stand here and have a meetin' wit' you. I have my respect in this city. Ace can vouch for me."

Mr. G. stared at Ace, who stood firm. I knew he was fearless.

"Does the mute talk?" he asked. He stood up and slowly approached us.

"I talk only when shit needs to be said," Ace replied.

"I've heard things about you, Ace, good things. Your reputation proceeds you. Why don't you come work for us, huh? I pay good money for men like you to be on my team. I'll give you the honor of murdering this bitch right now, and you can run things in Atlanta," Mr. G. said to him.

I kept quiet, allowin' the situation to play itself out. I wasn't sure if Ace thought it was a good opportunity or not.

"You like working for a bitch, huh? Or are you fuckin' this bitch, which one?" Mr. G. asked.

Ace returned Mr. G.'s hard stare and kept his composure. "I belong with my crew, here," was his only reply.

Mr. G. finally smiled. "I respect a man that's loyal to his crew."

"As I was sayin'," I chimed in. "I can boost business here in Atlanta by twenty percent. I have a strong team behind me, and I don't run my mouth like your past employees. I have Ace by my side, I don't get high so you don't have to worry about me using the product. Within one month I'll push fifteen kilos for you, more than what Donte was ever doing. And the most important, thing I'm a loyal chick."

"How about I throw you on that bed and see how loyal you truly are," he suggested.

I smiled and moved closer to him. "Whatever it takes to prove my loyalty, so be it."

I returned his gaze, never lookin' away. He smiled again. "Even though you're a woman, you got balls to come up in here and demand to come work for me after you put two of my men in the ground. But I respect that."

He moved away from me and sat back in the chair. He pulled out a cigar from his suit pocket and one of his men immediately pulled out a lighter. "I'll give you a trial period. You both have a month to make me happy, but if I'm not happy with business, then my men aren't happy. And if my men aren't happy, both of you will have problems. And I don't like problems. I make problems disappear. What do they call you, Mya?"

I nodded my head.

"Well Mya, I will personally make your face into a human jigsaw puzzle and have all of my men rape you if this business arrangement turns out to be a mistake," he warned.

I didn't let his threats bother me. "It won't, you can trust me on that."

"I don't trust anybody. For your sake, it better not be. Now, in a few days, I have a shipment coming in. I want twenty percent up front, and the rest I'll give to you on consignment. Please don't make me look for you, because I hate looking for people."

"Not a problem, Mr. G.," I replied.

With that, I had my new connect in place and things were starting to happen for me. Now it was time to take out the trash and do some spring cleanin'.

$ $ $

Establishing my new connect with Mr. G. gave me the green light to continue with my plan. Those who were against me had to go, and the first one on my list was that coke head, Donte.

A week after our meetin' wit' Mr. G, Ace was on his job and finally tracked Donte down at his new girlfriend's house in Decatur. He was tryin' to keep a low profile, but he was still getting high and sloppy as usual. Word around town was that he was tryin' to get a shipment of high powered guns, because he was paranoid and wanted the extra fire power to protect himself. He knew his time was up and a new dominant power was comin' to take over what he thought was his. I wanted his death to be a message and didn't want it to be discreet or unknown. I wanted to kill him out in the open for all to see and be warned.

That night me and Ace were parked outside Donte's girl-friend's house waitin' for him to arrive and meet his fate. I sat in the front passenger seat of the rented car we drove, holding onto a Mack 10, waitin' to cut him down like the annoyin' fuckin' weed that he'd become.

Ace was his normal quiet self, sittin' behind the driver's seat starin' out the windshield. He had his Glock in his hand and held a warrior look in his eyes. I loved the way Ace kept his cool and had my back in the meetin' wit' Mr. G. He could've easily betrayed me, because his reputation was fierce, and a lot of crews wanted him, but he gave his word to me that he would have my back. I felt invincible with him by my side.

"You okay, baby?" I asked.

"Let's just do this," he replied, without even turnin' to look at me. I guess he was preparin' himself for the hit.

Why does he turn me on so fuckin' much? I asked myself so many times. I eyed him for a short moment, and then got myself back into a killin' mode. I gripped the sub-machine gun in my hand and held it tightly. It wasn't my first time handlin' the weapon. I'd practiced numerous times with Ace at the hidden shooting range we went to at least once a week.

I'd picked the Mack 10 as my new gun of choice because it could easily mow down anything standin' within seconds, and we weren't sure how many men Donte would be with. I wanted everything to stop breathin' when the rounds went off.

Suddenly, a sliver Chrysler 300 with tinted windows slowly made it's way toward Donte's new home. Finally, it was show time. I put on my platinum wig and dark shades to hide my identity.

We were parked behind a van and some shrubberies, tryin' to be out of plain view and not easily noticed. The Chrysler pulled up to Donte's house and three men and a woman stepped out of the car, one of them being Donte.

He exited from behind the passenger side with his companion, along with two bodyguards. I'm sure they were concealing guns.

That must be his new bitch ass girlfriend," I said, as Donte patted her ass.

Ace looked at me like he was offended. "Are you jealous or some shit?" he asked.

Damn, he finally said something. "No, baby, I'm not jealous at all," I lied. For some reason I hated seeing my former men with other women even if I didn't want them anymore.

Donte looked around, observin' the area, and after he felt everything was safe, he pulled the girl close to him and threw his arm around her. He whispered somethin' in her ear as they began walkin' toward her house with his armed bodyguards trailin' not too far behind.

Seeing that they vulnerable to attack, Ace put the car in drive and peeled off, toward our marks. With the passenger side window down, I leaned out the window, west coast style with the gun gripped tightly in my hands ready to lullaby all four targets.

Hearing the sudden screechin' of tires, caused Donte and his goons to turn around quickly, only to be violently greeted with a heavy burst of rapid gunfire. I hit both of his goons first as dozens of hot metal slugs tore into them. They violently spun around with impact and instantly dropped dead to the ground.

I then hit Donte and his new bitch, and within seconds, they dropped like fuckin' flies. The gunfire was loud, chaotic, and intense, which turned me on.

I wanted to make sure Donte was dead, so I told Ace to stop the car. He looked at me like I'd gone insane, but followed my demands. When he did, I quickly jumped out the car like Ice-Cube's character, Doughboy did in Boyz N Da Hood. With the powerful gun still in my hand, I walked up to my former lover like I was on a mission. Both of his goons and his bitch were already dead, but Donte wasn't. *Shit, I need to work on my aim a lil' more.*

Donte was layin' on his side, clutchin' his wounds. He was in pretty bad shape. I'd hit him multiple times in the abdomen, and he was bleeding heavily.

"You fuckin' bitch," he cried out. His hands were desperately tryin' to cover the many gunshot wounds that I'd inflicted on him. But it wasn't helpin'. "Fuck you, Mya!" he shouted and then looked up at me. Even though I had on my disguise, he knew exactly who I was.

I stood over him, with my gun pointed at his forehead and smiled. "New day, new management mutha-fucka! Your services have been expired."

With that, I opened fired on him again, and the hot powerful rounds violently ripped into his skin and flesh. It was ugly, but the job was done. Donte lay dead in a pool of blood, as his eyes remained open in a mindless stare. It was a massacre.

I ran back to the car and quickly jumped in. Ace looked calm as usual and kept a blank look, as he quickly pulled off. He never seemed worried about anything.

"It's done baby," I said. I leaned over and gave him a kiss on the cheek.

He drove off as fast as he could, trying to get out he neighborhood before the cops arrived.

After we got on the expressway, I became so horny I couldn't even think. I guess the sight of my targets lying on the ground and my man handlin' business was a complete turn on for me. I tossed the gun in the backseat and moved closer to Ace

"I want you, baby," I said, lifting up his shirt, I began lickin' on his abs, as I pulled on his pants and belt buckle.

My hormones were ragin' and I needed some dick bad. With his pants unzipped and his big dick exposed, I kissed and sucked on his stomach and worked my way down to the prize. I slowly shoved his huge erection down my throat, and then began to suck it at a rapid pace.

"Mmmm," Ace moaned, tryin' to keep control of the car.

I jerked him off and sucked on his shaft simultaneously, feeling his hard black dick swell in my hands. For ten minutes I worked him over, and my pussy got so wet that it felt like I'd just gotten out of the shower.

"I want you in me, baby," I moaned. I was all over him, craving for his dick.

We ended up back at my place going at it like to two dogs in heat. Ace knew that I liked it rough, and he didn't hold back when it came to giving me some dick.

I was excited, I'd gotten rid of a major problem and was soon to get rid of a few more.

It was my finally my time. I was sendin' out a bloody message not to fuck with me. And with Donte's gruesome death, I dared anyone to come test the waters.

Chapter 16

Diamond

As soon as I exited the airport in Atlanta, I was met with a cool breeze and a heavy down pour of rain. I hoped this wasn't a sign of what being back in Atlanta was going to be like. I was starting to miss Scottie and the city of Miami already. I decided to take a cab home from the airport because I didn't want anyone to know that I was back in town yet. I needed some peace and quiet for a moment, especially from my loud month clients who were probably going crazy by now.

When I got home, my apartment was a mess. Apparently, I'd left in quite a rush because there were shoes and clothes everywhere. When I checked the voice mail on my cell phone, I had about two dozen messages. Most of them were from clients trying to get their hair done, and surprisingly two were from Mya.

"Yo, Diamond I see you ain't in town, what's up wit' that? Did you skip out on your girl? I know I ain't scare you off, but anyway, get at me, holla," Mya said, on my voice mail.

That bitch is crazy, I said shaking my head.

But her next message was even crazier "Yo, Diamond, where you at girl? I'm tryin' to holla at you, and you just up and disappeared. Why the fuck is your cell goin' straight to voicemail. What's up wit' that? I wanna get at you about somthin', but your ass is probably in Miami wit' that mutha-fucka, Scottie. What the fuck is wrong wit' you? Why did you hook up wit' that damn dude? I can't believe you sold me out like that. For real, Dimond you need to get back at me soon."

She sounded high or drunk. I erased both of her messages and closed the phone. I hadn't been back for twenty-four hours and Mya was already getting on my nerves. I began to unpack all of my clothes and went from room to room cleaning up my apartment. Being around Scottie's spotless homes, motivated me to start keeping my place a lit better cleaner. Besides, if I ever wanted him to marry me, I had to start getting myself together.

$ $ $

Early Monday morning I was at Trust Bank on Spring Street, in downtown Atlanta, to apply for my loan. I sat in front of Jonathan Frazier in my black St. John business suit and Dior pumps, looking like a true business woman. I had to represent for myself and my man.

Jonathan was a white guy, who was a bit overweight with a receding hairline. As soon as I arrived, we talked about Scottie for a brief moment, and then got straight to business. Like Scottie promised, he walked me through the application process step by step and told me exactly what to write down. Within an hour, all my paper work was signed and I'd gotten an approval on a hundred thousand dollar loan to open up my salon.

I stood up and shook Mr. Frazier's hand, thanking him for everything.

"Tell Mr. Morales I said hello, and that he shouldn't forget about me," Mr. Frazier said.

I gave a huge smile. "I will."

He returned the smile and gave his congratulations. Seconds later, I walked out the bank door the proud owner of a business. *Ma, if you could see me now, you would be proud*, I thought as I put on my sunglasses and walked back to my car.

It was a nice sunny day, so I put the top down and headed home to get on the internet. I had to find a space for my salon quickly so I could start getting things in order. I called Scottie and told him that everything went through. He sounded so happy for me, even though he knew all along that the loan was gonna be approved. He then told me that he was gonna send someone from Miami to meet me and go through the game plan. When I asked him who I should be on the look out for, he said his people would find me first. The less I knew about the person the better. I didn't stress it. I was so happy that I was finally gonna have my own hair salon he could've said Tupac was coming and I would-n't have cared.

$ $ $

Two months later, I opened up *DIAMOND'S* in Buckhead, a block away from the Fox Theater. It was a classy place, and everything in the shop was top notch. I had eight stylists working for me, paying three hundred dollars a week for booth rent. Two nail techs, and a receptionist. I'd even hired freaky ass, Alaina to be one of the shampoo girls. The shop had marble floors, three flat screen televisions, and a Bose entertainment system so we could listen to all the latest music.

I was the girl to go to if you wanted your hair done right, and had the best stylists in Atlanta working for me. My clientele ranged from around the way girls, to celebrities who wanted their hair done correctly. Soon, my name was ringing out all over the city, and I loved every minute of it.

Because I was the new kid on the block, all the other salons quickly became my competition and everybody seemed to hate on me. I guess it was because I took customers from every one of my rivals, and didn't mind doing it. That was more money for me. I knew a lot of people wanted me out of business, and quick-ly started crazy rumors. Some said I was into drugs, some said I was fucking a drug dealer to pay the mortgage, while others said I was selling pussy in the back next to the shampoo. Whatever illegal activity that was going on in Atlanta everyone said I was involved. But I didn't give a fuck what people had to say, even though some of what they were saying was indeed the truth.

Scottie was my silent partner and laundered his dirty money through the shop. The advantage to that was I never fell behind on any of my bills because he always made sure everything was paid. With eight stylists and two nail techs, I was pulling in over ten grand a month, and because Scottie took care of all the expenses, all the cash went directly into my pocket. Not to mention, the money I made off my own endless list of clients. I'd landed on a legit gold mine, and would've traded the dangerous game of robbing men for my dream any day.

However, behind closed doors, I was moving at least ten kilos a month for Scottie. Like he requested, I put a crew together that consisted of my older cousin, Marquez to work for me. Growing up I didn't see much of Marquez because he was always in and out of jail and probably had a rap sheet longer than I-95. Since my brother wasn't around to help me, I knew Marquez was the next best thing. He was always a nickel and dime hustler out in Charlotte pushing a little weight here and there, but once he accepted my job offer, moved to Georgia and started working with me, he instantly stepped up his game. Soon, Marquez brought in a couple of trust worthy soldiers from Charlotte that had his back at all times and mine. My cousin was all I needed to put the city on lock and hold shit down for my man. Marquez was my muscle, and his soldiers killed like murder was just a game for them. All I had to do was supply Marquez with the coke that I received from Scottie, and he took care of the rest. He was the hustler locking down the streets, while I maintained the salon. I was making a fortune by getting money from both ends.

The only thing that I asked of Marquez in return was to stay out the shop because he couldn't control himself around the ladies, and I didn't want my clients to think I had gangstas running around all the time. I wanted a shop with class, not a ghetto hang out.

Marquez would always try to push up on my employees, especially my best stylist, Michelle and my receptionist, Carol. I loved Michelle because she did her work with perfection and always had her booth rent on time. She also wasn't a gossip queen like all the other stylists or Carol, who we called mouth of the south. She seemed to know everybody's business and was a major flirt in the shop.

I knew Marquez was fucking some of my stylist, and I warned him and my girls to leave each other alone, but Marquez loved pussy, and I heard through Carol that my cousin was holding it down in the bedroom. But more importantly, the main reason why I didn't want Marquez coming around the shop was because he and his crew had gained a lot of attention lately and already had a beef with some dudes from Kimberly Court Projects.

It was known all over town that Mya was the ring leader of the crew and that she'd muscled and murdered her way to the top with a fierce thug named, Ace watching her back. Mya and her crew were getting serious drug money in the city, so between my cousins' crew and Mya's the murder rate had doubled over the past several months.

I hadn't seen Mya since that day she confronted me about Scottie, and honestly didn't want to. We made sure to keep our distance, but I knew sooner of later we would eventually bumps heads. We were both involved in the same game. However, unlike her, I kept a discreet profile, and to some I was just an average hair stylist. But to those who really knew, I was a rising kingpin with the help of my man. I knew if Mya ever found out, things would get really ugly. I heard that she'd stepped it up a notch by murdering one of her ex-lovers to get to the top, so trying to come after me would be a piece of cake. In my eyes, Mya was out of control and it was only a matter of time before her date expired.

Chapter 17

Diamond

Thursday evening in my shop was always crowded with ladies getting their hair done for a night out on the town, or a fabulous weekend. My girls and I were all busy with clients and worked effortlessly to a *Lyfe Jennings* CD. I turned up the CD player when my favorite song, '*Must Be Nice*' started playing. I let the words, Lyfe's voice, and his style serenade me as I took out the last roller in my client's hair.

"You know what must be nice, is to get a man with a job, no kids and some good dick," Carol uttered out, stirring the shop with laughter.

"I agree. I'm tired of all these damn wanna be ballers," another stylist added.

I smiled. *Too bad none of you ladies has a man like mine*, I thought.

"Well, I have all that and then some waitin' for me at home right now," Alaina said, pouring some conditioner on a client's head.

"Well if that's the case then why your trifling ass keeps having different niggahs pick you up from work all the time? It must be nice not gettin' caught," Carol replied, putting Alaina on the spot.

"Please girl, I'm just havin' some fun, and beside, my man ain't put a ring on this finger yet, so I'm just doing me. Let's just say I'm spreadin' my love around until the right one comes along," Alaina said.

"Well, you've been doin' a lot of spreadin' lately and it ain't been your damn love either," Carol replied.

The entire shop roared with laughter, but Alaina didn't look too pleased with Carol's smart comment. She sucked her teeth, and rolled her eyes. "Well at least I got a man at home waitin' for me, you still just a hoe waitin' around for one!"

"Oh, no she didn't," I heard a girl utter out.

"Carol, just go back up front. We don't need this today," Michelle said.

"Please, look who's talkin'. This is comin' from a hoe who fucked two brothers in their van right after work last week. I peeped you out there gettin' that two for one special, Alaina," Carol responded with her hands on her hips.

"Oh shit," someone shouted out.

"See Carol, you need to mind your fuckin' business, before you end up gettin' fucked up in here!" Alaina shouted, washing the client's hair even harder.

"I'm sorry, did I hit a nerve, boo? Don't you know I see and know everything that goes on around here? I'm like a mutha-fuckin' surveillance camera," Carol bragged.

"Well did you see my man fuckin' that bitch?" one of the customers said, who was under the dryer.

I laughed to myself and shook my head. Everybody was putting their two cents in.

"Well since you see so much Carol, why don't you see your ass over to the damn phone. Aren't you supposed to be the receptionist? I hear AT&T callin', bitch," Alaina responded.

The shop erupted with laughter again.

"Alaina, shut your nappy ass head up. You sweat your two dollar weave out every night under a different niggah, and then try to get one of your broke ass dudes to replace it. Well here you go," Carol said, handing Alaina two dollar bills.

Everybody in the shop loved it when Carol and Alaina had

their daily Jerry Springer moments. They had a love hate relationship, so everybody knew by the end of the day both of them would be giving each other high fives.

"You know what's fucked up, is that you always in a bitch's business," Alaina countered.

"Oooh, somebody's gettin' called out," another stylist yelled.

"Fuck you, shampoo girl. Just shut up and bust those suds," Carol joked, then stuck her tongue out.

Alaina gave her the middle finger, trying not to laugh at Carol's funny comment. She turned off the water and grabbed a towel to dry off the client's hair. Carol was a riot and always had to have the last word.

"Okay ladies, playtime is over, let's focus on getting our customers out of here so they can enjoy the rest of their evening," I finally intervened.

"Whatever you say, boss lady," Carol joked and walked back to the front of the salon.

I smiled. I loved my girls because even though they talked shit, they were all a good group of women. I enjoyed coming to work with them everyday.

"Diamond, girl I give it to you, you doin' your thing up in here," Alaina said, walking up to my station. She'd finished with one client and was waiting around for the next person who needed to be washed.

"I try," I humbly replied.

"You try…shit, you went from doing hair in your kitchen, graduatin' from hair school, to openin' up your own shop. That's a hell of an accomplishment. Hell, that's more than tryin', where we're from. You know that's either a miracle from God, or you're one hell of a hustler," Alaina said.

I looked at my friend and smiled because she was right, I'd worked very hard to get what I had. "I'm just a hard worker."

"Um-mm, right," she muttered.

"What's that supposed to mean?" I asked.

"Oh, nothin' at all, Diamond."

For some reason I didn't believe her. I knew how much these women ran their mouths. "What, have y'all been hearing shit about me?" I asked.

"Well, I ain't the one to gossip like that bitch, Carol, but word around town is that you in bed with some Cubans from Miami and they fronted you some cash for your shop. Also, that money is being laundered through here to clean drug money," Alaina informed.

"Alaina, you talk too damn much," Carol interrupted as she walked past us.

"I know you're not talking, bitch. You're the one who fuckin' told me!"

"Alaina, I swear, you worse than a fuckin' snitch," Carol responded.

"Well, first of all, don't believe everything you here, and get your facts straight first before you start telling people's business," I said, with a stern expression. "And that shit, goes for everybody up in here!"

"I ain't sayin' anything personally about you, Diamond. But your cousin Marquez has been coming in here a lot lately, and everybody in town knows what that cutie is about," Alaina replied.

"All of y'all need to shut up and mind your damn business around here," Michelle warned.

"Nah, it's cool, Michelle. But I want everybody to know that Marquez is my cousin, and he only comes here because we're family, that's it. My shop is legit so y'all ain't got anything to worry about," I lied. "Now just shut up and get back to work!" I yelled to everyone.

Both Carol and Alaina sighed and then went back to doing their job. I was upset with both of them a bit, but didn't show it. I knew people always had their speculations about me, but it was nothing but talk. I kept my business with Scottie very low-key and professional. Money was being made, and everybody was employed, so they should've been happy for that.

After I finished styling my client's hair, I was about to head into my office to get some time alone, when I heard Alaina ask the shop, "Yo, did y'all hear about those murders over by Decatur the other night?"

"Nah, what happened?" Michelle asked.

"Shit, it was all over the news," Alaina continued. "They found four bodies butchered to death in an apartment. One dude was almost decapitated. They were tied, mouths duct-taped and mutilated."

"Damn, that's fucked up," Michelle uttered.

"I bet you that shit got sumthin' to do wit' Mya. Yo, that crazy bitch is sick in the head. I heard she gunned down her own man in front of his crib. She ain't mentally right," Alaina replied.

"I heard she got everybody scared of her," another stylist added.

"That's because she got that crazy ass niggah by her side...what's his fuckin' name, clubs, spades or somethin'," Alaina said.

"Ace," Carol corrected, as she walked toward the back of the shop. "I've been around him once, and he don't talk much. He got this constant cold look about him and it creeps me out."

"Man, that Kimberly Court crew is wild as hell," another stylist replied.

"All of those assholes can stay the fuck away from me. They're making this city so damn hard to live in," Michelle responded.

I remained out of the conversation, and just listened. None of the girls in the shop knew that I used to run with Mya and that we were best friends at one point. I wanted that part of my life to remain quiet. Ever since I came back from Miami, her reputation had become more intense so I never wanted to be associated with her again. It was best that Mya and I stayed away from each other.

The girls continued to run their mouths about Mya and her crew, and gossiping about how much money she was getting and how many people they thought she'd killed. I was sick of hearing about that shit and turned to head into my office, when I heard Carol say, "Now who is this pulling up in the white Benz?"

When I turned around and looked out the large glass window in the front of the shop, I let out a huge sigh. I had dreaded this day since I came back from Miami. *Damn, I'm not in the mood for this.*

"Oh shit, speak of the devil," Carol said.

Mya stepped out of a white CLK with the words, PAID on the license plate and strutted toward the shop in her normal sleazy attire. I was surprised to see that she'd cut her long hair into a cute stylish bob that hugged her chin.

She entered the shop with a frown on her face along with a huge guy with dreadlocks by her side. Everyone's face suddenly became flushed with panic, not knowing what was about to go down or why she was here. Five minutes earlier, the shop was filled with drama and laughter, now everybody was quiet as a mouse. The only thing that could be heard was the humming of the hair dryers. Someone had even turned the music down.

Mya glared at me and clenched her jaw. "Damn Diamond, you've been back in town for months now, and I can't get any love from you," she said, looking around. "I see you doin' your thing, finally set up your own salon and shit. It looks good."

"Same to you," I returned halfheartedly.

Mya then turned to look at everybody in the shop. "Y'all bitches gotta problem wit' me since you keep staring in my fuckin' face?!" she barked.

Everyone's eyes quickly diverted from her, and back to what they were doing. She spread intimidation so quickly, that you thought it was a plague.

"As a matter of fact, I need some privacy wit' my girl. All ya'll get the fuck outta here and wait outside so me and my friend can talk in private," she demanded.

I gave her an evil look. Maybe everybody was afraid of her, but I wasn't. "Mya, don't talk to my employees and customers like that. We can talk in my office," I replied.

"Nah, I need something done to my hair, and I want you to do it while we talk," she ordered.

"That's okay, Diamond, we all could use a quick break anyway," Michelle said, leaving the shop. I knew Michelle hated drama, so it wasn't a surprise to see her leave first.

Soon everyone else followed along with her, customers and all. When everyone was out the shop, Mya took a seat in one of the chairs and looked at herself in the mirror. I walked up to her, frustrated about her presence in the shop and how she'd forced everyone out just to talk to me. But I kept my cool. She didn't intimidate me like she did everyone else around her. I knew Mya more than anyone, and deep inside her bark was bigger than her bite. I guess she kept forgetting that we came from the same background.

"So what do you need done to your hair?" I asked.

"Just a trim, nothin' spectacular," she said, leaning back in the chair.

"Is he gonna stand there and look at us the entire time?" I asked, pointing to her bodyguard. "I thought you wanted to talk in private."

"And?"

"So why is he still in here?" I asked with a smart tone.

She turned and looked at the dude, who hadn't said a word. "Its okay, Ace, I'm good."

Ace nodded and headed outside with everyone else.

"Does he ever talk? Or does he have to get your permission first?"

"He's about business and makin' sure no harm comes to me. His Glock does all the talkin' for him," she informed.

I sighed and picked up a pair of shears and began trimming her edges.

"So, when were you gonna let me know that you came back to town. I mean, I had to hear through the grapevine about you and your success. I thought that after our little dispute, you had moved down to Miami and shacked up wit' that cracker."

"Scottie," I corrected her.

"I know his fuckin' name," Mya spat back. "Did you forget that I was the one who told you about him in the first fuckin' place?" She looked in the mirror and stared at me.

I should cut all her shit off, I thought. "Look, can you get to the point?"

"So, Diamond I see you doing good for yourself wit' this shop. Got marble floors and fuckin' flat screen TV's everywhere. Did that cracker give you the money to open this place?"

"If you must know, I took out a loan," I replied.

Mya let out a huge laugh. "Yeah, right. Who the fuck do you think is gonna believe that stupid shit? If I didn't know any better, I would think you were back in the game and movin' weight in this city," she said, in a nonchalant tone.

I stopped cutting and looked at her. "What do you want, Mya?" I snapped.

"You think I don't know about you steppin' on my toes in this city. You think I don't know about your cousin, Marquez setting up shop here wit' his crew without my permission. You think I'm stupid bitch," she barked slightly.

"Mya, what the fuck do you think, you own the city or some shit? Besides, this is a big place, my cousin does what he wants to do."

"I know you're behind him, Diamond and I know Scottie's supplying you and you're supplying Marquez. Did you forget that I had your back, and without me, you would be dead? I helped you out."

"If you came into my shop to threaten me, then you need to get the fuck out. I'm my own woman. Me and my cousin aren't scared of you and your so called crew," I countered. "What the fuck do you want me to do, back down?"

She chuckled. "Back down, bitch, we can end this right now, you and me. You used to be my best friend and now you're stabbing me in the back; well I'm ready to return the favor."

I was tired, and wanted to let her know that if we had to go to war to end all this shit, then so be it. "You really wanna go there, Mya? You and your bitches may have this town locked down with fear, but me and Marquez don't give a fuck about you. You got guns, we got guns. You got soldiers, we got soldiers too," I said.

I held the scissors tightly in my hand, and stared back at her reflection in the mirror. If I wanted to, I could've taken her life then and there, but I knew the repercussions that would follow, especially with her goon, Ace outside the door with my girls.

I relaxed my anger and heard Mya respond with, "You know I'm a crazy bitch and don't give fuck about you, this shop, or anyone else. And cuz we used to be home girls, I decided to show you some respect and talk to you about this matter in person, woman to woman, rather than have my niggahs run up in here and shoot you and everyone else. Now, you gonna spit in my face and shout out threats to me, especially wit' your pale face boyfriend still down in Miami. You think he's close enough to have your back in time?"

"I think it's time for you to leave," I ordered.

"You really wanna do this? I'm only givin' you one warnin' and after that, if you still wanna play this game, then I'll no longer look at you as a friend, but as my enemy," she warned.

"I stopped being your friend the day you stepped to me about that bullshit before, Mya."

"And what did I say to you then, get in the way of my money again, and blood will spill between us."

"So let it be then," I spat back. "I'm tired of you talkin' shit!"

She smirked at me. "Tell your cousin Marquez if he's still in town by tomorrow night, then I'm gonna send my dogs out to play wit' him and it won't be pretty."

"Don't threaten my family, bitch!"

"I already did."

With the scissors still clutched in my hand, I wanted to thrust the sharp object into her neck. But I held my composure and stared at her. "Scottie sends his wishes."

I knew that would get under her skin. She stood up and walked out the door without saying another word.

As soon as Mya walked out of my shop, she got into her car and drove off, as my customers and employees made their way back inside asking a million questions. Everyone looked at me with a suspicious stare, wanting to know the connection between the two of us, but I just wanted to be alone. I walked into my office and closed the door behind me, knowing the gossip would start before I could even blink. But I could care less. They could talk until they were blue in the face. I had more important things to worry about, like how I was gonna protect the only family that I had and cared about.

Chapter 18

Mya

The next day, I held a metal baseball bat in the palm of my hands, ready to send a violent message to a very stubborn bitch. She thought that she could go against me without any repercussions, so I was about to show Diamond how vicious these streets could get.

With Ace and a few goons coverin' my back, we stepped out of a rented Chevrolet Trailblazer dressed in all black jumpsuits, ready to hit one of Marquez's inconspicuous drug spots with force.

Before he had a chance to react, we grabbed one of Marquez's workers who stood guard outside for a decoy to get inside the building. We warned him that if he wanted to live, then he had to do exactly what we told him. With a gun to his head and fear grippin' his heart, he led us to a steel door. The drug spot was on Simpson Road, in a rundown house surrounded by trees and abandon cars. I got word from a good source that they were pullin' in some serious paper and I wanted them shut down.

I went along with Ace and a member of my crew, because not only did the thrill of killin' people excite me, but this hit was personal. I wanted to see Diamond's cousin pay for her disrespectin' me.

"Knock niggah, and let 'em know you here," Ace instructed our decoy, as he hid behind him, but kept his gun aimed at the decoy's head.

I knew Marquez was inside, and I wanted to kill him for myself. Within a month he'd taken business out of my pockets by thirty-five percent, and that was a major problem. Also he had been going head to head with my crew, over territory so the body count in the city was at it's highest. It was hard to do business when you were disputin' with another crew over territory and clientele. But I knew we had to be careful because like Ace, he was a cold-blooded murderer who didn't take shit from anyone. His reputation was growin' strong, and I couldn't have that. He was killing my business so both he and Diamond had to be killed to send out a strong message that I was in control of this city.

Our hostage knocked twice on the door. We waited for an answer.

"Yo, who is it?" we heard a voice say.

"Gettin' money," our hostage said. I knew that was their code name to get in the house.

"Everything good?" the other person reassured.

"Yeah," our hostage returned, playin' along.

Soon the door unlocked and the other person came into view. That's when we sprung into action and pushed our decoy to the side and rushed our way inside with heavy artillery catchin' our victims by surprise.

"Yo, it's a hit!" the decoy shouted, tryin' to warn his crew.

I let off four hot rounds with the silencer on the tip that sent rapid hot steel through his back, dropping him face down to the floor. There were two more in the room and seeing us barge in unannounced, they tried to scramble for guns and cover. But unfortunately live rounds quickly tore into them and every last niggah dropped like pourin' rain. The gunfire was quiet, because we all had silencers on our guns, just to make sure nobody got away.

With a few enemies already taken care of, we moved stealthily through the first floor and began makin' our way downstairs to the basement where the product was being packaged. I gripped the bat and my gun tightly in my hand and followed behind my crew.

The steps were squeaky and we moved as quietly as we could toward the bottom of the steps. When we finally reached the bottom, the basement was dark and concrete. We began to hear voices as we moved closer. When the people were finally in view, it was a girl in her bra and panties and a niggah in his jeans, and a dirty wife-beater. It looked as if they were takin' a break or some shit. They looked heavily engrossed in their conversation and didn't notice that they had company until Ace suddenly loomed into view and popped off two in their heads with the silencer.

When we moved the bodies out the way, I quietly walked up to an open doorway and looked in. What I saw was shockin'. It was an assembly line for packaging crack cocaine and ecstasy for distribution onto the streets. There were a dozen women in their underwear and two men watching over them. *Damn, this mutha-fucka think he's Nino Brown from New Jack City up in this bitch.*

The resources about one of Marquez's spot was on the money. I displayed a devilish smile and prepared myself for the slaughter. *You hit us, and we hit you back harder until you finally collapse.* We had the element of surprise and I loved every second of it.

When we prepared ourselves for entry, I heard Onyx's, '*Last Days*' playin' from the small portable radio in the next room, and I thought how ironic that was for that particular song to be playin' as death was about to happen.

My crew member stepped forward with a Glock gripped in one hand and a wooden baseball bat in the other. He glanced at me and Ace, to let us know he was ready, and then entered the room like mutha-fuckin' Rambo. Soon, there was panic, followed by loud screams, and several people runnin'.

Ace shot one of the guys in the head, droppin' him near the door and then we went to work on the rest in the room. He stood near the door with his weapon exposed for everyone to see, making sure no victims could escape what was inevitable, death.

The women were horrified, and began beggin' for their lives, and callin' out the names of their children to spare them from being slaughtered. But I didn't give a fuck; a violent and strong message had to be sent, and what better message to send out than a bloody massacre.

I came across my first victim, a petite woman in black panties, a lace bra, and a do-rag on her head. Her eyes became filled with terror, as she backed herself toward the wall and screamed out, "Please, I'm only doin' this to support my kids. I have four kids. Please!"

"You know who I am?" I asked.

She nodded.

"Good," I exclaimed, before swingin' the bat and strikin' her in the head with a heavy-duty blow to her temple.

I felt her neck snap because her body was so small and fragile. She collapsed to the ground after the first hit. The side of her face was coated with blood, but I didn't stop. I hit her numerous times, leavin' her in a huge pile of blood.

I went after my next victim who was trying to hide under a wooden table. "Are you tryin' to hide, bitch!" I asked flippin' the table over.

She stood up and tried to run, but the sudden blow to the back of her head with the baseball bat, split open her head and dropped that bitch to the floor. "Don't you ever fuckin' run from me, bitch!" I shouted, and continued to beat her in the head with the bat, focusing on nowhere else but the face and skull.

I broke her nose in numerous places and damn near had her eye protruding out the socket. Me and my crew beat Marquez's bitches relentlessly, huntin' each and every one down and sprayin' the room with blood. The loud screams soon began to fade, and the cries for mercy came to a halt.

After the chaos, a total of five women and three men lay dead. My metal baseball bat was covered with blood, along with my hands. Bodies were layed out everywhere and we went through the each one of them, shootin' or beatin' whoever clung on to life. It looked like a scene from a horror film, but the message couldn't be any clearer.

I was disappointed though, because Marquez wasn't anywhere to be found. We searched from floor to floor, and room to room, but there was no sign of him. But I'm sure the blood bath we left for him downstairs said enough.

"Come on, we gotta go," Ace said.

We stole four keys and fifty thousand in cash before leavin' the dead and silent room. I walked out the back exit still holdin' both murder weapons in my hand. We dumped the guns and the bats in the back of the truck onto plastic coverings to make sure no blood stained the interior. We also took off the jumpsuits that had our regular clothes underneath and put them on top of the plastic as well. I wiped my hands and cleaned off any blood that may have splattered on my face then jumped in the passenger's side.

Minutes later, we quickly pulled off after committing one of the worst massacres in our city's history. Soon, I knew everyone would be lookin' at me and my crew, but I didn't give a fuck. My respect and reputation would be solid and I would have domination over this city and the drug trade. I wasn't scared to take it to the next level, and after tonight's actions proved just how far I would go.

Chapter 19

Diamond

When am I gonna see you again?" I asked Scottie, with a small plea.

"Soon, baby. I know it's been a while since we saw each other, but I think about you everyday," he replied.

"I miss you."

"I miss you too," he replied.

It had been months since I'd seen Scottie and got to spend some quality and intimate time with him. I needed to see my man soon because I was tired of using my faithful vibrator and I didn't know how much longer I could hold out.

I was in my office at the shop, on an early Friday morning. So far, Michelle and I were the only ones in the shop trying to get ready for another busy day. I loved hearing Scottie's voice when he called because he always made my day.

As I was on the phone, Marquez abruptly walked into my office. "We got a fuckin' problem," he said, not even caring that I was on the phone.

"Don't you see I'm on the phone, fool," I spat at him.

He picked up the remote to the T.V. in my office and turned to the early news. With the phone still to my ear, I stared up at the flat screen mounted on my office wall and read the words, "Breaking News" that flashed across the screen. My eyes became

wide when one of my cousin's drug locations was displayed
behind hundreds of police cars, paramedics and news crews.

"Baby, let me call you back, something came up," I said.

"Is everything okay? Who was that dude talking?" Scottie
replied.

"That was Marquez, he's about to get a beat down from one
of the girls, so I needed to put out the fire," I lied.

"Oh, well call me back when you're done. Love you."

"Love you too," I responded quickly and hung up the phone,
so Channel 3 news could finally have my full attention.

"We're live here on Simpson Road, where police came across
a gruesome discovery early this morning," the newscaster
announced, as she stood behind the yellow police tape.

"We're not sure as how many people have been found dead in
this prime drug spot, but police say there are several men and
women who have murdered. Two of the victims were even pregnant. They were found in the basement of this location at this
appalling scene. The murders seem to be drug-related, because
detectives found six kilos of cocaine in the same room where
some of the bodies were found. Once again, several victims have
been found dead inside of this location on Simpson Road, which
only adds to the murder rate that continues to climb. We'll keep
you updated with any new information that becomes available,
until, this is Roslyn Joyner, for Channel 3 news."

"Oh my God," I uttered, turning off the television.

"That bitch is fuckin' crazy. Damn near all of my men are
dead. She's gotta go. Did you see that shit? This is bad business.
Now police and the feds are gonna be all over us because of that
bitch. I'm putting a bullet in her fuckin' head myself because she
seems to think she can fuck wit' me!" Marquez ranted.

I couldn't believe it. What was Mya thinking? A gruesome
crime like that brought the feds into play and made business bad
for everyone.

"And didn't you hear the newscaster say, detectives found six
keys of coke. Well I know for a fact that it was ten keys over

there, so that means either the cops took the other four, or that bitch Mya did. My guess right now is Mya took the shit, and I'm pretty sure they took the fifty grand in cash too," he said pacing the floor.

I didn't know what to do. I was at a lost. What I did know was that Mya had completely lost her fuckin' mind, and we both needed to watch our back more than ever. I was trying to run a business and didn't need this shit in my life.

"Baby girl, you need to take your ass back down to Miami and chill out for a moment, until this shit blows over. You're in danger wit' that bitch still alive and running around. She knows where to find you and that ain't safe," Marquez said, calling me by my childhood nickname.

"No, I have a business to run. I can't keep running away from that girl," I replied.

"Well, are you at least strapped?"

I nodded. I kept my .380, in the office, and my new faithful .40 Caliber at home.

"I can't let anything happen to you. So from now on, I'm assigning a personal bodyguard for your protection," Marquez informed. I knew he wasn't taking no for an answer.

"Fine," I replied.

We had taken a huge lost with four keys and fifty thousand in cash. Not to mention all the men and women who were now dead. I had to give it to her, Mya knew how to strike and how hard to hit, but she still didn't put any fear in my heart.

I knew I needed to call Scottie and inform him about the problems that I was having, but decided against it, because I knew Marquez was capable of handling the situation.

I walked out my office with Marquez and told Michelle to hold down the shop until I returned. I needed to go home for a moment and get some rest and time to think, something I could-n't have done in the shop. I needed to come up with a solution before Mya took this shit any further and made this city too hot to do business in. She was out of control and was about to bring a ton of trouble down her way, and if I wasn't careful, mine too.

$ $ $

After a long day at the shop, I drove up to my house and eyed the fresh cut grass. A month ago, I'd moved from my second apartment and purchased a modest three bedroom home in Marietta that was nothing too extravagant. I wanted to keep a low profile with the neighbors. I still drove around in my Toyota, filed taxes, and tried not to act like I wasn't a rising kingpin with a murderous crew at war with a rival crew for the drug trade in ATL.

The past several months had been good to me. I had a man, money, cars, my own business and a proper level of respect in the city. But with all that, I still felt empty. I always thought that once I had everything I wanted, life would be better for me, but things were getting complicated. *How soon until my perfect little world starts to crumble with me underneath it all?*

I missed Scottie, and loved everything he did for me, but he was miles away, so I knew even though he claimed that he loved me, he was still messing with other women. Men need attention at all times, and when they don't get it from one person, then you're quickly replaced with someone who can. But I tried to look past all negative things and focused my time on work.

When I walked in the house, I went straight to the bathroom and stared at my reflection in the mirror. For some reason, I immediately thought about a family. I'd always wanted a family, a husband, and a rich life. I always thought that my life was rich growing up with my brother and the wealth he'd acquired through the drug trade, but in reality, that shit didn't last forever.

I thought about my mother, and remembered the talks we used to have when I was young, before my brother died. She loved her family, her children, and always made sure we lived in a stable home even after my drunk ass father walked out on us when I was only a year old.

She warned me never to get pregnant so young, or by just any man, because life would get harder. She never regretted having me or my brother, but told me she hated having us so soon. She had given birth to my brother at fifteen and had me three years later. Her advice always stuck with me, so I was always cautious when it came to sex. I wanted to make sure I didn't make the same mistakes my mother did. That's probably why she always hated the fact that Mya was my best friend. I guess she knew Mya was fucking every boy in the neighborhood and would warn me about her. I guess I should've listened to my mother's intuition because now the girl, who I used to call my sister, was now my biggest threat. I would've never thought that things would turn out like this between us. I couldn't help but think at what point did her life go in the complete opposite direction. It was almost as if she wanted to die. I'd always known for Mya to be a little crazy, but now she was letting money and power go to her head, and she needed to be stopped.

I found one of my favorite songs and pressed the play button on my CD player before turning on the water in the tub, and filling it with my favorite coconut scented bubble bath. I needed a nice soothing bath to help me relax. When the water reached the top, I slipped off my clothes and slowly made my way into the warm water. I closed my eyes with my back against the tub, as I listened to fine ass, *Tyrese* sing, *Sweet Lady* in the background. As the water began to calm me a bit, I had to laugh at myself because I always had dreams of marrying Tyrese one day. But the man of my dreams still existed, because now I had Scottie. I laughed to myself again because I'd gone from wanting a sweet dark chocolate man to a rich warm vanilla.

Chapter 20

Diamond

A week later, I was in the shop working on a client listening to several stylists talk about all the murders that had happened over the past few days. Marquez had managed to get a few dudes from Mya's crew, but they had retaliated, and killed a few more of his soldiers.

I would've been lying if I said that I wasn't scared. I'd thought that I was cut out for this type of life, but obviously I was wrong. Several police had come into the shop a few times asking about Marquez, and probably terrorizing my customers, so this drama had to end soon. Again, I thought about calling Scottie, but decided to leave him out of it. This was my problem, so I needed to fix it. The problem was I didn't know how. On the outside, I seemed so strong and acted as if I had everything together, but on the inside, I was crying for help.

"Michelle," I called out.

"What's up, Diamond?" she asked.

"Can you finish her up for me? I need to take care of something in my office?" I replied.

"No problem," Michelle said, taking the hair extensions out of my hand.

When Michelle took over, I quickly went into my office and

closed the door behind me. I lay across my couch, and started regretting bringing my cousin into all this, and taking a shortcut with Scottie to open up my own shop. At this point, I knew it was going to cost me. Tears began to form in my eyes as I thought about Marquez and the danger I was putting him in. At the end of all this there were two inevitable things that was soon to come, death or prison. Marquez was the only family I had left, so the last thing that I wanted was to cause him any harm.

I continued to think about my life for a few minutes, then I heard a knock at the door. "Who is it?" I asked.

"It's me, Carol."

"Come in," I replied wiping away my tears.

The door swung open and Carol peeped her head in, but before she could say anything I spoke up. "I'm not in the mood for any gossip, so if that's what you want then shut the door."

"No, that's not what I want. You got some dude out here looking for you."

I looked at her with confusion. "Who is he? What's his name?"

"He didn't say."

I sighed. I hoped it wasn't another damn cop because I wasn't in the mood for their shit today either. Then again, it could've been Mya or one of the dudes she ran with, so I began to get a little paranoid.

"He's really cute," Carol informed.

"Okay, give me a minute."

When she closed the door, I got up and went over to my desk to pull out the gun that I'd purchased to keep at the shop. I was a marked woman, and knew how crazy Mya was, so I didn't want to take any chances. I also didn't want to risk the lives of any of my employees.

I stuffed the gun down in the pocket of my smock, dried my tears and straightened my outfit, trying to look presentable. I then walked out my door and my face suddenly became flushed when I saw my former lover standing in the center of my shop. It had been almost a year since I'd seen or heard from him, and now here he was, back in my life all of a sudden.

He smiled at me, holding a bouquet of white roses in his hand. He was dressed in a black Hugo Boss button-down shirt, baggy denim jeans, and a fitted Chicago White Sox hat tilted on his head.

"Oh my god, Rashad," I uttered. I was lost for words.

"Hey baby, how you doing?" he greeted, never taking his eyes off of me. "I know it's been a long time. And I'm sorry, but give me a chance to explain myself."

It felt like I was seeing a ghost, but he looked so good. His goatee was neat and trimmed and his full lips looked so soft. *Snap out of it, this dude left you and never came back*, I thought.

"It's been almost a year," I said, suddenly feeling angry.

"I know, but…,"

"I thought you were dead," I replied cutting him off.

I looked around and realized that we weren't alone, and noticed the entire shop staring at us. The ladies smiled and batted their eyes at Rashad, admiring his six-three frame and smooth caramel skin. "Let's talk in my office."

He followed me and I closed the door behind him, knowing that the gossip would soon start when I was out of the room. When we were finally alone, Rashad handed me the flowers. "Here, these are for you."

"Thanks," I said taking them reluctantly. I couldn't believe he'd decided to show back up in my life after all this time. *Did he forget that he'd just disappeared from my life like I wasn't shit*? I needed an explanation.

"I know you're upset," he stated.

"Really, what would make you say that?" I replied sarcastically.

"I'm sorry Diamond. When I went New York that day, things got rough for me. I caught a charge and they locked me up. So I wasn't able to contact you, baby," Rashad began to explain.

I looked at him, like he was full of shit.

"Don't look at me like that, Diamond. Shit went bad for me and my crew. I'm sorry for not calling, but your number was in my phone."

"So, you couldn't remember any of my numbers?"

"I know it sounds like a lie, but I couldn't. Then when I finally caught up wit' somebody down here, I told them to go by your crib, but they said you had moved."

"It's been almost a fuckin' year, Rashad. You had me thinking that you were dead, or just didn't give a fuck. Do you know what that fuckin' felt like? It was hell for me," I shouted, as tears ran down my face.

"Baby, I'm so sorry. If I could, I would do things different, believe me. I thought about you everyday. I missed you," he said, walking toward me with his arms open.

I didn't want to give in too easily, so I moved back a few steps, rejecting his embrace. "Why are you here?" I asked.

"I came for you."

I didn't respond. I just looked at him as thousands of thoughts raced through my mind.

"Baby, I've been away from you for a long time, and I know it's too soon to have things go back the way they were, but I want to try. I don't wanna lose you again," he informed.

I wanted to tell him that I had somebody in my life, but couldn't get it to come out. He looked around my office. "I see you did really well for yourself while I was gone. You came up for real, and I'm proud of you. I always knew you were a hustler," he said.

"Thanks. So where are you staying?" I asked.

"I don't know yet. I was hoping you would let me stay at your place for a few nights, until I can get back on my feet. Is that gonna be a problem?"

I wanted to tell him yes, but once again it wouldn't come out. All of my common sense went out the door when I said, "Sure it's not a problem." *Why the fuck did I just say that? Scottie is going to kill me.*

He smiled and moved toward me again for another embrace, and this time I didn't refuse. I stood there, waiting to feel his touch. "Baby, I missed you. It's gonna be different this time around. I promise you," he said, holding me softly in his arms.

I know I should've pushed him away and told him to leave, but it was like I was in some sort of trance, almost paralyzed in a way. As if I didn't have enough drama going on in my life, I knew this unexpected reunion wasn't going to help.

$ $ $

That same evening, Rashad came back to my house to stay a few days. I had to admit that I was kind of excited. He made me feel like a young school girl; and with him around, I forgot about my beef with Mya.

"This you, baby, that's what's up," Rashad said, as we walked through the garage.

I smiled. "Yeah, I came a long way from that one bedroom apartment in the projects.

We both made our way inside, and I quickly gave Rashad a tour of the place. When he arrived in the guest bedroom, I told him that's where he would be staying.

"Thanks, Diamond. I really appreciate this," he said, dropping his duffel bag.

"Are you hungry?"

"Yeah, I sure am," he responded.

"Cool. Feel free to get comfortable while I fix us something to eat," I said, as I turned around and walked out the room. Within minutes, I could hear the shower running, so I guess he'd already taken me up on my offer.

I went into the kitchen and started preparing a small meal that consisted of steak, baked potatoes and string beans. I tried not to get too carried away with the meal.

About an hour later, Rashad made his way downstairs and

joined me in the kitchen. He was dressed in some baggy sweat pants, a wife-beater, and some fresh white socks.

I smiled at his presence. *He looks a little too comfortable.*

"Damn that smells good, Diamond. You still can burn, baby," he praised.

"I never lost it."

I told him that dinner would be ready in another half an hour, so that gave us time to chill. I met up with him in the great room, and he put in a movie for us to watch on my 40" flat screen.

I nervously took a seat on my sofa beside him, and waited for the movie to start. He smelled so good, and when I looked at him, his piercing brown eyes seemed to burn a hole in my heart and sent chills through my body. *Damn, I missed him*, I thought.

The movie began to start and it felt good to be home with a man, with dinner preparing in the kitchen. This was the life I wanted; this is what made me truly happy. Even though Rashad was a thug, he always knew how to make me feel so good, and no matter how much I tried to suppress my feelings, I knew I loved him.

The crazy thing was I loved Scottie as well, especially the way he took care of me, but there was something about Rashad that I loved more. We talked a little bit while watching, *Crossover.* He told me about what went down when he went to New York that day and how he'd ended up doing six months at Rikers, until he finally made bail.

"So how were you able to leave town with you out on bail?" I asked.

"I got my ways. My PO, is good people. I told him about you and how I loved you, and wanted to bring you back to N.Y with me," he responded.

I laughed. "Are you serious?"

"Diamond, since the day I left, I couldn't stop thinking about you. I'm only here for a little while because I have a court date in two months. That's why I want you to go back wit' me," he explained.

It all sounded good, but I couldn't do it. I had a business to run, and also had some unfinished business with Mya to take care of. Plus I had Scottie to consider. He loved me, and had also helped me with my salon. I knew having Rashad come back into my life wouldn't sit well with him. With Scottie's status, I knew he could find me even in New York and have me killed if he felt I betrayed him. I saw what he was capable of doing before I left Miami. But then again, when you're in love, you're willing to take risks. I gave Rashad a hug and told him I would think about it.

Suddenly, I remembered dinner and rushed into the kitchen to remove the bake potatoes out of the oven. Several minutes later, we ate, talked and laughed about everything. I held a smile on my face as Rashad continued to praise my cooking all throughout dinner. It had been a while since someone enjoyed my food. After dessert, we then found our way back on the couch to finish watching the movie. I decided to get a little closer to him this time, so I snuggled my body up against his chest, with my eyes glued to the television. I loved the feeling of his warm embrace. Suddenly, I felt his hands start to travel slowly across of my body, with his fingers slightly brushing against my breasts. My breathing became deep, as I felt his hands slowly going up my shirt, sending sensual chills throughout my body.

"I missed you so much, Diamond."

"I missed you too," I replied.

Once he made his way under my bra, he slowly took his fingers and massaged my nipples. I closed my eyes as he brushed his finger back and forth causing my nipples to become stiff. Suddenly, I felt his other hand unbuckling my jeans, and then bury its way down into my pants. I let out a slight moan as he neared my pussy. He began kissing me on the back of my neck, and sucking on my earlobes while he played in my kitty at the same time. I moaned again letting him know that I enjoyed his touch, which was sensual and soft, but also aggressive.

Almost immediately he jumped up and looked at me with

uncontrollable desire. He went for my jeans and began pulling them off slowly, and I raised my legs giving him easy access to slide them off without difficulty. After my jeans were tossed on the floor, he went for my panties, which he removed with ease and tossed them next to my jeans.

With my bottom half exposed, he admired me for a moment. My kitty hairs were trimmed down neatly like a fresh hair cut, and my lips were poking out waiting for his entry.

Rashad leaned forward and began kissing me on my stomach, sucking on my belly-button and then worked his way between my legs, kissing in between my thighs during his tour downtown. His tongue tickled my lips, then penetrated its way through me effortlessly, and sank deeply into my drowning pussy.

"Aaahhh," I moaned, as my fingers clutched his head.

His tongue seemed to do tricks with my kitty as it darted in and out and occasionally did laps around my clit. I could feel my juices oozing out when he lifted my lips to gain even better access. I began to moan so loud, I almost drowned out the movie.

I couldn't take it anymore, I had to have him. "Fuck me," I cried out.

I didn't have to say it twice. He lifted his face from between my legs, and quickly removed his sweats, came out his boxers and lifted his wife-beater over his head. His abs were ripped and his chest swollen with muscle. He positioned himself on top of me, spreading my legs as wide as they could go. His thrust inside caused me to let out an even louder moan than before, as I clutched his body near mine, and sank my teeth into his shoulders. I clawed at his back as his dick sank deep inside me feeling like the length was endless.

He grunted, taking control over my body. It felt like our heartbeats were one, as he lay pressed against me, making my body shake with pleasure.

It had been a while since I felt like this. I savored every second as he continued to make love to my body. We kissed each other excitedly like we couldn't get enough.

"I'm cumin'," he moaned.

I wanted to fill him explode inside of me. I hugged him tighter as our love making became more intense and my body also began to approach an orgasm.

"I love you," he said.

Rashad's thrust became more extreme knowing that a nut was brewing. His dick was so hard it felt like a huge piece of stone. I didn't want us to end. His body soon became rigid, and he clutched the couch firmly, like he was hanging on for dear life.

"Shit, I'm cumin'!" he yelled, with his face twisted with pleasure.

Suddenly, I felt him explode as his dick began to jump. My legs also began to quiver, so I knew I was cumin' as well. I wrapped my arms around his back and didn't want to let go. Rashad continued to shake as he probably let out six months worth of sperm that he'd been holding onto.

Afterwards, he lay nestled in my arms like a baby. Once we finally got ourselves together, we tried to focus on the movie for the third time. I smiled as I rubbed my hand back and forth against his face and thought about how happy I was that Rashad was in my life. However, my smile quickly faded, when I begin to think about Scottie. How was I gonna explain this to him? No matter how hard I tried to get away from it, drama clung to me like a leech. I'd been dealing with it all my life, and now I was beginning to think that I was cursed.

Chapter 21

Mya

The Simpson Road massacre was startin' to bring some serious heat from the Feds and local authorities. It had been in the paper several times and even made national news. The streets knew who was responsible for the murders, but shit never linked back to me. People talked and gossipped among themselves, but no one really talked. Snitchin' was a no-no and the number one rule on the streets, no mater what city you were in.

But there was pressure buildin' in the city and it was hard to do business because cops were posted up everywhere. Apparently they had been ordered by the mayor to do a full investigation into the murders because the two pregnant women who were beaten to death didn't sit too well with him. Even the Governor was on TV pleadin' for someone to turn us in. They wanted arrests to be made and indictments to be handed down, at whoever was responsible for the gruesome killin'. They were even pushin' for the death penalty.

But none of that shit scared me. The Mayor, the Feds all those assholes could talk all they wanted. I owned this town, so I was more than certain that nobody was gonna do anything to me.

However, there was one person who was beginnin' to make me lose patience and that was Diamond's cousin, Marquez. He was still a fuckin' headache and wouldn't back down even after we'd killed damn near all of is crew. I wanted to cut his fuckin' throat and watch him bleed like a gutted pig. He was becoming a thorn in my side that I couldn't pull out, so I placed a fifty thousand dollar bounty on his head, giving niggahs the green-light to take his ass out wherever he stood.

But Marquez was just one problem; the cops were becoming such nuisances by arresting and harassing my crew that business had dropped tremendously. I also suspected that I was pregnant with Ace's baby, because not only was I two weeks late, but my breast felt like a ton of bricks and the nausea was kickin' my ass in the morning. But I'd been pregnant before, so it was nothing new to me. Normally when I found out I was pregnant, I would be the first person at the abortion clinic, but this time I wasn't so sure. This was the first pregnancy that I hesitated to get rid of, which was weird to me. Besides, I didn't like kids anyway, so I didn't know why I was contemplating about keepin' it. I hated pregnancy because it always made me weak, and now wasn't the time. With a war going on and the feds tryin' to crack down on my organization, I needed every ounce of strength I had, so I kept my pregnancy a secret.

$ $ $

Mr. G. was back in town and he wanted to meet with me and Ace because he'd been hearin' about all the problems goin' on and wanted to see me in person. Hopefully he didn't come at me in a bad way because I'd made his ass a lot of money over the past few months. I showed him that a woman could be as ruthless and business minded as any man, so I wanted my respect. I'd earned it.

Around eight that evening, me, Ace, and one of our goons pulled up to *Azio*'s a fine Italian restaurant in downtown Atlanta. I'd only come with one goon tonight because I felt safe knowin' that he was extremely skilled and observant.

When we arrived, the hostess greeted us with a skeptical look. "Can I help you?" he asked in a snobbish tone. His eyes looked past me and landed on Ace and our goon, who were the only males in the entire restaurant without a suit and tie.

"I'm here to see someone," I said.

"His name, please?" the hostess responded.

I gave him a smirk. "He's expectin' me."

"This is a formal affair, and your guests do not have on the proper attire," he replied.

"Look here, man. I don't give a fuck about attire," our goon barked, causing people around us to gasp and stare at us with a disgusted look. "What da fuck y'all lookin' at!" our goon shouted.

Of course, Ace never said a word.

Suddenly, the hostess wiped beads of sweat off his forehead. It clearly showed that he was intimidated by our presence, and I couldn't blame him. If his faggot ass was caught in our part of town, he would've been robbed and probably left for dead.

"They're here with us," we heard a man say.

As we turned around and looked, it was one of Mr. G.'s men coming to escort us to the table. The hostess looked at us, and then nodded his head for approval, like we really needed it.

On our way to Mr. G.'s table, we noticed the stares of disapproval about our ghetto presence among the upper class. I probably had more than enough money to run with the big dogs, but by the looks in their eyes, I was nothin' but black ghetto trash lingerin' in their part of town. I wasn't even in their league with all the expensive jewelry I had on.

Mr. G. was seated at his private table when we arrived. He was distant from the rest of the crowd with one of his male bodyguards standin' a few feet away as he ate his meal.

He sat in a correct posture, dining in his five thousand dollar tailor made suit and designer shoes. When we approached he looked up at us, and gestured for me to have a seat.

"You needed to see me," I said sittin' down.

He didn't respond to me right away. He continued eatin' his linguine and drinkin' wine, before sayin' a few words to his bodyguard in Italian. The bodyguard smiled and then glanced at me.

I looked at them and replied, "What the fuck did you say about me?"

"Watch your tongue," his bodyguard warned.

"Relax, she's just expressing her concern," Mr. G. replied.

He then looked at me. "But please, no cursing in this establishment, so leave that ghetto nigger shit at home. You already caused a scene out front."

I reluctantly held my tongue and focused on business. I knew now wasn't the time or the place to get violent and ghetto. Even though he was a powerful and a made man, I still wasn't gonna let him or anyone of his goons disrespect me like that.

Mr. G. took another sip of wine. "Mya, what did I tell you about bringing me problems?"

"Ain't no problems, everything is still under control."

"I saw the papers and read about these murders. You made headline news, and now the Feds are involved," he stated.

"It's nothin' that I can't handle."

"Little girl, once the Feds get involved, they don't go away," he informed.

This pasta eatin' mutha-fucka was startin' to piss me off. "So what are you sayin', Mr. G.?" I asked.

"How does your generation say it, you're hot right now, too hot for business. You've attained quite a name for yourself over the past few months, murders, extortion, and killing pregnant women. I like things to be quiet."

"I can't stop people from comin' at me. I gotta let everyone know who's in control, who not to mess wit," I replied.

He looked at me and laughed. "I can't believe you think you're tough. There are other ways to handle things. You gotta know how to be subtle. These headline murders, they bring heat down on you and me. Now, my partners are afraid to continue business with you."

"So are you backin' out on me?" I asked clenchin' my jaw.

"I told you that I didn't like problems or risks," he explained.

"I wasn't a risk over the past few months when I made millions for you and your people up north," I retorted.

"You nigger, bitch," his bodyguard shouted, looking like he was about to reach for me.

But Ace and our goon, stepped to him, but before anything could jump off, and Mr. G. spoke up. "Everybody calm the fuck down, this is business. No guns, no violence, especially here," he said, looking around the restaurant.

His boy backed off, and so did mine. "I told you, this city is mine to deal with, and I can handle it myself. Now I need that pipeline to continue business and cuttin' me off would be a mistake."

"Are you threatening me, Mya?" he asked with a confused look.

"Not at all, Mr. G. I respect you a lot, but you know that there's tons of money to be made in this city. You would be cuttin' your own throat if you stop dealin' wit' me. You won't have no one else to distribute for you. I'm feared everywhere," I explained.

He looked at me and laughed again. "Do you think you're my only customer in Atlanta?" he asked, taking another sip from his glass. "I have others who work for me, unbeknownst to you, Mya," he continued. "I never put all my eggs in one basket. You're nothing but one of many niggers I help make rich, and who help make me rich. I don't give a fuck about you; you're just a cash cow to me. I'm good to you niggers, and don't forget it."

His mockin' smile toward me made me nauseous, and I began to feel sick. I started to feel light-headed. "I need to use the bathroom," I said, feeling my forehead.

Mr. G. displayed a wicked smiled. "Inside, to your left, the waiter will direct you."

I rushed out of my seat and walked to the nearest bathroom as quickly I could. With my hand on my stomach, I darted into the ladies bathroom, and made a bee-line for the nearest stall. I dropped to my knees and threw up in the toilet.

"Oh God," I cried out. At that moment, I wanted to get a hanger and give myself a fuckin' abortion, but I quickly thought about Ace. The thought of us havin' a baby was startin' to sound good to me. Maybe I could be a good mother.

I remained hovered over the toilet for a few moments, makin' sure I got everything out. I didn't need anymore interruptions when I got back to the table. It was already embarrassin' to be in this condition during a critical moment in my life.

I lingered in the bathroom for a short moment, collecting myself, and then exited the stall. I went to the sink, washed my hands and face, and then stared at my reflection in the mirror. Even after throwin' up everywhere, I still looked good.

I began to think about my relationship with Mr. G. that was obviously startin' to become a problem. He didn't respect me, and all he cared about was me makin' him richer than he already was. In his eyes, I was still a nigger and would never be on his level of power. But the one thing that Mr. G. underestimated about me was that I was a bitch who took risks and didn't give a fuck. So in his eyes, I may be still a nigger, but this nigger wasn't a slave to anyone.

When I stepped out the bathroom, Ace was there to greet me. "You okay?" he asked.

"I'm good. Is he still at the table?"

He nodded his head.

"Good," I said, putting a mint in my mouth.

Before I could walk off, Ace grabbed me by my arm. "He offered me your position again. He wants you dead and for you to take the heat for everything that's happened"

"That mutha-fucka," I cursed. "Do you trust him?"

Ace shook his head. "No."

Before walkin' away he looked at me and said, "You haven't

heard any of this."

This time, I nodded my head. I loved the fact that Ace always had my back, and made sure that nobody fucked wit' me. He was the only person who I could trust.

We went back to the table and acted as if everything was still good between us. Mr. G. was still at the table nibbling on his meal like he'd never said a word to Ace.

I took my seat across from him, and tried to subside my anger. "Mr. G. I'm sorry that you're upset with the way I do business. You've made me a rich woman and I'm very grateful."

"You should be. I bring you niggers up from poverty and make the ghetto rich. But you bring problems, Mya, too many problems. But since I like you, I'll think about it. Now let me enjoy my meal in peace," he said, in a very arrogant tone.

I stood up, but as I walked away, I heard him say somethin' to his bodyguard in Italian causin' him to laugh."

I stopped walkin' and thought about murdering his ass, but decided against it. There were too many witnesses around anyway. So I went my way, thinkin' to myself, it was either him or me, and it damn sure wasn't gonna be me.

$ $ $

Later that evening, I was in my bathroom preparing to get in the tub when Ace walked in.

"You okay?" he asked.

"I'm straight."

I looked at his handsome features and was tempted to tell him about my pregnancy. I wondered if he wanted to be a father because I didn't want to be a mother to a bastard child.

"What do you plan to do about, Mr. G.?" he asked.

"Kill him," I responded harshly.

He smiled and shook his head. "If you do, it's gotta be subtle, because the Feds are around."

"That's cool. As long as he goes, I could care less how it's done."

Ace remained in the bathroom with me as I dropped my robe in front of him and slowly approached the tub. Leisurely, I dropped myself into the tub and took pleasure in the warm soothing water that overwhelmed my body.

Ace stood over the tub and stared at me. I wanted his arms wrapped around me to hold me for the night, which was a different affection for me. Since we'd been intimate, I hadn't cheated on him once. Somethin' I'd never managed to do wit' any other man. Ace fulfilled me with everything that I needed in a man. He was a gangsta, and his dick game was spectacular.

As I lay relaxed in the tub, enjoyin' a moment of peace, I looked up at Ace and asked, "Do you love me, baby?"

"I told you that I'll always have your back," he responded.

Hopefully, that's his way of tellin' me that he loves me too. I wanted to tell him that I was pregnant, but I remained hesitant. I didn't want to look weak and more importantly didn't know what his reaction would be. *It's still not the time*, I told myself.

Ace peeled off his shirt and tossed it to the floor. He then took off his jeans, followed by his boxers and stood naked with his gorgeous body. His dick hung low like a thick vine from a tree.

He walked toward the tub and slowly got in. His body always got me excited. Once he was in the tub, I straddled him, pushin' his back against the wall. I embraced him tightly when I felt him enter me. He gripped my neck tightly and pounded his dick deep inside my pussy. He grabbed my ass with a strong grip and fucked me even harder. He was a beast in the tub, and I wouldn't have it any other way.

As the night moved on, Ace was lying on my bed, snoring like he was about to lose his breath, but I couldn't sleep. I kept racking my brain, thinking about the hit on Mr. G. I knew everyone would think that I was crazy, but it had to be done. I knew he wanted to kill me, so I had to try and get to him first. That's how those greasy mob mutha-fuckas think. If he thought I was gonna make him tons of cash and then have me replaced so easily, then he was wrong. Mr. G. had made his move, but now it was time to make mine, and I wasn't going to miss.

I had enemies to get rid of, and a vendetta so strong, that these streets were gonna continue to be bloody, despite the Feds sniffing around.

Chapter 22

Diamond

With Rashad back in town, everything seemed to be going well, but I knew my happiness with him would be short-lived. We fucked like rabbits, and I had the ladies in my shop gossiping more than ever before.

To add to the drama, Marquez didn't trust him. He couldn't understand how Rashad had gotten locked up for only six months on a drug charge and was already out. I tried to explain to him that he was my first love, but once Marquez had his mind made up about someone, there was no changing it. Rashad wasn't the type of man to back down from my cousin, because he was a thug too, so I kept the distance between the two of them.

With Scottie still in Miami, our relationship was becoming more business than intimate. It had been almost two months since I'd seen him. We would talk on the phone, but was distant every time we talked. I knew that meant he was fucking another woman. I wasn't stupid. I even thought I heard a woman's voice in the background late night one while he was on the phone with me.

I asked him about it, but he got upset and told me to know my place. So what I thought was special with him, ended out being nothing more than business in the end. I'd made so much money pushing drugs, and trying to run a legit business that I knew the bottom would soon fall out from under me. I was scared. That's why I looked for comfort with Rashad. Being with him, made me feel safe and wanted, so hopefully when the shit hit the fan, I prayed that he would be by my side to protect me.

$ $ $

One Sunday evening, Marquez and I decided to have lunch together at The Cheesecake Factory. It felt good spending time with him. We'd both been so wrapped up with this street war, making money, and other bullshit that it was good to spend quality time with my family.

Seeing Marquez seated in front of me in one piece, brought tranquility to my heart. So far Mya hadn't been able to get close to him, and I was thankful for that.

My cousin looked so handsome in his casual button down shirt and black slacks. For once, he didn't look like a hustler. We both gave a toast to success and family.

"You know your mother didn't want this kind of life for you, Baby Girl," Marquez said.

"Yeah I know, but what was I supposed to do? I grew up around this mess and did what I had to do. Shit, I didn't fall through the cracks, I was pushed."

"Well, I know she wanted to see you in college, to see you become a lawyer or a doctor. She even made your brother put some money aside for tuition."

"Yeah, but that was her dream, not mine," I stated.

"Yeah, but becoming a lawyer would've been a whole lot better than dealing wit' this shit. I mean, I'm glad that you're doin' your thing wit' the salon; but Baby Girl don't let this lifestyle become you. I've been through it all, and this is who I am, but just to see you come up out of this and move on to something better, would probably make Auntie proud. And I ain't gonna lie, me too," he said.

I was quiet for a moment as thoughts of my mother entered

my mind.

"Why don't you call her?" Marquez asked. It was almost as if he was reading my mind.

"I'm scared. I tried calling her a few months ago, but as usual she didn't answer."

"Well keep tryin'. I know she'll come around," he replied.

"I hope so." I stared at my grilled chicken and tapped it slightly with my fork. "Do you know what I want more than anything? A family," I informed him. "Something I haven't had in a long time."

Marquez smiled. "Yeah, it would be nice to have some lil' ones runnin' around," he replied. "It would be cool if it was a lil' girl, so I could protect her too."

"Marquez, you are always on guard duty."

"Yeah I know, but that's how I get down when it comes to family, Diamond. Every since my mother died, I never really had anybody else to call family except the niggahs I was in jail wit'."

"Yeah, I miss Aunt Faye," I added. Seeing my mother's sister die of cancer was another devastating blow to the family.

"You the only family I got left, so I don't wanna see anything happen to you. Atlanta is hot right now, and I can handle myself out here on the streets, but you, I wanna see you happy and wit' that family you were talkin' about. I see it in your eyes, you don't want this anymore, you want somthin' better and it ain't too late."

"It's not too late for you either, Marquez," I countered, taking a sip of my Strawberry Daiquiri.

He sighed. "Yo, I got two felony convictions, and this is all I know. I committed my first murder when I was fourteen and got locked up for my first felony when I was sixteen. I mean, Mama tried to raise me right and teach me better about life, but when you got that street mentality, your morals be out the door," he responded.

"Marquez, both of us are still young. Don't you ever get tired of this shit? Don't you have the urge to try something different with your life?" I asked.

"I thought about it, but honestly, there ain't nothin' else out there for me. I know that I'm gonna die in this game."

I reached over and slapped his hand. 'Don't say that! If anything were to happen to you, I would lose it. I couldn't stand losing anyone else at this point."

"Yo, you know I'll always be by your side. The last thing I want to do is hurt you. But let's be real, the chances of me coming out of this happily ever after, are rare. If I'm lucky, I can just get another bid in prison."

"Marquez, don't talk like that. I hate those negative ass thoughts."

"Baby Girl, you gotta accept the truth. Chances are, I'm gonna go out the way I live. I've made my choice, and if my fate is to die in these streets, then so be it. I can't run from it." He got quiet for a short moment, like he was thinking about something. "Promise me that you'll step away from this shit."

I kept myself from tearing up. I knew this life wasn't for me, and I didn't want to end up like my brother. I knew if he hadn't gotten sucked into this life of crime, he could probably still be alive today. "I promise."

We continued to talk and reminisce about old times, throughout the rest of the meal. I loved spending time with him. Marquez brought up Rashad and warned me to watch my back around him. I found myself always defending Rashad, but Marquez was adamant that he was not to be trusted. After going back and forth, I finally told him that I would be careful, and he warned me that if Rashad ever disrespected me, he would kill him. I didn't take his words lightly.

After spending over two hours at the restaurant, we finally left and Marquez walked me to my car.

"I enjoyed having lunch wit' you. We need to do this more often. Shit, I even wish we could have a family reunion like normal people," he joked.

I smiled. "I know, right. I'll see you soon. I'm about to go home and take a nap."

We hugged each other tightly and he kissed me on the cheek. "You be safe out here, Baby Girl," he said.

"You too, Marquez."

After I got into my car, I watched him slowly disappear in my rear view mirror. I became teary eyed again, thinking about him, my mother and most of all, my beloved brother. After sitting in my car for a few more minutes, I started up the engine and slowly drove away.

On the way to my house, I decided to take Marquez's advice, and call the woman who I hadn't spoken to in years. Hopefully her number was the same.

I was nervous as I pulled down the sun visor, opened the small mirror and stared at myself for a few minutes at a traffic light. "You can do this, Diamond," I said to myself.

I pulled out my cell phone and dialed the number to the place I once called home. My hands began to shake as the call went through and started to ring. Suddenly on the third ring, I heard my mother's voice and my heart seemed to stop.

"Hello," she said in a groggy voice.

I couldn't speak. I sat in the car with my mouth wide open and tried my best to form some sort of word, but it wouldn't come out.

"Hello," she repeated.

I sat there for a few more seconds before closing the cell phone, instantly disconnecting myself from the person who gave me life. I knew I should've had the courage to say something, but I just couldn't do it. I wanted to talk to my mother when I got my life together, so she could finally be proud, so until then I had a lot of work to do.

Chapter 23

Mya

Atlanta was on its way to becomin' the city with one the highest murder rates in the country, next to New York and D.C. with both the media, and the cops pointin' their fingers at me and my crew.

The hoods and the drug game were becoming so violent that I heard the Feds were tryin' to put together a RICO case against me and my crew. Since everybody in my crew was criminals, we all knew that the RICO act was for people charged with racketeering, and carried lengthy sentences. I'd gotten wind of this through a few paid cops and city officials that worked in the court system who constantly kept me updated. But a RICO case against me or anybody I ran with was the least of my worries. With all the power that me and Ace had in the streets, and the people on our payroll, nothin' would've been able to stick.

I loved my reputation and the intimidation I put into the people who I didn't fuck wit'. I took pleasure in being the talk of the town. I knew once I was dead, my name would ring out in this city for years to come. And after what I had planned tonight, the city was about to get another major headline.

As I watched the movie Scarface in the hotel room where I was stayin', my cell phone rang.

"Everything's in motion, Mya," the caller stated.

"That's what's up. Y'all niggahs give this city somethin' serious to read about tomorrow mornin'," I replied.

I hung up and laughed to myself. I had just signed off on Mr. G.'s fate. He was still in town on business, so I hired three shooters from L.A. for the hit, who Ace highly recommended. Apparently, the west coat niggahs knew how to put in work. Me and my crew were already under investigation, so it wouldn't have been wise for us to do the hit. Being at the hotel all night was my alibi, even though I knew fingers would still be pointed at me.

Suddenly, I began to think about the seed I was carryin'. I'd gone to the clinic and found out that I was six weeks pregnant, but still hadn't mentioned it to Ace. I knew he was the father because every since we'd been having sex, I'd stop messin' wit' other dudes. Something about Ace had me thinkin' about settlin' down and finally just being wit' one man. I wasn't sure if it was his street power, or his dick that had me hooked, but either way I couldn't get enough. However, despite what I loved about him, I still couldn't make up my mind if I was goin' to keep the baby. I wasn't quite sure if I was ready to be somebody's mother. As I continued to think, I sat back on the bed and watched Scarface tear shit up on the TV.

Scarface was one of my favorite movies, and Tony Montana was my fuckin' idol. I loved the way he caused chaos in Miami, got paid, and didn't take shit from anyone. He reminded me of myself because I also came from nothin' and now I had the city on lock. But I also remembered that Tony's life came to a violent end, being gunned down numerous times in his mansion. I often thought about my own endin'. I wasn't sure if it was gonna be by the hands of the Feds, or if I was gonna be gunned down by an enemy in the streets. Either way, I was ready. Besides, I didn't have time to think about my fate. I had moves to make and streets to take over. Scarface was only fiction, and my life was reality.

An hour later, I got another call. "We had a problem," the caller said.

I looked at the phone and clenched my jaw before puttin' it back to my ear. "What do you mean, you had a problem?"

"Like, I said, we had a problem. We tried, but it didn't go like we planned."

"So, let me get this straight. I paid you for a job, but it didn't get done? Now what the fuck am I supposed to do?" I replied.

"Have your boy, contact us in a few days, and we'll go at the target again," the caller stated.

"I can't wait a few more fuckin' days!" I yelled. "I want this shit done, now!"

"If I were you, I would calm the fuck down and stop screamin' in my ear. Have your boy, get at us." CLICK...

My mouth instantly fell open. I couldn't believe one of the shooters had actually hung up on me. I punched in Ace's number as fast as I could. I needed to tell his ass about his so called fuckin' recommendation. After the second ring, he answered.

"What's up?" he said.

"There was a problem, that's what's up. Your friends couldn't handle their business."

Ace was quiet for a moment before he continued. "Let's talk about round two later, when I see you in person." CLICK...

I couldn't believe what had just happened. Here I was for the second time holdin' a phone with nobody on the other end. Furious, I grabbed the remote and threw it against the TV, causin' the small plastic device to break into several pieces. *Now what the fuck am I gonna do*?

That night I went to bed feeling defeated. Tryin' to take down a major figure like Mr. G. took some guts on my part, so now that the hit had failed, it was gonna be trouble. I knew repercussions from his crew were soon to come, so I had to get ready because there was a storm approachin'.

$ $ $

The next morning, I woke up to the news recappin' about what had taken place the night before. I turned up the volume and watched with a frown on my face.

From what I heard, they said that three masked gunmen rushed their way into the restaurant with Uzi machine guns, and fired intensely at Mr. G. as he was eatin' with friends. The media also said that one of Mr. G's bodyguards had been shot in the chest, but wasn't dead. Unfortunately for us, Mr. G. hadn't even received a scratch.

The media went on to say that the city was in shock, and the Mayor along with other city officials were outraged by the public shooting of a mob associate in his city, which also put other witnesses at risk. The Mayor claimed that justice would be served and the gunmen would be found, indicted, tried and given a maximum prison sentence. Of course it wouldn't be right if he didn't say that violence and drugs had plagued the city, and also put me and my crew on blast. The rest of the day, I laid low. Luckily, I had checked into a hotel out in Norcorss, to keep people from finding out where I laid my head. My cell phone kept ringin' back to back, but I ignored most of the calls. I had to get myself together and figure out how I was gonna handle the situation. Not only did I have Mr. G. to think about, but I still had Marquez's bitch ass to take care of.   But his time was soon to come.

$ $ $

A week after the attempted assassination of Mr. G. I started gettin' back to business on the streets. During my brief vacation, I had my crew makin' packages, collecting money and distributin' the product. Business was still slow because of the heat and the pressure from the Feds and local cops, but we still had to get money.

Now with Mr. G. being my new enemy, I needed a new connect. I knew that was somethin' I should've taken care of before I made my move, but I was a hot-head. I had tried to take out a major problem, but created another one. However, findin' a new connect in Atlanta was as easy as findin' a strip club, they were on every corner. I just needed one with reasonable prices and someone I could trust.

Diamond and her crew were on our asses when it came to gettin' money. With Scottie being her connect, he kept the shipment of coke and ecstasy flowin' into the city continuously. And with Marquez pushin' the shit into the streets and gettin' in the way of my business, my money was comin' in slow, and if it was one thing I hated, it was slow money.

Marquez needed to be taken out and was next on my hit list, but he was hard to get at. I had my crew always checkin' his whereabouts, and who he was with, but the niggah was unpredictable. He was never at the same place twice, and his shooters were always by his side. I guess he didn't trust anyone, but I couldn't blame him for that.

I knew with Marquez out the way, business for Diamond would slowly come to a crawl. Marquez was a get money, no nonsense type of niggah, and I respected that about him, but he was in my way.

This was about money and territory, and I wasn't takin' the backseat for anybody.

With my supply on low, I knew that there was only one way to re-up, and that was to take from Diamond, Marquez and their crew. But I knew after our hit on Simpson Road, their street team would be more cautious and fully armed. However, there was still a way to get at them.

I had men watchin' Diamond's shop everyday just in case Marquez showed up. I was also payin' out top dollar for information about him through my crooked cops, and for that amount of money, I knew it wouldn't take long before someone took the bait and started talkin'. Surprisingly the source of information on him came from within the courts and not from the streets. It seemed that the local Police Department in Atlanta had a warrant out for Marquez's arrest and were zoomin' in on him for indictments on gun charges, assault and an old traffic violation he received back in North Carolina.

With the help of a snitch, I found out a legit address to where he was stayin'. My source also said that we had to act quickly because the cops had planned on servin' a warrant for his arrest and were raiding his place in two days.

I quickly got my crew together and was soon on my way to cause demolition. Ace for once was skeptical. He was worried about there being a stakeout and the Feds settin' us up, but even though I didn't have a dick, I had a hard-on for Marquez and his cousin, and wanted to see him dead instead of locked up. With him dead, there weren't any chances of him of gettin' out, and tryin' to come back at me. Marquez was a major player, and I knew if I got him out the way, it would be a major blow to his crew, especially Diamond.

$$\$ \ \$ \ \$$

Two days later, we made our move. Marquez was stayin' at an apartment complex in Scottdale, which was a few miles from the city. We drove out there in a rented truck, heavily armed with automatic weapons. Unfortunately, Ace was not along for the ride. He still felt it was a risk, and said that it was stupid of me to go, knowing there was a warrant for Marquez's arrest, and a raid around the corner; but I was willin' to take the risk. *Shit, risks got me where I am today.*

We parked outside of the housing complex near N. Decatur Road and waited for our target. I knew I should've just sent some shooters for the hit like I did with Mr. G, but I needed to see the niggah dead in person, even if it meant by my own hands. And besides, it was business and personal with Marquez.

Like the hit on most of our victims, we parked a few yards from the house we were watchin', in a parkin' spot that didn't make us look too suspicious. We had a direct view of the door to his crib. I held the 9mm in my lap and prepared myself for another slaughter.

"Mya, are you sure this is the place?" one of my goons asked. He was my top earner from Chicago.

"My source never lies. He's in there," I replied.

Another one of my goons was behind the steering wheel, while the third one sat in the back with my top earner, waitin' patiently. The neighborhood was residential, quiet and peaceful, but with me and my crew out here, they were about to get a wake up call.

We waited for what seemed like an hour, until the door suddenly opened and a man stepped out. *It's probably one of his shooters*, I thought. Soon, another man stepped out, followed by Marquez, who walked out carryin' a black duffle bag. The sight of seein' him so vulnerable made me smile. He was dressed in all black from head to toe. *Damn, does he know he's gonna die today*? He was already dressed for a funeral.

"There he is, let's do this," I said, grippin' my weapon.

"You sure you don't want us to handle this, Mya? You're hot right now," my top earner mentioned.

"I don't give a fuck about no investigation or the Feds. I want that niggah dead!" I barked.

He shook his head up and down and cocked his Glock back.

We watched as all three men piled into a burgundy Dodge Magnum. Marquez was seated in the passenger side. When the car started and the driver attempted to back out of the parkin' spot, we drove up behind them, blockin' their exit. Our doors flew open, and we immediately jumped out.

I heard someone scream out, "Oh shit, it's a fuckin' hit!" A barrage of heavy gunfire tore into their car, shatterin' glass and piercing metal. Marquez rushed out of the car without one ounce of fear. He screamed, "Mutha-fuckas, y'all want some...y'all want this!" he shot back with the similar Glock that my top earner had. I'm sure the gunfire was chaotic and stirred up many people in the neighborhood.

Gunshots were exchanged, instantly injuring Marquez. He was bleeding from his shoulder and other places, but he didn't fall. The intensity in his eyes could have burned a hole in my shirt. Marquez ran and hid behind a parked car. Me and one of my goons approached him as we continued to fire. The men that were with Marquez lay dead in the Dodge that was riddled with bullets.

"You fuckin' bitch!" Marquez screamed out. It sounded like he was in pain.

"It's your time, niggah!" I yelled.

"Fuck you, Mya," he cried out.

"Fuck this!" one of my goons yelled. "We ain't got time for no damn stand off." He ran up to where Marquez was, but it turned out to be a great mistake. Marquez sprang from behind the car and fired numerous rounds into my goon's body, droppin' him to the ground. He died instantly.

Seeing one of my crew members fall, I squeezed off numerous rounds at Marquez before he could shoot me too. Every round tore into him brutally as he trembled and got pushed back by bullets of my nine. When the gunfire ended, Marquez lay spread out on the concrete, dead to the world. I walked up to him and squeezed off more rounds into his face, makin' sure he got a closed casket funeral, and to give Diamond even more grief.

I then went to the Dodge and stole the duffle bag Marquez was carryin'. As I quickly walked back to our truck, the look on my top earner's face showed that he was upset by the death of my other goon. His face was stained with anger.

"We can't do anything for him now," I said. "Let's go before the cops come because I know somebody called them."

We all jumped back in the truck, and my top earner drove off like a bat out of hell. A few minutes later, we were back on our side of town. News travels quickly in the hood because before I knew it, everyone was talkin' about what happened.

When we met back up wit' Ace, he look at me with a disapproving stare. I knew he was probably upset about losin' of our goons, but in this game, you win some and you loose some, that's just how it is.

"I told you, this was a bad idea," Ace said.

"He knew the life," I replied, and then walked off without sayin' another word about the incident.

Before the night was over, the shootout was on every news channel, and officials were pissed about the violence that poured out into the suburban neighborhood. And once again, they promised civilians and the city that they were gonna crack down on whoever was responsible for the murders that escalated in the city over the past few months. *Damn, aren't they tired of sayin' that shit.*

Without giving today's shootin', or the media's hype about the violence a second thought, I went into my bedroom, took off my clothes and said to myself, "one more to go." I knew Diamond was next.

I stared at my image in the mirror, and thought about the baby growin' inside of me for a moment and decided. *I'm getting rid of this shit.* I didn't need anything else slowin' me down.

Chapter 24

Diamond

Friday morning, I woke up to my house phone ringing continuously, with me trying my best to tune the shit out. I'd turned off my cell last night, because Rashad and I were spending some quality time together. It felt good being back in his arms. He had cooked a late night dinner for me, and when it was time for dessert, he placed a two carat princess cut ring on top of a big slice of cheesecake.

I was shocked and didn't know what to say. I knew I wanted marriage and a family one day, but I still wasn't sure if it was the right time, or even if I was with the right person. Scottie was flying into town in a few days and I wanted to see if I had anymore feelings for him, even though I knew in my heart what we had was over. At this point, our relationship was strictly business. I was nervous about seeing Scottie again, and with Rashad back in my life and wanting to get married, my love life was starting to get complicated. I told Rashad that I needed time to think about his proposal, and luckily he didn't trip.

I lay nestled next to Rashad as tons of thoughts danced in my head. At this point, I knew I was going to get out of the game because this life wasn't for me. It was time for me to leave the fast money alone and just concentrate on making my salon a success. I just hoped Scottie would understand. I also thought about my mother and how I hoped to get our relationship back in order. But most of all, I thought about Marquez. Our family did need to change for the better and it needed to start somewhere.

I was surprised that Rashad was still sleep with the phone constantly ringing, but who could blame him after last night. Even after I told him I needed time to think about marriage, we still fucked like the world was coming to an end. You would have thought we were never going to see each other again, they way we had sex until the sun began to peep through the window.

I'm not gonna be able to get any sleep, I thought as I got out of bed. I was tired of my phone ringing, anyway. I stood up and put on my robe to cover my naked body that still smelled like sex. When I picked up my cell phone and turned it back on, I saw that I'd missed ten calls and had eight new messages. Even though this was odd, I still didn't think anything of it. *It's probably somebody from the shop calling me because they need something done. What would they do without me?*

I smiled, staring down at Rashad, who was stretched out on the bed. He even looked good when he was sleep. His well defined back was a beautiful sight to see in the morning. I knew that he wasn't gonna wake up anytime soon, so I went down into my kitchen to make myself a hot cup of tea. As I poured the hot water into my cup, my cell phone went off again. I decided to answer it this time, but was unfamiliar to the number on the caller ID.

"Hello?" I answered.

"Diamond?" Carol said.

"What's up girl?"

"Are you okay?" she asked, sounding upset.

"Yeah, I'm fine," I said, preparing my tea. "What's wrong? Did something happen at the shop?" I knew Carol probably had some gossip to tell me.

"Oh my God, you haven't heard? It's been all over the news," she informed.

I held a look of confusion even though she couldn't see my facial expression. "What's been all over the news?"

There was a long pause and her silence started to worry me. Carol of all people, was never quiet, so if she was hesitant about saying what was on her mind, something was terribly wrong. "Carol, what's been on the news?" I repeated.

Her voice was low. "I'm sorry, Diamond," she cried out, "Marquez is dead. He was shot and killed last night."

Hearing the sudden news, I felt frozen. My cup fell out my hands, breaking on my hardwood floor, and the phone soon followed. I pressed my back against the refrigerator, and became overwhelmed with pain and grief.

I immediately began to cry, thinking to myself, not Marquez. *Maybe I heard wrong.* After the talk we just had a few days ago, he couldn't be dead. It had to be a dream. I slid down to the floor, with my back still pressed against the refrigerator. I was shaking and couldn't pull myself together. I wanted to scream, but felt mute. It was almost as if there was a hard lump in my throat.

I heard Carol shouting, "Diamond, are you still there? Please pick up. We need to talk. There's more…please pick up."

With all the strength left inside of me, I reached for the phone. I needed to know, what she was talking about. I put the phone to my ear. "Carol…what happened?"

"They gunned him down in Scottdale," she informed.

"But how? Nobody knew he stayed out there," I replied.

"Everybody is saying that it was Mya and her crew and that Marquez got set up." She paused for the second time then continued, "Diamond, is Rashad there with you?"

Now I was really confused. What the fuck did he have to do with anything? "Yeah, he is."

"Well, please don't take this the wrong way, but I believe Rashad is a snitch."

"What?" I asked in shock.

"I heard he's working wit' the Feds to bring you, Mya, and

everyone else down. Marquez dug up some info on him and found out he was dirty. He had planned on tellin' you, but I guess he never got the chance."

Tears continued to run down my cheeks. "I can't believe this, Carol."

"I know. Rashad is the reason why Marquez got killed. I also heard he caught a case in New York and took a plea for less time to be an informant. Yo, the cops were going to arrest Marquez for some warrants, and somehow Mya found out."

I was so fucked up by what Carol was telling me. *What's going on?* All I knew was that my cousin was dead, and now Rashad was supposed to be a snitch. My world seemed to be coming to an abrupt end.

"Diamond, I'm coming over," I heard Carol say.

But I didn't respond, I just hung up the phone. The thought of not seeing Marquez anymore, tore my heart to shreds. It was if I was reliving my brother's death all over again. It felt like I had failed and nothing mattered to me anymore, not my house, the money, my shop, even life.

The Rashad I knew wasn't a snitch. He was a die-hard nig-gah, making his ends and was a man you didn't want to fuck with. It made me sick to my stomach to think that he could be responsible for my cousin's death and working for the F.B.I to bring down my family and the woman he was supposed to be in love with.

I remained glued to the floor for a moment before drying my tears and slowly got up. It's funny how fast your life can turn around. In one second, your life can change for the better, or the worse. I started thinking, and did find it strange that Rashad had come back to Atlanta so sudden. I was gonna kill him if he was taking advantage of me to save his own ass. I felt myself zoning out, not giving a fuck anymore. I went into the next room and pulled out my .40 Caliber from the coat closet, knowing Rashad was still sleep. I went into the bedroom with the gun in my hand and fire racing through my body.

I stared at Rashad as I stood over him. *Is he a snitch?* I asked myself. *Is he the reason why Marquez is dead?* With my tear stained face, I raised my weapon and pointed it directly at him. *I can't believe he even wanted me to be his wife.* I trusted Rashad and had jeopardized my relationship with Scottie to be with him. If I found out that he'd stabbed me in the back, I swear, I was gonna take his ass out.

I tapped the nose of the gun lightly on his shoulder. As he began to wake up, he turned over only to be taken aback by seeing the gun pointed at his head. He instantly became wide-eyed, lifted himself up and moved back against the headboard.

"Diamond, what the fuck is going on?" he asked.

I stared at him, as tears began to fall again. "I need to know something, and don't fuckin' lie to me."

"What's up wit' the fuckin' gun?"

"I thought you loved me, Rashad?"

"Yo, I do love you. Have you lost your mind or some shit? Put the gun down," he ordered.

"Marquez is dead," I enlightened.

He looked at me with a strange expression. "Damn, I'm sorry to hear that, but why do you have that gun pointed at me?"

"Did you have something to do with it?"

"What? Are you serious? I barely knew your cousin," he answered.

"Why are you here? What made come back to Atlanta?" I asked.

"I told you before. I came back for you. I missed you, baby," he answered.

The thought of him lying to me again, pissed me off. I pulled the trigger on my gun, and the bullet whizzed by the side of his face, missing him slightly.

"Bitch, are you fuckin' crazy!" he yelled, clutching his right ear.

"That was just a warning shot, to prove I'm not fuckin' playing with you, Rashad. I missed on purpose, but I swear on everything that I love, if you keep lying to me, I won't miss again."

I moved a bit closer, bringing the barrel a few inches closer to his head. "Why are you here after you've been gone for almost a year?" I asked again in a stern tone.

His face tightened and he looked hesitant to speak. I knew then that he was guilty of something. "I didn't have a choice," he replied looking at the floor. "I fucked up and was looking at twenty-five years. The Feds knew about my trips up north, so when I got to New York they were waitin' for me. They wanted to know about you and Mya at first, but then they wanted information about Marquez. They had me under surveillance for a long time, and threatened to lock my ass up, if I didn't give them something. So to get a lighter sentence, I became an informant."

"How did you know Marquez stayed in Scottdale?" I asked.

"I overheard y'all talking one night and picked up on the conversation. Then I went through some information you had lying around on the kitchen table one day, and found his phone number, so I gave the police that too, but don't worry baby. I just gave them small stuff. I never knew anything major about you anyway. But they are after that white dude you were messing wit' named, Scottie, so you need to stay away from him."

I was extremely hurt. "How could you, Rashad. You used me and my family to save your own ass."

"What was I supposed to do, Diamond? Those mutha-fuckas were talkin' about givin' me life," he said, raising his voice.

"So you decided to jeopardize me and my people because you fucked up?"

"Well, I did think about it first," he replied. Do you know how hard this was for me. You know I love you, baby."

"Fuck love!" I shouted. I could tell that I was about to explode.

"Put yourself in my position, and you would've done the same thing," he replied.

"I'm not a snitch and will never become one. You're a fuckin' coward. I can't believe I fell for that bullshit story. I can't believe that I fell in love with you again. My fuckin' cousin is dead because of you!"

"It wasn't personal, Diamond. It's just how the game is played sometimes. I can't do prison for twenty-five years, sorry."

I felt so disgusted. After all this time, I thought he was a true thug and man about his business like Marquez and my brother, but I was wrong. Everyone I knew, never snitched, and took their punishment like soldiers. Didn't Rashad's bitch ass understand that there were consequences to this game?

It took everything that I had in me not to squeeze the trigger and end his life. He was a bastard and now the Feds were probably putting a case against me. I was in a bad predicament.

"It's over, Diamond. Once you're on the Feds radar, it doesn't disappear. But trust me, they don't want you, they want your connect, Scottie. And they'll use you, me, and whoever else to try and bring him down," he said. "Oh, and I forgot they want that crazy ass bitch, Mya too."

I couldn't stop shedding tears. "They're coming for you," I informed him.

He looked at me like I was on medication. "What are you're talkin' about?"

"Marquez's crew, they're on their way here right now and they aren't too happy with your bitch ass."

"So it's like that, Diamond? You gonna have me killed just that easy after everything we been through. It ain't gotta be like this, just cooperate with the Feds, give them what they want and you and me, can still be together. We can go somewhere and start over, leave far from this city and do us," he said.

It was ugly, watching him trying to snake his way out of the situation. I couldn't believe he wanted me to go down that road of becoming a rat, and defy everything that my brother and Marquez stood for in this game. Yeah, I wanted a change, and leaving ATL to possibly settle down and start a family sounded nice, but I wasn't bringing anyone else down just to save my own ass. I grew up on loyalty and trust, so to see this mutha-fucka try-

240   Talk of the Town

ing to stain my reputation made me sick to my stomach.

"C'mon Diamond don't be brainwashed like all these other stupid mutha-fuckas in the game. Fuck loyalty, I'm out for myself, and if you ain't down, then fuck you, your cousin and …"

I felt the gun suddenly go off in my hands, striking Rashad in the chest before he could finish his sentence. His eyes enlarged, as he clutched his chest where the bullet struck. His breathing became sparse as I witnessed him still trying to hold on for dear life.

My hands shook and the tears that ran down my face were endless. With the smoking gun still in my hand and aimed at him, I fired several more shots until Rashad slumped over. I slowly walked away and put the gun back in the closet, still in shock about what I'd just done. When I was out in the street with Mya, I'd pulled my gun out on several different people, but I'd never killed anybody before. The guilt that came along with taking someone's life immediately jumped on my conscience. I didn't know what to do.

I left him in my bed with his blood staining my sheets for almost an hour, until the doorbell rang. As soon as I answered it, Carol stepped inside and held me as tight as she could. "Diamond, I'm so sorry. Oh my God, are you okay?"

I felt limp in her arms, like I was about to pass out. "I'm okay."

She looked at me with a concerned expression. "Where's Rashad?"

"Upstairs," I said, not mentioning to her that he was already dead.

"Well I have somebody who wants to talk to you," she said, wiping away my tears. When Carol went to the door and stuck her head out, several seconds later, a man walked in who I never expected to see. I couldn't believe she had brought him to my home. Was this a set up? *Damn, is he gonna kill me?*

Chapter 25

Mya

The federal investigation on me and my crew was crackin' down hard, after Marquez's murder. They cops were becomin' relentless and began raidin' our spots and lockin' up everyone that was connected to us. I guess they were pissed off that we'd gotten to Marquez first and gunned him down before they could serve the warrant for his arrest. We had shut it down, and now they wanted to shut us down.

Me, Ace and my top earner, had stopped stayin' in hotels for a while in order to remain two steps ahead of the cops at all times, and were now movin' from one safe house to the next. We had to move around constantly. The safe houses were always provided to us by people Ace knew, so if he trusted them, then so did I. Lately, I'd been followin' his orders more often, which is something I'd never done. I guess a part of me was startin' to get tired of tryin' to run everything all the time. Besides, it was me who had gotten us in the situation in the first place. Maybe if I'd listened to him all along, we wouldn't have to keep hidin' like fuckin' Osama Bin Laden. I loved Ace, and after thinkin' about it, I'd decided to keep the baby, and had planned on tellin' him soon. I'd told myself that once Ace found out about the baby, I was gonna cut the streets back in a major way. I couldn't be a good mother runnin' around all the time. What kind of example would I have been setting for my child?

As I sat in the bedroom of one of the safe houses, I heard someone arguing wit' Ace in the next room. I got up and placed my ear against the wall to see who the other person was. When I realized it was my top earner, I crept out the room to hear a little clearer. It appeared that my earner was upset with what was going on.

"That bitch is bringin' us down, Ace. You see she got another one of our boys killed. Yo, she gotta go," my top earner said, with a bold tone.

"You need to chill,…relax my niggah," Ace replied.

"Nah, fuck that relax shit. Our man is gone, so Mya needs to be gone too," he continued.

I'd heard enough and emerged from the bedroom where I had been eavesdropping. I was so pissed, that I'd totally forgot, I only had on a pair of sheer panties and a short t-shirt. When I walked in the room where they were, both men turned around and looked at me with lustful eyes.

"You gotta problem wit' me?" I asked my earner.

"Fuck you, bitch, I got heat for you," he scolded. He walked up in my face ready to cause a problem. "I ain't the one scared of your ass."

I smirked. "Control your lil' puppy, Ace."

"Bitch, you talkin' to a true gangsta, you don't fuckin' control me."

"You're a long way from Chicago, homeboy," I responded.

"I don't give a fuck where I'm at, I'll still put my murder game down!" he yelled.

Instantly, I slapped the shit out of him and then backed away a bit. I hated the fact that I'd left my gun in the room, but I still had somethin' for his ass. When he realized what I did, he came at me, but I landed a hard right across his jaw. Unfortunately, it didn't faze him, and he grabbed me by my neck. "I'm gonna kill you!" he shouted.

I gagged, tryin' to fight him off, and then reached down into my panties and pulled out a small razor that I'd concealed.

Ace just stood there and watched the assault on me take place, which made me even more furious. He was supposed to be my man, but I guess he didn't feel the same way. Fightin' back, I freed my arms, sprung into action and quickly put the razor to my earner's throat and sliced him rapidly. Blood poured out everywhere and his violent hold on me was suddenly loosened. He grabbed his throat, and displayed a look of death in his eyes. His hands were covered with blood.

"You fuckin' bitch," he mumbled, as he staggered and fell against the wall.

I just stood there and looked at him. "I told you, niggah, you're a long way from home. I'm not the one to fuck wit'."

"Help me," he cried out to Ace. He slowly slid down to floor with his back pressed against the wall and within seconds, he was dead.

When I looked back at Ace, he had his Glock pointin' in my direction. "You've gone too far, Mya."

I looked at him with a huge frown. *Why is he pointin' his gun at me*? "What the fuck do you mean, I've gone too far? Didn't you just see that niggah was tryin' to kill me first?"

"I'm not talkin' about just with this incident. I'm talkin' about everything. You've gone too fuckin' far wit' everything. Even wit' Diamond."

The mention of her name, immediately pissed me off. *I know this mutha-fucka is not taking up for her*? "Fuck you and this baby," I screamed.

He looked at me with this puzzled look.

"Yeah niggah, that's right. I'm pregnant and it's yours," I informed him.

He smirked and never stopped aiming his gun in my direction. I loved Ace, and couldn't understand why he was doin' this to me. I'd made plenty of enemies in Atlanta, and apparently even in my own crew, but now it was boiling over. I was beginnin' to think that Ace was right, maybe I was out of control. If I was gonna be somebody's mother, I had to start gettin' myself together. I stared at Ace with the bloody razor still in my hand. "So it's come down to this? You always had my back and now I'm gonna end by your hands?"

"Don't you get it? You're outta control, Mya. It's over…there's no more for us," he replied.

"There is something for us and I'm carryin' it," I said, pointin' to my stomach. "I promise, I'll stop all this nonsense today if you want. I know you may not believe me, but I'm startin' to realize that I do need to calm down and…"

"I told you that I'll have your back till the end," he replied interrupting me. He then lowered his gun and smiled.

I was confused. "You can't kill the mother carryin' your unborn, child. I love you, Ace."

"Love will get you killed," I heard a voice say.

I turned to see who was talkin'. Suddenly, Diamond appeared from behind. Before I could react, she bashed me in the face with the gun. I stumbled and fell back, and then she hit me again until I collapsed on the floor.

"Yeah, bitch," she screamed out, as she stood over me with the gun.

I laughed and showed no fear. "Do you think I'm supposed to be scared of you?"

She was quiet, and her face was filled wit' anger. I began to wonder how she could've possibly found me, and then it hit me like a ton of bricks. It had to be Ace.

I looked at him as tears formed in my eyes. It had been years since I displayed, what I always thought was a sign of weakness. "How could you?" I asked Ace.

"He looked at me and gave a devilish grin. "Sorry baby, it's just business. Both O.C. and Mr. G. paid me top dollar to have you smoked, so I figured what better person to watch you die, than your friend, Diamond," he responded.

It felt like my heart and been ripped out of my chest. I couldn't believe the one person who I trusted had betrayed me. I continued to look at him as tears ran down my face.

"Nobody gives a fuck about those tears," Diamond said.

I gave her a look of death, "So you ready to step your game up, huh?" I shouted.

"Why did you have to kill Marquez?" she responded.

"I shoulda killed you first, but that's what I get for holdin' off for a *friend*," I joked.

"We're not friends."

"Yeah, now we ain't…you're a dead bitch," I replied.

"This city is so done with you," she barked. And then I heard the sounds of gunfire exploding in the air.

Chapter 26

Diamond

Like they say, everything comes to an end. Money, power, lives, even love and friendship. After I killed Mya, I took off in my car and drove back to my shop, but I still didn't feel any better after her death. Everyone who I once called family was dead, and I was suffering.

There are no true friends in this game and every since I'd stepped into it, I've learned that money changes people. It takes over your mind and eventually your soul. I offered Ace, all the money I had in order to get close to Mya and he willingly accepted my offer. I guess in the end, he'd gotten paid from three different people to get close to her. However, it was sad to see that he was still willing to watch Mya die even after he found out that she was pregnant with his child. Damn, this was a cold hearted business.

I arrived at the shop looking like a fuckin' mess. My hair was in disarray, my clothes wrinkled and spotted with some of Mya's blood, and I was overwhelmed with anger and grief.

When I walked into the shop, everyone turned and looked at me. I saw the look of shock among everyone's face by my crazy appearance, but I didn't give a fuck. I'm sure by now everyone knew about Marquez, and probably thought I was going crazy.

"Girl, what storm did you just step out of?" Alaina asked.

I ignored her and continued toward my office like everyone was invisible. As I passed by, everyone asked if I was okay, or did I need anything.

When I got in my office, I flopped down in the chair behind my desk and cried like a baby. At that point, nothing mattered to me anymore. Moments later, someone knocked on the door and then walked inside without my invitation.

"Diamond, are you okay? I was worried about you," Carol said.

"You need to leave now Carol, don't get caught up in my shit. You're a good woman, and shit is gonna get real ugly soon," I stated.

"Stop talkin' like that, you know I'm here for you," she replied. "Talk to me."

I looked at her and shook my head. "Mya's dead."

"What?" she said, looking surprised.

"I killed her a few hours ago," I said.

"Oh my goodness...are you serious?"

"Yeah, she had to go."

"If I would've known that's why Ace wanted to see you, I would've never brought him to your house. That asshole told me Mya was in trouble and needed your help." She let out a huge sigh. "Shit, now I feel bad."

"Stop that Carol. You know damn well, it's not your fault. Now for your safety, you and the girls need to get outta here. As a matter of fact, I'm firing everybody today. The Feds are coming for me, and I don't need y'all getting caught up in the bullshit that I'm in."

"Diamond, stop talkin' that nonsense. Whatever happens, I'm here for you. I know you're hurtin' right now, but you can get through this."

I chuckled, trying to keep my sanity. "How can I?" I cried out. Carol tried her best to console me, saying that she was going to be there no matter what.

A few minutes later, we heard commotion coming from the shop. There was several loud voices and then suddenly, my office door flew open. They had finally arrived. Several FBI agents with dark blue flight vest with F.B.I imprinted across in bold yellow letters stood in my office with huge grins on their faces.

"Diamond Pierce?" one of the agents called out, flashing his badge.

"Do you all have a warrant?" Carol asked.

"Its okay, Carol," I said, in a submissive tone.

"No, girl…you ain't do nothin', fuck them," Carol said.

One of the agents went over to Carol and warned her to calm down.

"Diamond Pierce, you're under arrest for murder, conspiracy, and money laundering," the agent informed me.

Two men stepped toward me and I slowly stood up from my chair. I looked over at Carol and noticed that tears had formed in her eyes. "Don't hurt her," she shouted as they put the metal bracelets around my wrists.

"Make sure you take care of the shop," I said to Carol.

It didn't matter if they had hurt me or not because I didn't have anything left inside of me. Not even life. I went with the Feds willingly. They walked me out of my shop in front of all the customers and my employees. I could see the awe on all of their faces, but I didn't hold my head down. I had made the mistakes, so I wanted everyone to learn from my stupidity.

When they put me in the back of the car, I continued to hold my head up. I had to except the consequences no matter how bad they were; and if prison was my fate, then so be it.

Epilogue

When it was all said and done they charged me with the RICO act, and for the murders of Rashad and Mya. Much to my surprise, the Feds had bugged my house and were listening to everything for quite a while. They were willing to be easy on me if I gave up Scottie, but I wasn't a snitch. I killed Rashad for that same reason and I would be contradicting myself if I went down that same route. Some may say that it was a stupid choice, refusing to give up one man in exchange for a lesser time, but I didn't roll that way.

I wanted to take my chances in court; even though my attorney informed me that it didn't look good for me. The Feds had a ninety percent conviction rate, and when they came for you, you didn't stand a chance.

It's crazy, because while in jail, I found out that I was two weeks pregnant, which meant the father was Rashad. As if I wasn't going through enough, now I was pregnant with a snitch's baby. Damn, when it rains it pours.

Crime does pay, until you get caught, and then that's when the real fun begins. My dreams of happiness, a family and a marriage went out the door, and I was looking at twenty years to life due to the charges against me. They didn't give a fuck that I was about to become a mother, all they saw was that I was being held accountable for the murders, violence, and drugs that were being poured into the city. Basically, I was their scapegoat with Mya dead and Ace on the run.

I'd heard from one of Carol's visits that Ace had disappeared and was on the run for multiple homicides and also from someone in Praise's crew, who had a hit out on him. I guess he was taking the heat from one of Mya's stunts as well. More than likely, he'd gone back to Chicago; some say he left the country for Jamaica, where apparently his mother was from.

I also heard from Carol that Scottie was still in Miami making millions. He had enough money to always pay people off, so

I'm sure he would never get locked up. It's sad because I thought it was love when I was messing with Scottie, but it turned out to be all a game. I started off playing him, and in the end, I was the one who got played. I wasn't anything to him, but a guinea pig, another way for him to make money. While I was locked up, he had a female inmate step to me and sent a message stating, that if I opened my mouth, I was a dead bitch. But they could keep their threats, I wasn't a snitch, and never gave it a second thought.

The best thing that came out of all this was four days after being in jail, I received a visit that brought me to my knees. After years of silently praying to God to bring her back in my life, my prayers were finally answered when I saw my beautiful mother waiting for me in the visitor's room. To say, I cried like a new-born baby is an understatement.

In the end, when you think you're winning, with the money, the cars, and the power, you end up losing. Gangsters don't retire or get pensions; they end up in jail or dead. When you finally wake up and realize the mistakes you've made, you're looking at twenty years to life and end up asking yourself, was it all worth it. For me, it wasn't because my baby will be born behind these walls. The father of my child is dead, and my best friend, sold her soul for a dollar, and betrayed our friendship to get rich.

Life is a gift, how we chose to live it, is a choice.

Who Needs A Job When You're A Paper Doll

As a young girl Karen Whitaker dreamed of becoming rich and famous, promising to buy her mother that huge house on the hill with a Rolls Royce parked in the driveway. Her desire for material things turns into a grown woman's obsession with money, power and sex. Now of age, Karen possesses the brains of a scholar, beauty of a diamond, and a body that a Coca-Cola bottle would envy. She knows how to get what she wants even if it means taking advantage of those who trust her most. Greed and passion for tantalizing sex throttles her into compromising situations that may destroy her career and crumble her picture perfect relationship with a multi-millionaire. Take a journey into her intriguing story as demons from her past strike to unravel her fairytale life thread by thread. In the end, will she escape her dark clouds or be exposed as one money-hungry, conniving vixen?

Visit Nicolette Online @ www.myspace.com/paperdollthebook

Available At Borders, Waldenbooks and Independent Bookstores Nationwide

ORDER FORM

MAIL TO:
PO Box 423
Brandywine, MD 20613
301-362-6508

FAX TO:
301-579-9913

Date
Phone
E-mail

Ship to:
Address:
City & State: Zip:
Attention:

Make all checks and Money Orders payable to: **Life Changing Books**

Qty.	ISBN	Title	Release Date	Price
	0-9741394-0-8	A Life to Remember by Azarel	08/2003	$ 15.00
	0-9741394-1-6	Double Life by Tyrone Wallace	11/2004	$ 15.00
	0-9741394-5-9	Nothin' Personal by Tyrone Wallace	07/2006	$ 15.00
	0-9741394-2-4	Bruised by Azarel	07/2005	$ 15.00
	0-9741394-7-5	Bruised 2: The Ultimate Revenge by Azarel	10/2006	$ 15.00
	0-9741394-3-2	Secrets of a Housewife by J. Tremble	02/2006	$ 15.00
	0-9724003-5-4	I Shoulda Seen it Comin' by Danette Majette	01/2006	$ 15.00
	0-9741394-4-0	The Take Over by Tonya Ridley	04/2006	$ 15.00
	0-9741394-6-7	The Millionaire Mistress by Tiphani	11/2006	$ 15.00
	1-934230-99-5	More Secrets More Lies J. Tremble	02/2007	$ 15.00
	1-934230-98-7	Young Assassin by Mike G	03/2007	$ 15.00
	1-934230-95-2	A Private Affair by Mike Warren	05/2007	$ 15.00
	1-934230-94-4	All That Glitters by Ericka M. Williams	07/2007	$ 15.00
	0-9774575-2-4	The Streets Love No One by R.L.	05/2007	$ 15.00
	0-9774575-0-8	A Lovely Murder Down South by Paul Johnson	06/2006	$ 15.00
	0-9791068-2-8	Changing My Shoes by T.T. Bridgeman	05/2007	$ 15.00
	1-934230-93-6	Deep by Danette Majette	07/2007	$ 15.00
	1-934230-96-0	Flexin' & Sexin by K'wan, Anna J. & Others	06/2007	$ 15.00
	1-934230-92-8	Talk of the Town by Tonya Ridley	07/2007	$15.00
	0-9741394-9-1	Teenage Bluez	01/2006	$10.99
	0-9741394-8-3	Teenage Bluez II	12/2006	$10.99
			Total for Books:	$
		Shipping Charges (add $4.00 for 1-4 books*)		$
			Total Enclosed (add lines)	$

For credit card orders and orders for over 25 books
please contact us @ orders@lifechangingbooks.net
(cheaper rates for COD orders)

*Shipping and Handling on 5-20 books
is $5.95. For 11 or more books, contact
us for shipping rates. 240.691.4343

BAD GIRLZ OF FICTION

COMING JULY 2007

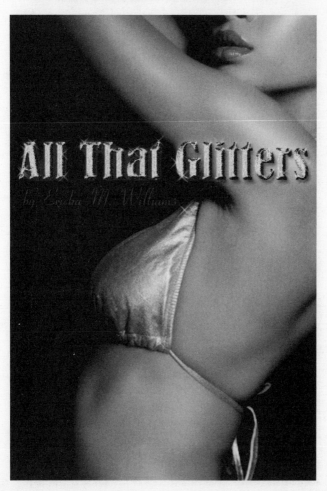

BAD GIRLZ OF FICTION

COMING SEPTEMBER 2007

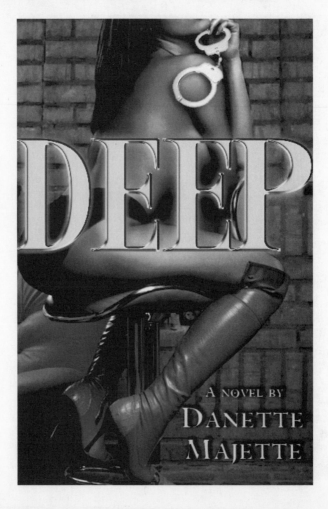